DISTURBING THE PEACE

ALSO BY RICHARD YATES

Revolutionary Road

Eleven Kinds of Loneliness

A Special Providence

Disturbing the Peace

The Easter Parade

A Good School

Liars in Love

Young Hearts Crying

RICHARD YATES

A novel

DISTURBING THE PEACE

DELTA TRADE PAPERBACKS

DISTURBING THE PEACE
A Delta Book

PUBLISHING HISTORY
Delacorte Press hardcover edition published September 1975
Delta trade paperback edition published April 1984
Delta trade paperback reissue / November 2008

Published by
Bantam Dell
A Division of Random House, Inc.
New York, New York

Library of Congress Catalog Card Number: 75-11628

ISBN 978-0-385-29332-7

Printed in the United States of America
Published simultaneously in Canada

www.bantamdell.com

BVG 12 11 10 9 8 7 6 5 4 3

FOR MONICA McCALL

DISTURBING THE PEACE

1

Everything began to go wrong for Janice Wilder in the late summer of 1960. And the worst part, she always said afterwards, the awful part, was that it seemed to happen without warning.

She was thirty-four and the mother of a ten-year-old son. The fading of her youth didn't bother her—it hadn't been a very carefree or adventurous youth anyway—and if her marriage was more an arrangement than a romance, that was all right too. Nobody's life was perfect. She enjoyed the orderly rotation of her days; she enjoyed books, of which she owned a great many; and she enjoyed her high, bright apartment with its view of midtown Manhattan towers. It was neither a rich nor an elegant apartment, but it was comfortable—and "comfortable" was one of Janice Wilder's favorite words. She was fond of the word "civilized," too, and of "reasonable" and "adjustment" and "relationship." Hardly anything upset or frightened her: the only things that did—

sometimes to the point of making her blood run cold—
were things she didn't understand.

"I don't understand," she said to her husband on the
telephone. "What do you mean, you 'can't' come
home?" And she glanced uneasily at their boy, who sat
on the carpet eating an apple and absorbed in the CBS
Evening News.

"What?" she said. "I can't hear you. You're what?
. . . Wait; I'll take this in the bedroom."

When she was alone at the extension phone, behind
two closed doors, she said "All right, John. Let's start at
the beginning. Where are you? At LaGuardia?"

"No, thank God; I finally got out of that son of a bitch.
Must've spent at least two hours walking around and
around out there before I figured out how to get a cab;
then I got one of these damn talky cab drivers, and he—"

"You're drunk, aren't you?"

"Will you let me finish? *No*, I'm not drunk. I've been
drinking but I'm not drunk. Listen: you know how much
sleep I got in Chicago? The whole week? Almost none.
One, two hours a night, and last night I didn't sleep at
all. You don't believe me, do you? You never believe the
truth."

"Just tell me where you're calling from."

"I don't know; some kind of stand-up phone booth,
and my legs are about to— Grand Central. The Biltmore.
No, wait: the Commodore. I'm having a drink at the
Commodore."

"Well, dear, that's practically around the corner. All
you have to do is—"

"God damn it, aren't you listening? I just got through
telling you I *can't* come home."

She hunched forward on the edge of the double bed with her elbows on her slacks, holding the phone tightly in both hands. "Why?" she said.

"Jesus. Hundreds of reasons. More reasons than I could possibly begin to—possibly begin to enumerate. One thing, I forgot to get a present for Tommy."

"Oh, John, that's absurd. He's ten now; he doesn't expect a present every time you—"

"Okay, here's another thing. There was a girl in Chicago, little PR girl for one of the distilleries. I screwed her five times in the Palmer House. Whaddya think of that?"

It wasn't the first news of its kind—there had been a good many girls—but it was the first time he'd ever flung it at her this way, like an adolescent braggart trying to shock his mother. She thought of saying What would you *like* me to think? but didn't trust her voice: it might sound wounded, which would be a mistake, or it might sound dry and tolerant and that would be worse. Luckily he didn't wait long for an answer.

"And whaddya think of this? All the way back on the plane I kept looking at my sweet little Air Transportation Credit Card. Know what I could do with that card anytime I feel like it? I could say the hell with everything. Climb into a big silver bird and take off to someplace like Rio; lie around in the sun and drink and do absolutely nothing, absolutely nothing until—"

"John, I'm not listening to any more of this. Tell me why you can't come home."

"You really want to know, sweetheart? Because I'm afraid I might kill you, that's why. Both of you."

* * *

Paul Borg, like the Wilders' son, was watching the CBS News. He said "Damn" when the phone rang because Eric Sevareid had just reached a summing-up about Senator Kennedy's chances of defeating Vice President Nixon.

"I'll get it," his wife called from the steaming kitchen.

"No, no; that's all right. I'll get it." His legal clients sometimes called him at home and they wanted to hear his voice right away, with no fooling around. But this was no client. "Oh," he said. "Hi, Janice."

"Paul, I hate to bother you at dinnertime but I'm terribly concerned about John . . ."

He listened, interrupting her with questions, and the questions were enough to bring his own wife slowly out of the kitchen, enough to make her turn off the television set and stand as close as possible beside him at the phone, her eyes round with fascination. When he said ". . . afraid he might kill you?" her cheeks turned pink and the fingers of one unsteady hand crept into her mouth.

". . . Well, of course I'll do whatever I can, Janice. I'll run up there now and—you know—have a talk with him, try to find out what the problem is. You just take it easy and don't worry, okay? I'll get back to you soon as I can. . . . Okay, Janice."

"My God!" his wife said when he'd hung up.

"Where's my tie?"

She found it and pulled his coat from the hall closet with such urgency that the wire hanger clattered to the floor. "Did he really threaten to kill her?" She looked radiant.

"Oh, for God's sake, Natalie. No, of course he didn't 'threaten'; apparently he's just going through some kind of nervous or emotional— I'll tell you when I get back."

He let the door slam behind him but she opened it and followed him halfway to the elevator. "Paul, what about dinner?"

"You go ahead and eat; I'll get something uptown. And listen, I don't want you calling Janice. I want her phone to be free so *I* can call her. Okay?"

They lived in one of the new, tall buildings of the northwest Village; Borg figured it would take him no more than ten minutes to get to the Commodore, and as he eased out of his parking space and headed uptown on Hudson he was pleased with the efficiency of his car and the fluid skill of his driving. He was pleased too at the way Janice's voice had gone from desperation to a renewal of strength and hope, pleased that she'd called him in the first place. Once at a crosstown stoplight he leaned over for a quick look in the rearview mirror, to make sure his hair and tie were straight and to admire the sober maturity of his face. Not until a horn blared behind him did he see the light was green.

He spotted his man as soon as he walked into the downstairs bar. John Wilder sat alone at a table against the far wall, staring into a drink with his forehead resting on his hand. But it was important to make this seem a chance encounter, which shouldn't be hard: they both worked in offices not far away; they'd often met here for a drink on their way home. To dispel any notion of conspiracy he slid one buttock onto a barstool and ordered a Scotch and soda—"make it light"—and silently counted to a hundred before he risked another glance at Wilder. No change. His hair had been raked awry by nervous fingers (that alone was odd because he was usually careful to the point of vanity about his hair), and with his face in shadow it was impossible to guess at whether he was drunk or exhausted or—well, whatever. From the head down, though, he was the same as ever: a short, composed, well-proportioned man in a well-cut business suit, fresh shirt and dark tie, with an expensive suitcase on the floor beside his knee.

Borg turned back to the bar, hoping Wilder might see him first; then he counted to a hundred again, carried his drink across the room in what he hoped was a casual stroll and said "Hey, John. Thought you were in Chicago."

Wilder looked up, and he looked terrible: very pale, beaded with sweat, and his eyes seemed out of focus.

"Just get back?" Borg said, pulling out a chair to sit down with him.

"While ago. What're you doing out so late?" At least he seemed to know what time it was.

"Didn't get out of the office till seven. Hell of a day. Meetings, phone calls; sometimes everything happens at once. You know."

But Wilder wasn't listening. He finished his drink greedily and said "How old're you now, Paul? Forty?"

"Almost forty-one."

"Son of a bitch. I'm not even thirty-six and I feel old as God. Waiter! Where the hell's that waiter?" When his eyes turned back they were clear and keen. "Tell me something else. Why do you suppose we both married homely women?"

Borg felt a welling of blood from his collar to his scalp. "Come on," he said. "You know that's a stupid thing to say."

"True, though. Hell, it's understandable in my case because I've always been a shrimp. Everybody said I looked like Mickey Rooney when I was a kid, and I mean it's no cinch to get good-looking girls with a handicap like that. I guess I settled on Janice because she had these wonderful big tits when she was younger; figured I could forget the rest of it, the short legs and the fullback shoulders and the face: I'd just bury myself in those tits forever and shut out the world. Jesus. But that's my story; what's yours? I mean you're *tall*. How come you wound up with an alligator like Natalie?"

"All right, cut it out now, John. You've had too much to drink."

"Hell I have. How do you know how much I've had to drink? Need sleep, is all. Absolutely no sleep, the whole week in Chicago. Thrashed around in that bed at the Palmer House with my nerves screaming and my mind going in circles like some crazy— I don't know. Had a nice little girl thrashing around with me part of the time and even that didn't help. But you know something? I learned a lot about myself. Sometimes when you can't sleep you figure things out; I did, anyway. Hell of a lot of things. Then coming in from the airport I got one of these damn talky cab drivers and you know what he said? He said—Oh Jesus, you're sore at me now, aren't you, Paul? You're sore because I called Natalie an alligator."

"I'm not sore; I'm concerned about you. You don't look well and you're not talking sensibly. Frankly, I don't think you're in any shape to go home tonight."

And Wilder gave a heavy sigh of relief. "Neither do I, old friend. No shape at all. Tried to tell Janice that and she didn't understand. Listen, you call her, okay? You explain it."

"Sure, John. I'll call her later."

"Because I mean she'll understand anything if you explain it. She thinks you're Abraham fucking Lincoln."

"All right, John."

"You're a lucky bastard, you know that, Paul? I mean a lawyer's a professional man, like a doctor or a priest: people *listen* when you talk. You're not some turd under everybody's feet like me. Cab drivers, waiters, all my life I've been victimized by slobs. Tyrannized by slobs."

"What did the cab driver say, John?"

"Ah, that smartass. He was driving like a maniac and I kept telling him to slow down, you see, and I was kind of jumping and squirming around in the back seat, and he said 'You better see a psychiatrist, buddy, you're a nervous wreck.'

"Another thing: you're lucky you don't have any kids. My God, if it weren't for Tommy I'd take my sweet little Air Transportation Credit Card, climb into a big silver bird and take off to someplace like Rio: lie around in the sun till my money's gone and then blow my brains out. I mean it."

"No you don't. Let's try to be reasonable, John. Nobody can go without sleep for a week. I think you need medical care; you need sedation and rest. Let me run you down to St. Vincent's."

"Listen, Borg. You're a nice guy and you've had a hard day at the office and I'm sorry I called your wife an alligator because she's nice too and she's probably got a dandy little chicken-noodle casserole waiting for you downtown, but I'll be a son of a bitch if you're gonna lock me up in any hospital."

"Nobody's going to lock you up. You'll check into St. Vincent's for exhaustion; they'll put you to sleep and you'll come out tomorrow or the next day like a new man. Like your old self. It's the only thing to do."

There was a pause. "Let me think about it." And thinking about it meant calling for another drink, half of which he finished in a swallow. "I got a better idea," he said then. "Take me down to Varick Street."

And Borg winced because he'd been afraid of that suggestion from the start. Several years ago the two of them had joined in renting a dirt-cheap basement apartment on Varick Street (a cellar apartment, really, the kind supposed to be condemned by the city) as a secret retreat from their married lives. They'd had it cleaned up and painted white, they'd equipped it with a double bed and a well-stocked liquor cabinet, a second-hand stove and refrigerator and enough other stuff to make it "nice," and an unlisted phone: the idea was that when either of them came across what Wilder called a windfall—an available, willing girl—he could disappear into the place for an afternoon or even a couple of nights, feigning out-of-town business, and be a happy if somewhat nervous bachelor again. But it had sounded better than it was: there'd never really been all that many windfalls.

"You don't want to go to Varick Street, John."

"Who says I don't? What's the matter, you going there yourself?"

"No. I haven't been down there for months. But if the

girl in Chicago couldn't help you sleep, what makes you think some other girl could?"

"Might be worth a try. You ever met Rita? Research girl up at Time and Life? Course, it's probably too late to call her. Or the sort of heavy one? What's her name? Married to the doctor? No, wait; she moved to Boston."

"Come on, John. Let's be realistic."

And Wilder gave up. "Realistic; right. That's my trouble. All my life, I've never been realistic. I ever tell you how I wanted to make movies? Jesus Christ." He finished his drink. "Okay, Borg; you're on. One more drink and I'll be realistic as hell. Waiter!" He thrust his glass as far into the aisle as his arm would allow and might have fallen out of the chair if he hadn't clung to the table with his free hand.

"No need to shout, sir," the waiter said.

"No need to be a little wise guy, either."

"Look, mister: I don't have to serve you."

"Yeah? Well then how'd you like to kiss my ass, greaseball?"

"It's all right," Borg said, laying many dollar bills on the table. "It's all right; we're leaving. Here, John, I'll take your suitcase."

"Whaddya mean, I can't carry my own bag? You think I'm a cripple?"

But the bag did give him trouble: he got it wedged in one of the plate-glass doors and said "Son of a *bitch*," causing people to turn and look at him; then as they walked the passageway to Lexington Avenue he stopped and put it down several times, once nearly tripping a woman, because he said it was killing his hand and breaking the hell out of his leg.

He was quiet in the car as Borg crept through cross-town traffic, but when they'd begun the long ride down Seventh Avenue he began to twist and writhe against the passenger's door and one hand flew up as if to shield his face. "Christ's *sake*, Paul, will you watch your *driving?* Will you slow *down?*"

"Try to take it easy, John. I'm going as slow as I can."

It was a busy evening at the St. Vincent's emergency entrance—stretchers on the floor with orderlies or interns crouched over them, a middle-aged woman bleeding from the face and groaning on an examination table —but Borg found a partitioned alcove where a young man in white sat behind a desk, apparently in charge.

"Doctor, this isn't really an emergency but my friend here's exhausted; he hasn't had any sleep for a week, and he needs sedation. Frankly, I think he may be going through some sort of nervous or—"

Borg could not afterwards remember how he'd finished that sentence: he was aware only of the doctor's eyes blinking through thick glasses at one and then the other of them. Wilder had opened his collar and tie long ago; now he clawed them open further and so roughly that a shirt button fell and spun on the floor. When the doctor told him to sit down he dropped his suitcase with a crash and sank into the only seat available, a big old-fashioned wheelchair of varnished yellow wood that made him look very small and helpless, especially when it rolled backwards and was caught by an orderly who'd appeared from nowhere.

"Would you please step outside, sir?" the doctor said, and Borg was quick to obey. His feet hurt. He was hungry and tired and wanted to go home. All this would be over soon. "Oh, I don't know how to thank you, Paul," Janice would say. "I can't imagine what we'd ever have done without you."

The partition was thin. He couldn't hear the words of the doctor's interrogation or Wilder's replies, but he assumed it was a routine interview for admission—name and age and occupation, next of kin, medical history, previous instances of insomnia—and then it all went out of control.

". . . You're God damned *right* I've been drinking. What the hell do *you* do when you can't sleep, sonny boy? Eat fudge? Watch 'The Late Show'? Pull your prick? Listen! Listen, you overeducated little snotnose, you faggoty little— Listen: I figured out a lot of things about myself this week. Things you'd never understand in a hundred *years*. . . ."

By the time Borg was back in the alcove there was a sound of splintering wood as Wilder stamped one shoe on the footrest of the wheelchair and broke it, and the orderly said "Easy, mister, *easy.*"

The doctor had stood up from his scattered paperwork, and Wilder was saying "I've been a turd under everybody's feet all my life and I've just now figured out there's greatness in me. There's greatness in me, and if you don't quit looking at me that way, if you don't let me into this fucking hospital I'm gonna take your glasses and shove 'em down your fucking *throat*. Is that clear?"

Then the orderly had turned him around and wheeled him down a hall and the doctor was explaining to Borg that there were no facilities for him here, that in his judgment the only course was to take him to Bellevue and that an ambulance would be provided at once.

"I'll call ahead now," he said. "They'll be ready for you."

And the next thing Borg knew he was cramped on a narrow bench of the ambulance with the suitcase between his legs. He had always thought that stretcher patients were carried face-up, but Wilder lay on his belly with the hands of three or four attendants holding him down, and he was still shouting in a monologue so nearly incoherent that only the words "fuck" and "shit" and "greatness" came through. In the dim pink and grey light Borg could see that his coat and shirt were rucked up to his shoulder blades; he pulled them down and rubbed the damp, trembling spine in what he hoped would feel like reassurance. "John," he said, whether Wilder could hear him or not, "you wanted a good rest and you're going to get it. Just relax now; you're all right." That was when the ambulance gained speed and its siren came on, growling low at first and rising to a scream as they swerved across town.

"Ow!" Wilder said over and over, as if the smooth ride were filled with bruising bumps and potholes. "Ow! . . . Ow! . . . Ow! . . ."

And Bellevue—or whatever part of the labyrinth of Bellevue they arrived at—was so bewildering that Borg's own mind went briefly out of focus. He stood around with his mouth open like a fool's, holding Wilder's suitcase, until someone handed him a printed form headed CITY OF NEW YORK, DEPARTMENT OF HOSPITALS, showed him where to sign his name, where to put his home and office phone numbers and told him to write "friend" in the space marked "Relationship." He did that quickly because they wouldn't let him see Wilder until it was done; then he found he couldn't see him anyway because Wilder's arms were slung tight around the necks of two big orderlies who dragged him still shouting toward a closed elevator, where a third orderly waited with a wheelchair, and they not only forced him into it but strapped him in. When the elevator door slid open they shoved him inside, and across the back of the chair was the stenciled word PSYCHO.

"Look," Borg said to the nearest white-coated man he could find. "Listen: what's the procedure here?"

The man smiled, shrugged and spoke rapidly in what could have been either Spanish or Italian.

"Are you a doctor?"

"Me? No. Doctor over there."

"This your bag, mister?" another voice said.

"No. I mean yes—wait—here, I'll take it."

Then he said "Doctor, excuse me, but I'm a little— What exactly is the procedure here?"

This man was very young too, like the one at St. Vincent's, but handsome enough to play the romantic lead in some movie about a great metropolitan hospital. "The procedure? Thanks, honey," he said to a nurse, or a nurse's aide, who had brought him a hamburger and a container of coffee.

"You're very welcome."

"What I mean is," Borg said, "could you tell me what they're going to do with Mr. Wilder?"

"Wilder." He set his coffee down, picked up a clipboard and squinted at it. "Oh, yes. And you're the man who signed him in, right? Mr. Berg?"

"Borg. I'm an attorney." And he pulled his coat straight as further proof of respectability. The warm brown smell of the hamburger was making him weak with hunger.

"Well, he'll be treated like any other patient, Mr. Borg," the doctor said with his mouth full. "They'll put him to sleep, first of all."

"And how soon do you think he might be released?"

"Hard to say. This is Friday night, and it's the Labor Day weekend. The psychiatrists won't be back till Tuesday, and it'll probably be Wednesday or Thursday before they can review his case. After that it's entirely up to them."

"My God. I'd forgotten about Labor Day. This is—the point is I'd never have signed that paper if I'd realized —I mean this is really very--unfortunate."

"I wouldn't worry about it," the doctor said around his chewing, spilling crumbs of meat and bread from his lips. "I'd say you've done the right thing. Look: you're an attorney; you deal with the police at all?"

"No. My clients are— No, I don't deal with the police."

"Well, okay; even so. You've seen the shape he's in." He wiped his mouth on one white sleeve and left a streak of ketchup. "Which is better? Having him safe in here for a while, or out walking the streets until the cops pick him up and book him for disturbing the peace?"

2

He woke up soaked with sweat, breathing stale and fetid
air. A naked light bulb shone in his eyes and he found he
was in a steel-framed bunk slung by chains from the wall,
like a bunk in a troopship or a jail.

". . . Everybody out," a voice called, and there were
other sounds: groans and curses, wretched coughing and
hawking, a loud fart, the creak and bang of bunks being
folded back and clamped against the wall. "*Let's* go, *let's*
go. Everybody out."

When he sat up a hand closed around his shoulder and
rolled him onto the floor. He was wearing grey cotton
pajamas that were much too big for him: the pants
tripped his stumbling bare feet and the sleeves hung to
his fingertips. Swaying and squinting under the lights, he
rolled up the sleeves first, disclosing a loose plastic brace-
let that read WILDER JOHN C. He bent over to roll up the
pants but was kicked from behind and fell to his hands,
and he looked up frightened into the angry face of a
Negro in pajamas like his own.

"Watch your ass, man. This here's the *corridor*. You got no business hunkerin' down playin' with yourself; get up and *walk*."

And he did. Steel-mesh panels were being drawn across the folded bunks to prevent anyone from using them: this was indeed the corridor, the place for walking. It was yellow and green and brown and black; it was neither very long nor very wide, but it was immensely crowded with men of all ages from adolescence to senility, whites and Negroes and Puerto Ricans, half of them walking one way and half in the other, the dismaying variety of their faces moving into the glare of lights and then into shadows and then into the lights again. Some were talking to one another and some talked to themselves, but most were silent. He felt warm grit under his feet until he stepped on something slick; then he saw that the black floor ahead was scattered with gobs of phlegm. A few of the walking men wore dirty paper slippers, and he envied them; a few were smoking, with packs of cigarettes in their pajama-top pockets, which puckered the roof of his mouth. Then he saw that some weren't wearing pajama tops but straitjackets, and he wanted to whimper like a child.

There were closed windows at both ends of the corridor, covered with steel mesh: the light outside was drab —either an early grey morning or a late grey afternoon —and there was nothing to see but air shafts and windowless walls.

Near the middle of the corridor stood a Negro orderly in hospital greens, and he hurried toward him with a mouthful of questions—Look: where're my clothes? Where's my money? Where's a phone? What's the *deal* here?—but when he confronted the man he felt small and shy and all he knew was that his bladder was about to burst.

"Excuse me," he said. "Where's the bathroom?"

"Over there."

And he followed the pointed finger into a bright stinking latrine where men squatted on toilet bowls or stood jockeying for position at a long urinal trough.

"Now this here," another orderly explained, "is your toothbrush. Way you can always tell is because it got your name on it. See that tape? Wilder. When you done with it, put it back here in this rack. Ain't nobody gonna use this toothbrush but you, and you never gonna use nobody else's toothbrush, understand? That way, nobody pick up no trench mouth or nothing like that. Understand?"

But nobody was allowed his own razor. The men stood four and five deep waiting to shave at a steamed-up mirror under watchful, official eyes.

". . . Soon's you done you rinse that razor and lay it on the shelf. Ain't no use foolin' with that razor; you can't get that blade out. That razor's *locked* . . ."

". . . Showers for the new men *only*. Showers for the new men *only*. Not you, Gonzalez, you come on back outa there . . ."

There was no soap in the communal shower room and no way of regulating the water: the new men slid around on greasy duckboards and tried to clean themselves until each was given a towel in one hand and his own wadded pajamas in the other.

"Can I have slippers?"

"Ain't no more slippers. Slippers all gone."

And then it was back to the corridor with nothing to do but walk. He passed a locked door with a small wired-glass window and peered inside to discover a padded cell. Canvas mats of the kind used by wrestlers and gymnasts were hung from the walls and spread on the floor. It was vacant, but the one next door was occupied: a man in a straitjacket lay face down in it, as still as death, with a dark stain of piss around his thighs.

". . . I don't care! I don't *care!*"

Both columns of walkers shrank aside to make way for the spectacle of a young white man shadowboxing down the middle of the hall. He was stripped to the waist and he'd neatly ripped off his pajama pants to the length of prizefighters' trunks; he was bobbing and weaving, jabbing and hooking in a swirl of yellow dust motes.

". . . Can't you idiots understand? I don't *care!* I *want* my father to see me like this!"

"All right, Henry; easy, now," an orderly was saying, coming up from behind to put a hand on his shoulder, but the shadowboxer spun and faced him with both fists cocked.

"Don't call me 'Henry,' you dumb black bastard—call me Doctor or I'll break every fucking bone in your—"

"You ain't gonna break nothin', Doctor," a second orderly said, and the two of them held his arms. Both orderlies were bigger than he; they had no trouble turning him around and leading him down the corridor. He didn't struggle in their grip but his shouting rose until he sounded on the verge of tears.

". . . God damn it, if I want my father to see me like this it's none of your dumb, black, ignorant, motherfucking—"

"Your father iddn't gonna see you no way, Doctor; come along easy now, 'less you want Roscoe to shoot you out."

"Yeah, yeah, shoot me *out*, that's all you know. Big deal! Ah, you poor, dumb— Whaddya do? Go home and tell your wives, 'Hey, baby, I got me a doctor today'? 'Got me a real white doctor right in the ass'? Well don't forget I'm naming both of you, and your little buddy Roscoe too, tried to send me up to Wingdale. I'm filing a mal— a mal— a mal*practice* suit against this hospital, and when the facts—when the facts are out you'll all be . . ."

He was out of sight now, and out of earshot because of the laughter and jeers and catcalls that broke in his wake. Another Negro in greens was hurrying down the corridor with a hypodermic syringe; he stopped and squinted at it under a light, holding it high while he thumbed the plunger just enough to make a drop of liquid appear on the point of the needle, then he went on toward the shouting man.

"Go get 'im, Roscoe," somebody called. "Fix 'im up good." And there was more laughter as the columns began to move again.

Wilder felt a light nudge at his elbow and thought he heard a voice say, "Want to kiss me?"

"What?"

A remarkably handsome Negro boy was smiling there, wearing a turban made of his pajama top, gently swiveling his shoulders to display the beauty of his naked torso and holding his half-erect cock in his hand. "Do you want to kiss me?"

"No."

"Oh, it's all right. It's all right. You can kiss me if you want, but only if you say 'I love you' first."

It was time for breakfast. Double doors were opened at one end of the corridor and both columns became a jostling crowd.

". . . All right, hold it; *hold* it now. Two at a time. Two at a time, or nobody gonna get *nothin'* to eat . . ."

The sense of entrapment was even worse inside the mess hall: once you'd been shoved crouching and sidling down the narrow space between a long table and its high-backed, immovable wooden bench, there was no way out. Wilder sat pressed between a toothless, ancient man and a fat boy whose wet mouth hung open as if in pain from the cramp of the table against his belly. Each of them received a plastic bowl of glutenous oatmeal with canned milk and a mug of lukewarm coffee, and Wilder didn't know he was hungry until he'd dug into the oatmeal with a big tin army-surplus spoon. If he could eat, if he could drink this coffee and find a cigarette and a telephone, there might still be a chance of the world's coming back to normal. But the old man couldn't lift the shaking spoon to the reach of his gums without spilling it, and the fat boy picked up his bowl in both hands and plunged his face into it, slobbering like a dog as the porridge slid down his chest; then a shrill voice at one of the other tables rose to panic: "Lemme *outa* here, lemme *outa* here, lemme *outa* here . . ."

When the mess hall set him free at last he found that the men who looked the least insane had begun to congregate at the head of the corridor where there was a little ell facing the locked front door. On a high bookkeeper's stool beside the door sat a policeman—not a uniformed hospital guard but a real New York City cop, complete with badge and dangling nightstick and holstered pistol. He chewed gum steadily and talked to no one, not even the orderlies, and he wore the kind of sunglasses whose lenses were silver mirrors on the outside: if you tried to look into his eyes you saw only a double image of your own craning face. Even so, this seemed the best place to be: the place where rational things were most likely to happen.

"Hey there, Shorty. How's old Shorty today?" The man who said this wasn't much taller than himself, and he was ugly—a sallow face with close-set eyes and a big humorless smile full of bad teeth—but his pajama pocket bulged with cigarettes. "I seen you when they brought you in last night. *Boy* you was high."

"I was?" He could remember nothing of last night after the ride in the ambulance with Paul Borg rubbing his back.

"Yellin' and screamin', talkin' a mile a minute; they shot you out and you *still* wouldn't shut up. I figured, Jesus, this is some tough customer we got here; this must be some *big* son of a bitch. Then I seen you was even smaller'n me, and laugh? I damn near died."

"Yeah, well, look. Could I have a cigarette?"

"I'll save you," the man said, and turned away.

" 'Save' me?"

"He won't save you," another voice said. "He never saves nobody. He's a prick."

The door opened then, letting in a rush of cool air—not fresh air, but cool and better-smelling if only because it came from some wider, cleaner corridor—and there was a loud, happy chorus of "Charlie!" . . . "Hey, Charlie!" . . . "How are ya, Charlie?"

He was well over six feet tall and built like a heavy-weight, a Negro dressed in greens like the others but dominating all of them, dominating everyone as he pocketed his key ring and moved slowly into the ward, trundling a medicine cart. "Good morning . . . Good morning," he said in a deep, rich voice, and even the cop said "Morning, Charlie," after making sure the door was locked behind him.

"Hey Charlie, can I see you a second?"

"Charlie listen: 'member yesterday I asked you about somethin'?"

They swarmed around him, coming from all sides as he wheeled his cart to a stop in the exact middle of the corridor, where he raised his head to address them all.

"Nourishment, gentlemen!" he called out to one end, and "Nourishment, gentlemen!" to the other. The trays of the medicine cart held many shot glasses filled with what looked like bourbon whiskey or maple syrup: it was neither, though it tasted a little like both.

"You bring my paper, Charlie?" said a man with a dirty bundle of newspapers under his arm.

"Oh, now, Mr. Schultz, you have plenty of papers. Use up the papers you have, then maybe I'll bring you a new one." And he turned to one of the orderlies. "How many admissions last night?"

"Eight. We got a hundred and seventeen on the ward now."

Charlie winced and shook his big head. "That's too many. And there'll be more coming in today, more to-morrow, more Monday. We don't have facilities for that many." With a jangle of his key ring he opened a door marked KEEP OUT, briefly revealing what looked like a snug little den—a table and chairs, shelves with cups and a hotplate and coffee-makings—and came out with two packs of Pall Malls in his hand.

"All right, one at a time, gentlemen," he said to the eager crowd that pressed around him. "Form a line to the right, please; one at a time and only one apiece. Not you, Mr. Jefferson, you've got a pack in your pocket. You know the rules: these are *ward* cigarettes . . ."

Everything was slightly improved with Charlie's arrival, with the "Nourishment" and the ward cigarettes: the lights were less glaring and the shadows less dark, and there were new discoveries to be made: a long wooden bench against one wall, other places to sit in a recess between sections of folded-up bunks and even a place to lie down—four dirty mattresses on the floor of an alcove at the far end, well away from the mainstream of walkers. But the padded cells were still there, six of them, and one now contained the twisted figure of the man who'd shadowboxed and screamed before breakfast. He lay with his mouth still open in the shape of outrage, as if ready to scream again in his drugged sleep, and his dark hair glistened with sweat.

"Who shot Dr. Spivack out?" Charlie's heavy voice inquired.

"Roscoe, Charlie. He was actin' up real bad."

"What happened to his pants?"

"Tore 'em off himself, tryna make like a fighter. Then he started yellin' about his malpractice suit and all that; wasn't no other way to handle it."

"I don't understand that. I thought he was coming along very well."

"He has good days and bad days, Charlie."

"Mm." And Charlie got out his keys again. "Well, the least we can do is open the door. I don't want him waking up with that door locked. Get him a new suit of pajamas, too."

"Okay, Charlie."

"Ah, Charlie, you're a prince," said a fragile, palsied man of seventy or more. "A prince among men. I swear to Jesus—I swear to Jesus you're a saint, Charlie."

"Well, Mr. Foley, I thank you for the compliment, but I've already given out the cigarettes and I happen to know you received one because you tried to take two."

"Ah, Mother of God, how can you think of cigarettes? It's spiritual help I need, Charlie. Spiritual help."

"I'm not the man to see about that. Why don't you go sit down awhile? I have other people to attend to. You, sir; are you one of the new men? What's your name?"

"Wilder. John Wilder."

"Did you take your Nourishment, Mr. Wilder?"

"Yeah, 'Nourishment,' " said the old man. "You know what it is? It's formaldehyde."

"That's enough, Mr. Foley; you go along now." Then he said "It's Peraldehyde, Mr. Wilder. You get it three times a day; it's very good for you. Settles your nerves."

"I see. And are you the chief orderly, or—or what?"

"I'm a male nurse. There's always a nurse on duty here; my shift's eight to five."

"Oh. Well, look: it's very important that I get to a phone as soon as poss—"

"Oh, no, Mr. Wilder; you won't be making any phone calls here."

"Well, how soon— I mean when can I see a doctor?"

That was when he learned it would be Tuesday before the psychiatrists came back, that it might well be Thursday before they could interview him and that the length of his stay thereafter would depend on their decision. "So meanwhile," Charlie said, "I'd suggest you try and make yourself comfortable."

He lumbered away, trailing other supplicants in his wake, and Wilder stood watching him go for what seemed an intolerably long time. " 'Comfortable,' " he said, and then suddenly he was padding after him, running, stepping in slime again and surprised by the shrillness of his own voice: "Comfortable in *this* fucking place? Are you outa your fucking *mind?*"

Charlie turned back, looming over the chattering men with one long forefinger raised in admonition. "Mr. Wilder. I'm telling you now to keep your voice down and keep your temper under control. I don't want to have to tell you again."

Yellow and green and brown and black; black and brown and green and yellow. The only way to shut out the sounds and the smells of this place was to concentrate on the colors, and to walk. Up past the latrine to where the cop sat; turn, back past the mess hall to the other end; turn. A small man could move unnoticed in a crowd like this if he kept his mouth shut and his eyes front and his arms close to avoid touching anyone. He could breathe at measured intervals and keep his own counsel; he could even burst into tears if he did so quietly; nobody would notice.

Instead of crying he sat down in the only vacant place on one of the corridor benches, and a brown hand slid onto his thigh.

"It's all right."

"Huh?"

"It's all right. You can kiss me if you want, but only if you say 'I love you' first."

He was up and walking again, and he'd made three circuits of the ward when he found an empty mattress in the alcove at the far end. Sitting was better than walking and lying down was better still, though it sank him deeper into the smells of sweat and feet. He squirmed and sprawled facedown in total collapse—the hell with everything—and he even slept for a while, or thought he was asleep, until his eyes came open and saw that the men who lay very close on either side of him were masturbating.

But after lunch there was another call of "Nourishment, gentlemen!" and another round of ward cigarettes, and he found himself walking with Dr. Spivack. He didn't recognize him at first because he wore fresh pajamas and had combed his hair and his face was free of hysteria: it was a tightly clenched, sardonic face.

"You come in last night?"

"Yes."

"Half these poor bastards don't even know where they are. You know where you are?"

"Bellevue."

"Gotta be more specific than that, buddy. Bellevue Hospital is a great public medical institution. It's—"

"Okay; the psycho ward."

"And you honestly think there's only one? My God,

man, there's an entire psychiatric *wing* in Bellevue. Seven floors, each one worse than the one beneath, and this is the top. The worst. This is the Men's Violence Ward. Are you blind? Can't you see these clowns in straitjackets? Can't you see that cop? There's got to be a cop on duty here because some of us inmates are police cases. Criminals. Nobody knows who; I don't even think the orderlies know. I don't even think Charlie knows." He had been walking briskly, making Wilder stumble and hurry to keep up with him, but now he stopped short, grabbed Wilder's arm and spun him around to face a stiff, jabbing index finger. "How about you? Huh? You a police case?"

"No. How about letting go of my arm?"

Spivack laughed and punched him on the shoulder. It seemed to be meant as a punch of camaraderie, but it hurt. "Hell, I'm only kidding; I knew you were okay from your face. Know how you look? Like some little kid's lost his mother in a department store. What's your name?"

And for at least an hour Dr. Spivack talked, steering Wilder through the crowds on either side of the corridor, pausing only to interrupt himself with little advisory asides— "Don't ever take a flop in there unless you *really* have to," he said of the alcove with the mattresses; "that's Jerk-off City"—and most of his talk was autobiography.

He came from what he called a medical family. All his male forebears had been distinguished doctors in Germany until his father fled with his own family to this country in the thirties. His oldest brother was "tops: a first-rate heart man at Cornell Medical Center," and the second was doing all right too, considering he'd never been the brightest guy in the world; he was a radiologist up at Mount Sinai— "*You* know, he's dumb, but dumb in a way that doesn't show. And he's married to the most glorious piece of ass you ever saw, this big blonde Wisconsin girl with legs like—legs like—legs that defy description." Then came his sister, who had married a psychiatrist—and wasn't that the God damnedest thing? His own sister, for Christ's sake, actually married to one of these Sigmund Freud freaks? And then came the youngest and the favorite, himself.

". . . Ah, I had my share of suffering when we first came over; my mother died; they called me the Katzenjammer Kike in junior high and I got a few bloody noses, but don't worry, I'm not trying to break your heart. I always knew I'd make it and I did. Never had any sex problems, either, don't worry about that. Never thought I was a fag or anything. Lost my cherry at fifteen on the beach at Far Rockaway and I've been wallowing in pussy ever since. *Wallowing* in it. You married, Wilder?"

"Yes."

"Well, maybe that takes care of it for some guys, but I'll be a son of a bitch if any broad's gonna hook me till I'm ready. What kinda work d'ya do?"

"Sales."

"Yeah? That's funny. You look smarter'n that. I always thought salesmen were slope-heads. Whaddya sell?"

"Space."

The doctor reeled away in astonishment. "Christ, isn't *any*thing free any more? You sell *space?* Which kind? Inner space or outer space? Huh?"

"I think you know what I mean," Wilder said. "Advertising space. For a magazine."

"Oh. Yeah, I get it. Advertising space. What magazine?"

The American Scientist.

"No kidding? Well, that's impressive. They run some pretty abstruse, sophisticated material. If you understand that stuff you must be fairly—"

"I don't understand it. I just sell it."

"How can you sell something you don't understand?"

"Isn't that sort of what psychiatrists do?"

And that earned him another of Spivack's painful punches and a bray of laughter. "You're okay, Wilder," he said. "Anyway, I always knew I'd make it and I did. Straight A's all through college and med school, did my internship at Johns Hopkins and came here as a resident two years ago. Internal medicine. Thought it was an honor to work in Bellevue Hospital; family did too. And I was damned good. That's not bragging: I happen to be an excellent physician, that's all. Then, *wham!* The old administrative double-cross, and look where the hell I wind up. Talk about irony, huh?"

Wilder wanted to hear more about the old administrative double-cross but thought better of asking; and when Spivack began talking again he had changed the subject.

"Speaking of fags," he said, "you notice how this ward's crawling with 'em? Fags, junkies, fall-down drunks. Another thing: you notice all this 'Save me' talk? 'Save me, buddy,' and all that? It's supposed to be about cigarettes—they want you to save 'em the butt when you're done—but it's really kind of a half-assed prayer: you hear guys say it that don't even smoke. They want to be *saved.* Find a lot of religious nuts in here. There's one guy thinks he's the Second Coming of Christ. Proba-

bly more than one—it's a common psychotic delusion—
but this guy's a riot. Keeps to himself most of the time,
then once in a while he puts on a show. Stick around;
you'll see him. Hey, and another thing: you notice how
they only hire spades here? You know why?"

"No. Why?"

"Why d'ya think? Because they're so 'gentle' and so
'kind'? Yeah, yeah, they've got a Natural Sense of
Rhythm too. They're scared of ghosts and they're just
plain crazy about watermelon. What the hell were you,
born yesterday? It's because no white man'd *work* here
for the kind of money they get. You know what kind of
money they get? Even Charlie there? Huh?"

"Excuse me, Mr. Wilder," Charlie said, blocking their
path. "Those pajamas of yours don't fit very well, do
they?"

"No, I— No, they don't."

"Sometimes the night people are careless. We have
Small, Medium and Large. A man of your size needs
Small. I'll see about it."

"Yeah, you do that, Charlie," Spivack said, "and while
you're at it why don't you see about your buddy Roscoe.
I want that little bastard put on Report, is that clear? If
he shoots me out one more time I'll have his nurse's
license. Is that clear?"

"All right; try to keep your voice down, Doctor."

"Charlie's the only halfway decent one they've got,"
Spivack said when they were walking again. "Know
something? This fucking place was built in the nineteenth century and it hasn't changed a bit. Look at that."
He pointed to a bench. "And you seen the benches in the
mess hall? Antiques! Antiques! Get some faggot antique

dealer up here and he'd pay a thousand bucks apiece for 'em. Listen. Little piece of advice. Watch out for Roscoe. First morning I was in here he let me sit in my own urine for an hour and a half. An hour and a half! And mind you, this was after I'd asked him for a urinal seven times. Bastard kept telling me to go to the latrine, go to the latrine, go to the latrine."

"Why didn't you go?"

Spivack struck his own head with the heel of his hand in a spasm of exasperation. "You're missing the *point*, Wilder! The point is, when a patient asks a nurse for a urinal he's supposed to *get* it. Ah, Christ, I thought you showed a glimmer of intelligence, but you're just as fuck-ing dumb as all the other fucking— Look: get lost for a while, okay? My father and my sister are coming to see me tomorrow and I happen to have a few things on my mind."

So he was alone again, but it wasn't long before he had his Small pajamas, which were heartening; then he joined a group huddled in one of the padded cells whose door had been propped open. The man with the newspa-pers was there—he had spread part of his collection on the floor for study—and among the others were two young boys, white and Negro, who sat deep in conversa-tion against the rear wall.

". . . So we was all fooling around this vacant lot up behind the Breyer's Ice Cream sign, see," the white boy was saying, "and see, I should of gone home when the other kids did; that's where I made my mistake. Any-ways, it was getting dark and me and this Kovarsky was just kind of sitting there talking and smoking cigarettes behind the sign, and then he—"

"Hold on a second, Ralph, you goin' too fast. Who's this Kovarsky?"

"I just told you. He's this big-shot kid in the neighborhood out home; all the kids are scared of him; I mean he's, you know, real big and he talks tough and he's got a Record. Breaking and Entering. He's nineteen. Anyways, he says for me to stick around after the other kids go home and I says okay. I mean I know it was dumb but I guess I was kind of—I don't know, kind of—"

"Flattered, right?" the Negro boy said. "Sure, I can see that. So then what?"

"So then he starts giving me cigarettes and telling dirty stuff about girls, telling the names of all the girls in the Senior Class he's had innercourse with, and like that. You know."

"Yeah, shit, I know those kinda guys. How old're you, Ralph?"

"Fifteen. I mean I'm fifteen now; I was fourteen then. So anyways, all of a sudden he kind of moves in close and opens up his pants and tells me to—you know. Go down on him. Blow him."

"Jesus."

"So I tell him no and I get up quick and start to run around the sign and he makes a grab for me and says he's gonna break my arm. That don't scare me—I know he can't do nothing like that on account of his Record—but then he says, 'Okay, kid, you got a choice: be nice to me and I won't tell nobody nothin'. Run on home, and I swear to God you're never gonna hear the end of this.'"

"Oh, Jesus," the Negro boy said.

"So I go home, and the next day at school all the kids start in on me. You know. 'Hey, Ralph, what's it taste like?' That kind of stuff. Dirty stuff. Or they'd grab the front of their pants and say 'Wanna go up behind the Breyer's Ice Cream sign, Ralph?' And then around the candy store they start calling me Hot Lips Volpe. That's my last name, Volpe. Even the big kids, Juniors and Seniors. Even the *girls*. 'Cause see, what he did was, this Kovarsky, what he did was, he told everybody it was *me* wanted to suck him off."

The other boy looked puzzled. "How come you didn't tell 'em the truth?"

"I did! I did! I told 'em and told 'em, and everybody just laughed. 'Cause it was just my word against his, see? And this Kovarsky's such a big shot, who's gonna believe me?"

"Mm. Man, that's a tough story."

"And then my father hears about it."

"Your father? Your father didn't believe you either?"

"Well see, he got it from the other kids' fathers. He says 'Ralph, I want you to tell me exactly what happened up behind that sign.' So I tell him and he says 'That's not the way *I* heard it,' and I says 'I *swear!* I *swear!*' He just sits there and looks at me like I'm some kind of—some kind of—I don't know. And ever since then, ever since then—" Ralph couldn't finish; he turned his face against the wall mat, wholly expressionless, and began fingering his pimples. All his fingernails had been bitten to the quick.

"Man," said the Negro boy. "I mean, that is one tough story. Hey listen, though; I got an idea. Let's play a game. Let's play pictures. You know how to play pictures, Ralph?" Ralph didn't answer. "How 'bout you, man? What's your name?"

"John."

"I'm Francis, John; this here's Ralph. You want to play pictures? It's easy. I say somethin', you all try and tell me what picture it's in. Here's an example. I say 'Frankly, my dear, I don't give a damn.' What picture is that?"

"Well, I guess I don't—"

"You don't know? Shit, man, that's *Gone With the Wind*. Clark Gable says it to Vivien Leigh. You want another one?"

"Okay."

"Here's another one. Wait a minute." Francis screwed up his eyes in concentration. "You got another one, Ralph?"

"No."

"You got one, John?"

"Not yet."

"Well, wait a minute. We'll think of one. Plenty of good pictures." But his downcast, brooding face had begun to suggest that there weren't plenty of them at all. "Some pictures I don't like," he said. "I don't like that *Psycho*, you know? Anthony Perkins? I mean that's a bad picture, know what I mean?"

"Mm."

"Yeah."

"Well, let's think." He thought for a while and then he said "Shit, I don't want to play pictures any more. You like music, John?"

"Sure. What kind of music?"

"Any kind. You like this?" He bunched himself into an athletic squat and began slapping his flexed thighs as if they were bongo drums; when the rhythm was established he threw back his head and closed his eyes as he sang, or rather wailed and howled, in what could have been an ultra-progressive style of jazz or an African tribal chant. Ralph seemed to like it: his own eyes glazed over and he wagged his head to the drumming.

"Hey," said the man with the newspapers. "Take a look at this." He had neatly torn out a sports headline from the *New York Post:* CAN MARIS TOP THE BABE? "Got that?" he said. "Well, watch. Wait." Out of his raddled sheaf came half a dozen other scraps of newsprint, which he shielded from view. "Wait," he muttered over his work, carefully tearing and smoothing and adjusting, and then "Look now," he said. "Look at there."

He had laid out a big photograph of Marilyn Monroe. The headline above it read: CAN pARIS sTOP THis BABE? And beneath it, in many different typefaces, ran the caption: Tired Blood? TALK ABOUT SUMMER VALUES! *IKE VOICES 'CONCERN' AS Thousands Flee City's Heat;* F.B.I. Joins State, Local Police in Massive Effort to *FLY AIR FRANCE.*

"Well, that's—quite something."

"Ah, it's not a very good one. I'll do a better one. Wait."

Francis's music had grown louder and seemed to have put him in a trance. The effort of singing had brought up two gouts of phlegm from his throat, but he'd caught them both without missing a beat, one on the back of each flying hand.

"Mr. Wilder?" Charlie called from the corridor. He was holding Spivack close by the upper arm, either in restraint or affection, and Spivack glowered with narrow eyes, breathing so hard through his nose that his head wobbled slightly with each breath. "Mr. Wilder, Dr. Spivack would like you to join him for supper this evening."

". . . Okay, you can eat with me, Wilder," Spivack said as they filed into the stifling mess hall, "but no more questions; no more fucking *talk*, is that clear?"

On Sunday morning Wilder was shot out.

It happened so quickly that he could never afterwards put it straight in his memory: there was no coherent pattern of helplessness and resentment and anger rising to rage. He'd had his breakfast and his Nourishment and his ward cigarette; he was standing alone at one of the grey windows looking out on nothing, and he heard the shouted word "Shit! . . . Shit!" before he recognized his own voice. He stepped back from the window, raised the sole of one dirty foot and slammed it against the steel-mesh grid, denting it, and the sight of that dent was so invigorating that he hauled off and slammed it again and again, making it deeper, while his raw throat burned with the cry of *"Shit! Shit! Shit! . . ."* He was only dimly aware of other voices around him—*"Watch* it, fella"; "Easy; *easy"*—and not until two orderlies grabbed his arms did he know he was in trouble. "Hey, Charlie!" somebody called. "Charlie!"

And there he came, lumbering down the corridor with his face pressed into a frown. He paused under a light to squint at his upraised needle until the drop gleamed on its point; then the orderlies tore down Wilder's pants and Charlie sank the shot into one buttock. "I did warn you, Mr. Wilder," he said. "I told you to watch that temper of yours." The door of a padded cell was opened just enough for Wilder to be flung inside; it slammed shut and he heard the lock click. He couldn't breathe and it took a great deal of work to pull up his pants and secure them while scrabbling on all fours around the soft floor; then the drug went to work in him—heavy waves of sleep as deep as drowning—and the last thing he knew as he turned and floundered and sank was that nothing in his life had ever been as bad as this. This was the worst.

". . . Wilder? Hey, off your ass, man."

It could have been ten minutes or ten hours later. "Wilder?"

"Mm? . . . Wha'? . . ."

"Get up outa there, man. You got visitors."

Visitors.

He stumbled up the corridor like a drunk, colliding with other men, reeling against one wall for support and then against the other. Even when he found his balance he had to stop and run furtive fingers down the fly of his pants to make sure it was closed while his free hand clawed hair away from his eyes.

The mess hall had been transformed into a visitors' room—tables shoved out of the way, benches hauled around in conversational groupings—and he stood blinking in the doorway for some time before discovering his wife and Paul Borg. He tried not to wobble as he sat down with them and said hello.

"Oh, this must be awful for you, John," Janice said, putting her hand on his knee. "This *place.*" She looked troubled and affectionate—she had even worn what she called his favorite dress, a blue-and-brown print that emphasized her breasts—and for a second or two he could see the girl who'd made all other girls unnecessary long ago.

"Yeah. Well, how've you been? How's Tommy?"

"We're fine. Except that we miss you."

"What'd you tell him?"

"I said you'd been held over by business in Chicago."

"Well, but the trouble is you can't possibly say when I'll be back. I won't even see a doctor till Thursday, and God only knows what'll happen after that. Might be two weeks, four weeks, six weeks, and I mean whaddya gonna *tell* him?"

"Sh-sh." She squeezed his knee. "Why don't you let me worry about Tommy? He'll be fine; I promise. You just concentrate on getting rested and getting well."

"And I can't even call him because there's no phone here. Look, you better call the office Tuesday; tell George I've got the flu or something."

"Oh, of course, dear. That's no problem."

Paul Borg had been gazing around at other patients as if trying to assess the degree of insanity in each case; then he turned the same cool scrutiny on Wilder for an instant before they both lowered their eyes, and that was when Wilder saw a carton of cigarettes on Borg's lap.

"Jesus, are those for me? Can I have 'em?"

". . . One thing I still fail to understand," Borg was saying, "is this nuisance about the Labor Day weekend."

"Yeah."

"An institution of this size, a public institution; surely it's reasonable to expect at least a partial psychiatric staff to be on duty over the holidays."

"Yeah. Sure is." With a cigarette in his mouth, a pack in his pocket and a carton under his arm he was ready to forgive anybody for anything.

At the end of visiting hour they went out into the pressing, overheated crowd near the front door. Borg shook his hand and Janice put her arms around him to kiss him goodbye. "John?" she said. "You know what I thought we might do? When you do come home? I thought we might drive up to the country with Tommy —he can skip a few days of school—and just relax and be together and have a little vacation. Maybe a whole week. How does that sound?"

"Sounds fine. I— Yeah, that sounds fine."

And the door was locked behind them.

"Hey, save me, buddy, okay?"

"Save me, man."

"Save me . . ."

He was the center of attention, passing out cigarettes, until Charlie said "Mr. Wilder? Will you come with me, please?" and led him to the KEEP OUT room. "That carton won't last very long if you carry it around," he said. "What we generally do when a man gets a carton, we keep it for him in here. I'll write your name on it." And while writing he said "Was that lady your wife, Mr. Wilder?"

"Yes."

"A very nice-looking lady; very well dressed. You have children? . . . Well, that's fine; a son. I have three little girls, myself," he said when they were back in the corridor. "Seven, eight and nine years old. They're the joy of my life."

"All right, how d'ya like *that*, Charlie?" Spivack demanded. "Explain *that* to me if you're so fucking smart."

"Explain what, Doctor?"

"What the hell d'ya think? My father and my sister. I gave 'em every chance. I waited at that God damned door for a solid hour and neither *one* of 'em showed up. You know what *I* think?" His eyes were as wild as when he'd been shot out for shadowboxing. Charlie laid one hand around his shoulder as if to guide him away for a private talk, but he held his ground. "You know what *I* think? That jerk-off spook of a husband of hers's got 'em *both* by the short hairs. He's got 'em *both* convinced I'm a dangerous lunatic and they've written me off! They're gonna let me *rot* in here!"

"Oh, now, I imagine there's any number of reasons why they couldn't make it today, Doctor. One thing, you have to remember your father's getting on in years and it's a long trip for him, all the way down from White Plains. Your sister has her family to look after, and she's probably—"

"Charlie, you're a great big chocolate sweetheart but you don't know shit about human nature. Even a dumb little asshole like *Wilder* knows more'n you. Gimme your pen."

"I don't believe I'll give you anything, Doctor, until you apologize to Mr. Wilder and to me. For your language."

"Ah, Jesus fucking Christ. Language. Apologize. All right, all right, I apologize. Let's try it this way. Nurse, would you please be so kind as to lend me your invaluable twenty-nine-cent ballpoint pen for approximately twelve seconds?" He tore a dirty scrap of paper from his pajama pocket, held it flat against the wall and wrote a set of numerals. "Here. Now listen carefully. This is my sister's phone number. When you get off work tonight I want you to call this number and give her the following message. Tell her—"

But Charlie was shaking his head. "You know I can't do anything like that."

Spivack backed away three steps and stood there—legs apart, fists clenched and eyes blazing. "So what the hell *can* you do? Smile? Preach? Make everybody's ass feel good? What the hell *can* you do, you big, dumb, motherfucking—"

"Doctor!"

"Yeah, 'Doctor.' Shit. Why don'tcha just shoot me out and get it over with?"

"I've considered that," Charlie said, "but I believe you're playing games with me. You know I don't play games. What's more, you've taken up too much of my time. There are a good many other patients on this ward besides yourself." He turned and walked away into one of the shuffling columns, soon surrounded by other talking, favor-seeking men. Spivack slumped alone against the wall, and that gave Wilder a chance for escape.

He ducked quickly into the latrine. He had a comb in his pocket now—another gift from Paul Borg—so he dampened his head and restored it to the carefully casual shape of everyday: a clean part on the left, short front hairs combed sideways across the brow, longer side hairs back and down. It was a style he had copied from the actor Alan Ladd after years of experimentation, and it looked all right. He had to admit, studying himself from several angles in the dim, white- and red-flecked mirror, that this was a sound, manly, reliable face. Troubled, maybe, but not openly neurotic and certainly not mentally ill. It was nothing less than absurd for him to be here, in the Men's Violence Ward, and the absurdity made him toss his head with a wry, amused little smile.

"Hey, what the hell you doin', man?" said a voice behind him. "You tryna look pretty for yourself?"

". . . I mean it may be understandable in my sister's case," Spivack said, coming up beside him in the supper line. "She lets that slippery bastard *fuck* her every night. He works the old cock up in there and shoves it around till she screams, and I guess you can't blame her for believing all the Sigmund Freud horseshit he gives her in the daytime. But my father; that's something else. *And* my brothers. They're intelligent men! They're medical men! They *know* I was railroaded in here on some half-assed, trumped-up charge of— Ah, never mind. Let's go eat up our goody-good macaroni and cheese."

One of the new patients brought in on Monday—or was it Tuesday?— was a grey-haired Negro so badly injured around the head and face that bloodstained bandages covered his eyes. They couldn't make a blind man walk, so his bunk stayed down and he lay on it all day as the column on that side of the corridor detoured around him. Wilder passed him twice before noticing that his wrists and ankles were secured to the bunk by heavy restraining bands. He writhed constantly, groaning and muttering; several times he struggled up to a half-sitting position and screamed.

"D.T.s," Spivack explained.

"How can you tell?"

"Obvious. Anyone with medical training can spot 'em. Lot of the drunks in here have 'em all the time. Hear what he was yelling just now? When Charlie went over to him?"

"No."

" 'Ah! Ah! Ah got lucidations! Ah got lucidations!' Didn't you hear that? He means hallucinations. Bastard's been soaking up a quart a day for twenty-five years and now his brains have turned to shit. You drink, Wilder?"

"Some."

"How much? Four, five, six drinks a day?"

"I don't know."

"Eight? Ten? Fifteen? More'n that? Huh?"

"Look, Spivack: in the first place I don't think it's any of your fucking—"

"Wow! Boy! Talk about hitting a *sore* spot— So *that's* your trouble. Well, it figures: you do look like a lush; funny I didn't notice before."

"Yeah, funny," Wilder said. "Fuck you."

And Spivack's reply was to thrust a triumphant middle finger high in the air and say "Fuck *you*" as he turned and disappeared into the column of walkers.

For the rest of that day—Tuesday?—they avoided each other. Wilder tried to renew his acquaintance with Ralph and Francis, but Ralph didn' 'eem to recognize him and Francis didn't want to play pictures even when Wilder fed him a good one—"Hey, what picture is this: 'Play it again, Sam'?"

He helped the newspaper man lay out a spread that didn't work at all, and after that he kept to himself, walking the corridor, peering at his double image in the cop's sunglasses, smoking cigarettes and saving people, wondering in a quiet panic if he really might be out of his mind.

But sometime during the next afternoon he heard the blind man saying "Oh! Oh! Oh!" and found Spivack crouching low over his bunk.

"What's the matter, Sambo?" Spivack inquired softly. "You got them old lucidations again? You want a drink?

Well, I'm afraid that's tough, Sambo, because we don't got no drinks in here."

". . . Oh! Oh! Oh! . . ."

"No, we don't got nothin' here but Peraldehyde and straitjackets and shots in the ass and . . ."

"Why don't you cut that shit out?" Wilder said.

Spivack straightened his spine and turned around in a great display of surprise. "Well, I'll be God damned." His gaze ran from Wilder's eyes to his bare feet and back again. "Look who's preaching at me now. I thought I'd taken just about every kind of holy-Joe shit there is, from every kind of fool; and now some pipsqueak, some drunken little salesman starts telling me 'kindness,' starts telling me 'compassion,' starts telling me—"

"You're an arrogant, insolent, overbearing son of a bitch, Spivack. You're a prick . . ." Wilder walked backwards, letting Spivack advance on him, but it wasn't a retreat; he was withdrawing to a wider part of the corridor where the crowd was thin and he could take a stand.

"And whaddya think *you* are? Some Boy Scout? Some faggot social worker? Some saint? Christ himself? Huh?"

They both stopped, three feet apart, glaring fiercely and ready for anything. Neither of them took up a fighting stance—their hands hung loose—but Wilder squared his shoulders and said "How'd you like a punch in the mouth, Spivack?"

"From you? Funny little alcoholic creep? Shit; I'd wipe up the floor with you in five seconds and you know it."

"Don't be too fucking sure of that, Spivack."

"Wanna try it? See what happens?"

Then the KEEP OUT door swung open and Charlie was

smiling there, happy with welcome. "Gentlemen?" he said. "Would you care to join me for a cup of coffee?"

Going about the cordial business of arranging chairs for them and measuring out instant coffee while the pan of water bubbled on the hotplate, he seemed unaware of their red, hard-breathing faces and trembling limbs. "I generally enjoy a little coffee at this time of the day," he said, "and once in a while it's nice to have company. If you don't mind I think I'll just shut that door. Makes the air a little close in here, but I don't want to give the impression I'm holding open house. Sugar and cream, Mr. Wilder?"

"Yes, please."

"It's only a powdered cream substitute, of course, but it's very tasty. You, Doctor?"

"No, thanks. Black."

At first Charlie did all the talking as they sat and sipped and smoked in this unaccustomed luxury. Wilder kept waiting for his monologue to turn into a lecture (". . . Now, I don't want to see any more trouble between you two . . .") but it didn't, and soon they were able to relax. They could even exchange bashful, half-smiling glances of complicity, like bad little boys who'd managed to raise hell without getting caught.

". . . Well, I'm certainly glad the holiday's over," Charlie was saying. "These long weekends are always difficult. We get badly overcrowded; we don't have an adequate staff; it's good to have the psychiatrists back. Oh, now, never mind, Doctor, I know *your* opinion of psychiatrists; we needn't go into that. All I mean is, from my point of view, it's good to have them back because they make decisions. Some of the men here have to go home to their families, right? Some have to be sent to alcoholic or narcotic facilities, some have to be sent up to Wingdale or Rockland or wherever, and some—well, it's no secret—some have to go to criminal court. And I mean, those decisions have to be made, right?"

Spivack frowned over the careful stubbing out of his cigarette. "Charlie," he said, "will you tell me the truth?"

"I'll do my best."

"Who was it—which of these big decision-makers of yours—exactly which one of them told you I was a paranoid schizophrenic?"

And Charlie leaned back for a delighted peal of laughter, placing one great white shoe on the edge of the table. "Ah, Doctor, you tickle me. It wasn't *any* of 'em. It was you yourself! You came out of an interview—what was it, two, three weeks ago?—and you said 'Better watch out for me, Charlie, I'm a paranoid schizophrenic.' It was you yourself told me!"

But Spivack was not amused.

When Charlie's laughter dwindled he put both feet on the floor and leaned earnestly forward. "I do know one thing, though, Doctor. Mind you, this isn't criticism, but I imagine every time you see those psychiatrists you go in with a negative attitude. I imagine you tell them about filing your malpractice suit and so on, and of course that's understandable. You're a physician too and you've been placed in a difficult situation here. All I mean to suggest is this: why don't you surprise them next time? Walk in there and answer their questions, make a good appearance, show a little sense of humor, let them see the kind of rational, agreeable man you *are* most of the time, the kind of man you are with me, or with Mr. Wilder here."

"Yeah, yeah, okay," Spivack said. "I'll turn on the old charm. Hey, here, I forgot to give your pen back." He unclipped it from his pajama pocket and slid it across the table. "Don't suppose you've got an envelope, do you, Charlie?"

"An envelope? No."

"Doesn't matter. Even if I had an envelope I'd still need a stamp. Thing is, I wrote a letter to my sister. Want to read it?"

"Oh, I'd rather not, Doctor, if you don't mind; I don't really enjoy reading other people's personal—"

The door shuddered with pounding and a voice called "Charlie! There's a turd on the floor! Some son of a bitch dropped a *turd* on the floor . . ."

"Excuse me, gentlemen," he said as he escorted them quickly back into the corridor. "I'll have to lock up here. It's been a pleasure."

Would there now be a resumption of their fight? Evidently not. Spivack walked moodily but not angrily, and soon he made shy, tentative efforts at conversation. "*There* goes a Wingdale man," he said as they passed a muscular, dull-eyed Puerto Rican wearing work clothes: high-top shoes, denim shirt, green twill pants with wide, old-fashioned suspenders. "When they dress 'em up that way it's Wingdale every time. And oh Jesus, look at that."

A very old white man stood crying like an infant—"Wah! Wah! Wah!"—as an orderly approached him with a straitjacket. He twisted away and tried feebly to escape; in the tussle his pajama pants fell and revealed genitals so shriveled and small that they might have been an infant's too, and he clutched them either in shame or anxiety.

"Hey there, sexpot," Spivack said in passing.

"Save me, buddy," the shuffling men were saying of their cigarettes, "save me . . ."

"Yeah, yeah, we'll save you. Hey, look, Wilder: there isn't a soul in Jerk-off City. Want to sit down?" And they sank onto the stained mattresses. "Want to read my letter? I mean I worked like a bastard on it; seems like *some*body ought to read the damn thing."

"Okay; sure." He accepted the smudged, much-folded sheet of paper and opened it.

Dear Sis; dear Miss Priss:

If you are languorously glancing through *The New Yorker* and sipping an ever-so-extra-dry martini when you receive this letter, or if you are changing from a terribly sweet little cocktail dress into something svelte and provocative for evening, or if you are dabbing a delightfully subtle Parisian scent at your throat in preparation for prolonged and exquisite dalliance with your husband tonight, then don't bother to read it. Drop it among the crushed gardenias and the empty Liebfraumilch bottles and the Tiffany invitations to parties you've chosen not to attend.

If, however, this letter finds you on your knees in your dungarees scrubbing the kitchen floor, or scouring a pot so badly encrusted with last Saturday's *Boeuf Bourguignonne* that your fingers bleed into the Brillo, or better still sitting and grunting and raising a stink on what I believe your husband calls the "john," then read the hell out of it, baby. This is important. This is reality.

1. —Call Dad.
2. —Call Eric and Mark.
3. —Tell your husband he is a simpering, pretentious little fool.
4. —GET ME OUT OF HERE.

HENRY

"So whaddya think?" he asked.

"Well, it's pretty funny, but the general tone does seem a little—"

" 'Hostile,' right? That's every psychiatrist's favorite word."

"I wasn't going to say that; I just mean it seems a little on the self-defeating side. Doesn't seem very likely to accomplish its purpose."

Spivack sighed and stuffed it back into his pajamas. "Ah, I guess you're right. Purely an academic question anyway. Haven't got an envelope; haven't got a stamp."

Wilder's name was called on Thursday morning. He stood by the cop at the door, combing and recombing his hair while Spivack gave him last-minute counsel.

"It's an inquisition. They ask you questions—loaded questions, the kind that'd never stand up in a court of law—and when you answer they don't listen to you: they listen *at* you. They let everything you say slide past and hang in the air while they study it. Because it's not the substance they care about, it's the style. You can almost *see* them thinking 'Mm; interesting. Why did he make that slip? Why that particular choice of words?' Oh, and they watch you like hawks too. Not just your face—it's very important to keep a straight face and look 'em in the eyes—but everything. Squirm around in your chair, cross your legs, put your hand up to your head or anything like that and you're dead."

"Okay, Wilder," an orderly said. "Let's go."

There may have been less than a dozen white-coated men in the interview room but there seemed to be twice that many. They sat row on row in chairs with writing-panel armrests, like students, and Wilder faced them alone in an ordinary chair with his sweating hands on his thighs, as if he were their teacher. Nobody smiled. A bald, heavy man in the front row cleared his throat and said "Well. What seems to be the trouble?"

It probably lasted a quarter of an hour. First he did his best to tell them about the business trip to Chicago, about the week of insomnia and heavy drinking, about Paul Borg and St. Vincent's and the poorly remembered events that had brought him here.

Then came the questions. Had Wilder ever been in a mental hospital before? Had he ever been under psychiatric care? Had he ever sought treatment for alcoholism? Had his drinking ever gotten him into trouble? With an employer? With his family? With the police?

No, he kept saying, no; no; no—and through it all he held his face straight, sat still and didn't gesticulate. But after the questions they stared in silence; they seemed to expect him to make a summing-up in his own defense, and that was when everything went to hell. One hand leaped to his wet brow and clung there. "Look," he said. "Listen: I know if I say 'I'm not crazy' it'll probably just convince you I am; but even so, that's my—that's my position." The hand fell back to his thigh, but he knew he was squirming because he heard his chair creak. "I *don't* think I'm crazy, or mentally ill or emotionally disturbed or whatever the hell, I mean whatever you people call it." His mouth was so dry he could feel every movement of tongue and teeth and lips in their laborious effort to form speech. "I know I was behaving erratically or whaddyacallit, irrationally last Friday, but that was last Friday. After the first couple of nights' sleep and the first few doses of formaldehyde, I mean *you* know, Peraldehyde, I think I was all right again, and I'm all right now; so the point is— Christ's *sake*, is anybody *listening?*" The spastic hand flew to his head again, messing up his hair, and his eyes closed to shut out their faces.

"What makes you think nobody's listening?"

"Because I've been locked up in a God damned— because this place is enough to drive anybody out of their—I don't know." He opened his eyes, but nothing could be done about his hand. "Look. Listen: I don't think I belong here any more and I think I ought to be discharged. That's all I've got to say."

He was reminded again of a classroom—this time of one whose students are embarrassed because their teacher has made a fool of himself—so his face twitched into an apologetic little grimace and he said what teachers often say at such moments: "Are there any—questions?"

"Okay, Wilder," said the orderly, and he was escorted back and locked into the ward, where he wanted to smash his fist against the wall or scream or kick a window again with his filthy foot. Instead he walked and smoked, promising to save people.

"How'd it go?" Spivack inquired.

"Shit, I don't know."

"Slimy bunch of bastards, aren't they? Make your flesh crawl. And when you think of the *power* those fish-eyed fuckers have over a man's life—I mean talk about your FBI; talk about your CIA; talk about your Nazi secret police . . ."

But an hour later Charlie beckoned him aside for a hushed, private talk near the KEEP OUT door. "You did very well in there, Mr. Wilder."

"I what? I did? How do you know?"

"Well, now, never mind; I just happen to know you gave a good account of yourself. Matter of fact I understand they'll be taking you down to Rehabilitation after lunch. It's very nice there, very clean; they seldom keep a man more than twenty-four hours. Give you a little counselling, finish up your paperwork, get your clothes and you're free to go. But look: it's a busy day and I may not see you again, so I'll just say goodbye and wish you well"—he held out a big hand to shake—"and another thing. I think it's very nice the way you've been so friendly with Dr. Spivack; talking with him, taking your meals with him. Dr. Spivack didn't really have any friends here till you came. He's a fine man, as you know; only trouble is he's a little—disturbed. Well. Good luck, sir."

"Thanks. Thanks, Charlie."

And he watched him move away to bear down on the beautiful boy in the turban. "Gail! Now, Gail, how many times have I told you to take that pajama top off your head? And put your penis back in your pants where it belongs. Nobody wants to look at that thing."

They called six or eight men to stand by the front door after lunch, and Wilder was among them.

"Well, look at you," Spivack said, advancing on him. "Wudga do in there anyway? Bribe 'em? Blackmail 'em? Crawl around and kiss their asses? Hey, wait a second. Got something for you." And he probed in his pajama pocket, to which Charlie's pen was clipped.

"What's this? Another letter?"

"No, shitface. My address and phone number. If I ever do get outa here I might buy you a drink sometime."

"Well, that's very— Sure; thanks."

"So here's the pen: wanna give me yours?"

And Wilder did so. "I'll look forward to it, Spivack," he said.

"Yeah, well, don't hold your breath. I may forget your fucking existence in an hour and a half. Anyway, keep a tight asshole, Wilder."

"I'll try. You too."

The door opened, not to let the men out but to admit an elderly female nurse trailed by a dozen very young girls in fresh blue-and-white striped smocks and white stockings.

"My God," Spivack said. "Student nurses. Beautiful little student nurses on a training tour." He stepped back into the corridor and stood with his arms flung wide, like a master of ceremonies. "Girls, I'm delighted to see you. It's nonsense for them to send you up here because once you graduate you'll never get near this place, but even so you might learn something— Oh, it's all right, Nurse," he said to their leader, who seemed to have been stricken dumb. "I'm a staff physician; I can handle this. Girls, what we have here is a relic of the nineteenth century. This isn't a 'psychiatric ward,' you see; it's a madhouse . . ."

Some of the girls looked bewildered and a few looked scared, but most had begun to giggle behind their hands to show they found Spivack "cute."

"Officer," the nurse was saying to the cop, "who's the charge nurse on this ward?"

"His name's Charlie, ma'am. I can't leave the door, but I'll send somebody to get him—just a second. Hey, uh—"

". . . We have psychopathic criminals here, girls, and we have men in advanced stages of madness caused by venereal disease and alcohol and drugs, and we have at least one Second Coming of Christ; then we have men who don't belong here at all. Take my own case: I'm what you might call a political prisoner. Hospital politics, that is; medical politics. I don't suppose they teach you girls about medical politics, but I really think they should because believe me it's a very real, very treacherous—"

"Doctor!" Charlie came loping up the corridor in a swarm of laughing men. "Doctor, I want you to leave those girls alone . . ."

The door opened again to let Wilder's group out, and then it was locked behind them.

Rehabilitation was very nice and clean indeed: real beds, chrome-and-leatherette armchairs, good showers with soap and a kind of shampoo guaranteed to remove lice. The talk was quiet and most of it courteous: nobody wanted to make trouble.

"Counseling," the next day, meant being taken into a roomful of cluttered typewriter desks—it might have been a state unemployment office—and sitting down beside a pale man who looked like an underpaid clerk but was said to be a psychiatric social worker.

". . . and you'll be seeking psychotherapy after your release, right?"

"Well, I don't know; I haven't really thought about it."

The interviewer stopped typing, closed his eyes and ran pale fingers over his face. "You know something? I don't understand some of you people. You're a mature, well-employed man with family responsibilities. You spend a week as an involuntary patient in the tightest lockup in the city and you 'haven't really thought about it.'"

"Okay. I will, then."

"You damn sure better, mister. Now. Can you afford private care, or do you want to apply for outpatient treatment here?"

"Private care."

"What about your drinking? You gonna quit?"

"Frankly, I think that's my own— Well, look: if you're filling out a form there, just write 'Yes.' That'll take care of it."

"Oh, you *are* a little wise guy, aren'tcha? I don't know; I don't know. Some of you people." He finished typing, ripped the forms from the machine and tore out the carbon paper; then he stapled them, banged them angrily in several places with a rubber stamp, and the business seemed concluded.

"Can I get my clothes now?"

"You're kidding. You've gotta be kidding. You think the City of New York's just gonna let you walk outa here, after the way you came in? You can be discharged," he said, "only in the custody of Mr. Paul R. Borg; only after he has personally met and talked with me; and *only* if he agrees to sign these papers." He reached for his phone. "Now you go back inside and wait. I'm tired of your face."

It didn't take very long. Paul Borg came walking into Rehabilitation with an anxious smile, carrying a mimeographed slip. He had signed the discharge papers, he said; this was the one for the clothes. "It says Room 3-F. You know where that is?"

They found it only after walking down wrong corridors, taking wrong elevators and asking directions of people who didn't speak English; and when Wilder was dressed (an incredible pleasure: his own clothes and shoes, his own wristwatch and walletful of money), he said "Listen, Paul. Something I've got to do. Got to find the canteen, or the gift shop or whatever they call it."

"Why?"

"Never mind. Come on. Must be on the ground floor." It was, and Wilder bought a carton of Pall Malls. With his own pen he wrote "For Charlie with many thanks," and signed his name. "Now," he said. "Where's the Psycho elevator?"

"John, what *is* this?"

"Never mind. It's important."

" 'Men's Violence Ward?' " said the puzzled elevator man. "Ain't no ward by that name."

"Well, that may not be the official name," Wilder said, "but it's the men's ward on the seventh floor."

"Can't take you up there anyway. Ain't no visiting hour today."

"I'm not a visitor, I'm a— Well, look. Just take this up

to the ward, give it to the cop at the door and tell him it's for Charlie. Will you do that?"

"Oh. Sure, okay." And the door slid shut.

"Son of a bitch'll keep 'em for himself," Wilder said, "or else he'll give 'em to the cop and the *cop*'ll keep 'em. I should've insisted on going up. I should've *demanded* to go up."

"John, it doesn't matter. Can't you see it doesn't matter?"

"It does matter. Some things *matter*, that's all."

But at last they found their way through corridors and waiting rooms and doors into the abrupt, fresh air of First Avenue, and Wilder said "Wow." Then he said "My God."

It was midafternoon on a fine September day, and nothing had ever smelled so sweet. Tall buildings rose in a deep blue sky and pigeons wheeled and sailed among them; clean cars and taxicabs sped uptown bearing sane, unfettered people to the sane, unfettered business of the world.

"I'm parked right around the corner," Borg said as they walked. "Have you home in no time at all. John? What's the trouble now?"

He had stopped to read a torn scrap of paper from his pocket: *Henry J. Spivack, M.D.*, with an address and phone number lettered underneath. "Nothing," he said, and let it flutter from his hand to the dirty street. "It's nothing. It doesn't matter."

3

What the Wilders called "the country" was a clapboard bungalow on half an acre of ground, fifty miles up the west bank of the Hudson. It would have been exposed to a great many other bungalows except for the dense shrubbery and trees shielding it on three sides and a high rustic fence along the fourth—that gave it the seclusion they prized, and there was a small lake for swimming close by.

But the best and most bracing part of the country was getting there: the trip across the George Washington Bridge and the long pastoral ride up the divided highway. As with certain other family pleasures, expectation topped fulfillment.

". . . I think this is my favorite time of year," Janice was saying, "when it's just beginning to get fresh and cool again. Oh, I suppose it'll be even nicer in a few more weeks when the leaves really turn—all those lovely yellows and oranges and reds and browns—but even so, this is marvelous."

"Mm," he said. She had done a great deal of talking since he came home from Bellevue yesterday—most of it serving no purpose except to fill silence—and he knew that was because he'd said so little himself: he had mostly drunk bourbon and looked out of windows, or sat blinking in bewilderment along the shelves upon shelves of tightly packed books. "Well," he said now, doing his best, "it'll sure feel great just to lie on a blanket in the grass."

Tommy, in the back seat, had been silent since leaving home. He was methodically pounding an unused regulation baseball into the oiled pocket of his fielder's glove, and he wore a New York Yankees cap. The Yankees were far ahead in the American League pennant race, and Tommy liked winners.

"How do you want to work it, Champ?" Wilder asked him. "Take a swim first and then play catch, or play catch and then go swimming?" And he instantly regretted calling him "Champ." He used that nickname, or "Buster," or "Slugger," only in times of family tension when it seemed urgent to be hearty (on mornings, for example, when he knew the boy had lain awake and heard his parents fight the night before), and he knew that Tommy knew it too.

"I don't know," Tommy said. "I don't care." And the flawless surface of the road sped along under their tires.

The way they worked it was to play catch first, while Janice, wearing a big floppy hat, knelt and squatted in the sun to weed her vegetable garden.

It wasn't a good game of catch—no warm, sweat-raising pull and release of muscles with each exchange, no clean flight of the ball to a satisfying *pock* in the glove, no easy laughter and congratulations ("Hey! . . .";

"Nice! . . ."). Well over half of Tommy's throws were wild and sent his father racing breathlessly over the grass or down on all fours under the bushes, where twigs whipped his face and mud soaked the knees of his clean chino pants. Once a pine needle stabbed him in the eye.

Then his own throws began to go wrong, making Tommy do the running, and if nothing else, that gave him a chance to get his wind back. "Let's try—let's try a couple of grounders," he called, hoping to make it easier on them both, but there was nothing easy about grounders on this lumpy ground: the ball jumped and flew in crazy directions; they ran and went sprawling and Tommy's Yankee cap fell off.

"Haven't you two had enough?" Janice inquired, smiling up from the garden. "Don't you want to go for a swim?"

"How—how about it, Tom? Feel like calling it—calling it quits?"

"I don't know; I don't care."

Things didn't go well at the lake either, but that was to be expected. Janice was an excellent swimmer and Tommy was good too, for his age, but Wilder had been afraid of water—and afraid to admit it—all his life. Through boyhood and youth he had done his best to avoid swimming; when it was inevitable, he'd endured it as a kind of aquatic clown, thrashing and dog-paddling, helplessly gulping and inhaling water, scared of putting his head under but taking hilariously graceless flops from springboards to win laughs he never heard as he struggled blind and terrified back to the air. This was one of the first things Janice had learned about him, before they were married, and had caused one of their first quarrels

("But that's silly, John; anybody can learn to swim."
"Okay, okay; I'm silly, then. Let's shut up about it").
When Tommy was a baby and even until he was five or
six, it hadn't mattered much: he could wade in deep with
the boy wriggling and squealing on his shoulders, and
he'd greatly enjoyed the trusting grip of small thighs
around his neck and fingers in his hair—it had been
especially good in heavy ocean surf where nobody really
swam anyway and the whole point was to jump and
shout in the breakers—but over the past few years, here
at the lake, Janice had taught Tommy to swim. She had
done it tactfully: if he'd ever asked why Daddy didn't
teach him, she'd probably said that Daddy was too busy
or too tired, or that Daddy didn't really enjoy swimming
as much as other things, like—well, like playing
catch.

The lake was crowded today—people from neighbor-
ing bungalows out for a last chance at summer—and that
made him less conspicuous as he hung back to fuss over
the careful arrangement of blanket and towels and shoes
and wristwatches while his wife and son struck out for
the white raft that always seemed an impossible distance
away. Nobody in a crowd this thick was likely to notice
that he waded up to his nostrils before starting to tread
water and only then began the desperate flailing and
kicking, with tightly held breath, that enabled him at last
to reach out and grasp one of the wet chains securing the
raft to the steel drums beneath it. Once he had that
chain he was all right; he could rest, maneuver for purchase and heave himself up, shedding water and whipping back his hair with a gasp of relief that might have
been a victorious athlete's sigh.

"Hi," Janice said as she and Tommy made room for him. There was no way of telling whether they'd watched his journey out here.

"It's a little chilly, don't you think?" she said. "Look, I'm all goose pimples." He looked, and she was. She lowered her voice. "And it's so *crowded*. I don't think I've ever seen quite so many people here before, have you?"

No; he hadn't.

Nor had he ever seen anything quite so lovely as the slim young girl who walked alone among the huddled bodies on the raft at that moment, murmuring "Excuse me" as they moved aside for her. She wore her bikini with a sweet combination of shyness and pride, and when she stood erect at the base of the diving board she seemed unaware of anyone watching. She took three gracefully measured steps, then both arms and one splendid thigh rose up, the thigh came down, the board shuddered under her powerful spring and she was airborne, parting the water with almost no splash at all.

He expected a pair of heavily muscled arms to reach out and help her back to the raft, but none did: she *was* alone. She climbed back herself and sat shaking out her long black hair, talking to nobody. Except for a young couple absorbed in each other, the raft was filled either with children or with adults of middle- and post-middle age: bald heads and sagging flesh and varicose veins.

"Let's go back in," Janice said. "I want to put on some clothes and get warm, don't you?"

"Okay. You two go on ahead. I'll be along in a minute."

He watched their precise four-beat crawl to the shore, watched them gather up their things and disappear into the bushes; then he gave his whole attention to the girl, who had stood up in readiness for another dive. When she came back from this one he would speak to her. He wouldn't try to help her onto the raft—that might spoil everything—but it would certainly be easy to sit beside her as she dried off (if they were sitting, she wouldn't see how short he was; then later when they stood up it might turn out that she wasn't really very tall), and now as she gravely advanced to the board he allowed his mind to fill with a happy rehearsal of their talk.

"You know, you're really very good at that."

"Oh?" (Shaking her hair, not quite meeting his eyes.) "Well; thank you."

"Live around here?"

"No; I'm visiting my parents. They have a little . . ."

"You in school?"

"No; I graduated from Holyoke last June; now I work for an ad agency in the city."

"Which one? Thing is, you see, I'm in the same business."

"Really? Well, it's . . ."

She had executed her three dancer's steps now, performed her wonderful thigh-flexing and her leap, and his secret dialogue raced ahead.

". . . Maybe we could meet for lunch sometime."

"Well, actually, I—yes, that might be nice."

And later: "Oh, this has been such fun, John; I mean I'd *heard* of expense-account lunches, but I've never really . . ."

And later still, after their first brandy-flavored kiss in the taxicab downtown: "*What* street? Varick Street? Is that where you live?"

"Well, not exactly; just a little place I think you might like . . ."

The bubbles had long vanished from her splash, and he waited for the water to break again with her surfacing, but it didn't. He stood up (Who cared how short he was?) and watched for her on all sides of the raft like an alert, conscientious lifeguard. Only after what seemed a full minute did he see her moving far away, her slender arms stroking as smoothly as Janice's as she made for the shoreline and the trees, going home. And then, sitting hunched until his heart had slowed down and the ache of disappointment in his clenched jaws relaxed, there was nothing to do but slide into the cold water and fight his way home himself.

One good thing: there was plenty of bourbon on the kitchen shelf. As soon as he was dressed he got out the ice and made himself a double that was more like a triple.

"Feel like a drink?" he asked Janice.

"No thanks." She was sitting on a tall kitchen stool in her slacks with a colander in her lap, snapping string beans for dinner, and didn't look up. "It's a little early, isn't it?"

"Seems late enough to me."

And not until he'd gone outdoors for the first few greedy swallows did he figure out why he was so angry. It wasn't because of the girl on the raft (the hell with the girl on the raft), or because Janice had asked if it wasn't a little early, or because her crisp little snap-snap of string beans had always been an irritating sound; it was because the stool she sat on, with her tennis shoes hooked over its middle rung, was exactly like the cop's stool at the door in Bellevue.

"Son of a bitch," he whispered aloud, and his free hand made a trembling fist in his pocket as he walked around the yard. "Son of a bitch." Because this was the funny part, the neurotic part, the crazy part: he was still furious. Wasn't it supposed to be true that if you could isolate the cause of an irrational anger it would go away? Didn't everybody know that? Then why wasn't it working? All he wanted now was to go back into the kitchen and say "Janice, get off that stool."

"What, dear?"

"You heard me. Get your ass off that fucking *stool.*"

She'd look as astonished as if she'd been slapped; the colander might fall from her lap and if it didn't he'd grab it up and send it clattering against the wall, spraying string beans.

"I swear to Christ if you don't get off I'll *knock* you off! Is that *clear?*"

"John," she'd say, standing up and backing away in fright, "John, what's the— John, are you—?"

He'd get the stool then, swing it high and bring it down in so mighty a crash that its splintered legs and rungs would skate across the floor, and as she cowered against the wall the very sight of her would enrich his voice with a thunderous rage: "Whaddya think you are, some cop? Some cop in a madhouse? Huh? You think you're some broad-assed, bull-dyke cop keeping the lunatics in line? Huh? Huh?"

By this time Tommy would be crying in the kitchen doorway, helplessly clutching the fly of his pants (as the ancient man had clutched his shrunken genitals in Bellevue and caused Spivack to say "Hey there, sexpot"), and in the momentum of his fury he would turn on Tommy too. "Yeah, yeah, yeah; you better take a good look, kid, and don't forget it. Wise up. I'm your father. This is your mother. I'm a certified lunatic and she's a cop, do you understand that? A *cop!* A *cop!*"

None of that happened, but only because he stood whispering it all to himself, breathing hard, with one arm tight around the trunk of a tall rustling tree in the silence of the yard.

The next morning was bright but too cool for the lake, so he did what he'd said on the highway would sure feel great: he lay on a blanket in the grass.

Well before noon he was getting up to stretch every twenty minutes or so, aiming a congenial smile at Janice in case she happened to look up from the garden, and going inside to pour a quick, deep shot of whiskey which he downed like medicine at the kitchen sink. Several times, when the drone of Tommy's transistor radio in another room seemed to guarantee that he wouldn't be seen, he had two or three.

After lunch he took a nap; when he awoke very late in the afternoon he struggled heavily up to sit on the edge of the bed and called Janice, and she came to sit beside him.

"Look," he said. "I know you were planning to spend a few more days up here, but I want to go home tomorrow. The thing is I've got to get back to the office."

"Well, it's hardly a question of 'got to,' dear," she said. "George Taylor can wait."

"Of course he can wait. It's not him, it's me. I just think the sooner I get back into a normal working routine the better I'll be, that's all."

RICHARD YATES

He knew he couldn't expect her to say "You know best," or anything like that, but at least she didn't argue. She studied the leaf-mottled rectangles of sunset on the floorboards for a while; then she patted his knee and said "All right."

He was in the kitchen, fixing the first of what he vowed would be his only two drinks before dinner, when he heard her announcing the change of plans to Tommy. "Dear, Daddy and I've decided to go home tomorrow. You won't mind that very much, will you?"

And Tommy said he didn't know; he didn't care.

"Well, hey, stranger," George Taylor said, lumbering around his big desk with his hand held out. "Janice said you might be laid up another week."

"Yeah, well, you know how the flu is; sometimes it hangs on, sometimes not." And Wilder allowed his knuckles to be crushed in welcome back to work.

"You did a great job in Chicago; got some good reports on that."

"Well, that's—fine." But it was strange, too: he could remember almost nothing of Chicago.

"Like to go over some of that stuff with you today; then there's a couple new things coming up. You free for lunch?" He was back behind the desk now, punching one of the many buttons on his complicated telephone. "Honey," he said, "Mr. Wilder 'n' I'll be wanting a table for two at Rattazzi's, twelve thirty. Right."

And so at twelve thirty they presented themselves to the headwaiter in the upstairs room, who called them "Gentlemen" like Charlie in Bellevue. The martinis here came in stemmed glasses, but the stems were only an inch high and the glasses as deep as tumblers. Well before George Taylor had finished his first it was clear that he'd grown bored with going over the Chicago stuff and the new things coming up: as his voice trailed away in incomplete sentences and his eyes wistfully roved the crowded tables he seemed bored with the very idea of *The American Scientist*, with advertising, with business and with money itself—and who could blame him for that?

He was fifty-six and burly, with a healthy crop of red hair just beginning to turn grey. As vice-president in charge of advertising sales he had risen as high as he ever would in the corporate structure. His excellent salary and stockholder's dividends accounted for less than half his income; the rest came from shrewd investments. He lived in an exclusive Rockland County village; all his children were grown and he was a grandfather of three. Another man might have turned obsessively to golf or sailing or collecting antique shotguns, but George Taylor's avocation was young girls. More than a few of his lunches with Wilder in the past had featured stories of girls who found it impossible to leave him alone, who hounded him and begged for him and fought for his favors, of how at least one had wept in his arms all night after her formal engagement to some recent graduate of Harvard Law.

"Hell, I'm about ready for another one, aren't you, John?" he said now, raising his empty glass.

"Yeah; I'm ready."

And the second round launched him into a confessional monologue. ". . . Jesus, if you only knew what's been going on with Sandy. I mean talk about a sweet little package of trouble; talk about a sweet little nest of rattlesnakes." Sandy was a laughing, full-breasted girl who'd been his secretary for six months. "Bad enough when she worked for me, but it's been even worse since I got her outa there. Told you I got her a job up at Drake and Cornfield, didn't I? This new agency up on Fifty-ninth? You know, one of these swinging little shops where everybody says 'creative' all the time; they've got girls running around the office barefoot; got a lotta bright young studs on the make; I figured she'd fit in there. But son of a bitch, John, she can't quit. Worst part of it is *I* can't quit. Three, four evenings a week, half my vacation —Jesus. Crazy child. Twenty-two years old and all sex. All sex. Says she can't stand boys her own age. Says I fulfill her. Last week my wife said 'Pajamas? What're you wearing pajamas for?' And you know why I was wearing pajamas? Because my back was all raw welts from where Sandy'd clawed me. Crazy, crazy child. Couldn't stand her apartment. Had this apartment with another girl, didn't like it because she didn't have enough privacy with me, so I got her a new one by herself—oh, she pays the rent and everything—she's very strict about that— but now if I don't show up there damn near every after-noon she's calling me on the *phone*. Then about a month ago she said 'Drive me to Philadelphia.' I said 'Why should I drive you to Philadelphia?' She said 'Because I want to blow you while you're doing eighty miles an hour on the Jersey Turnpike.' "

"And did she?"

"Damn right she did, buddy. Eighty miles an hour. Jesus."

There was a third round of drinks and finally some food, which grew cold before they began to pick at it;

then there were gulps of coffee and the promise of a long and dismal afternoon. Taylor grumbled about having to arrange the God damn December Issue Sales Conference; Wilder's desk held an indecipherable batch of expense-account vouchers from Chicago that would somehow have to be put in order, and after that he'd be on the phone trying to set up a week's worth of calls.

The office was better than Bellevue. Its walls were white and its lights indirect; it contained women as well as men; everybody wore clothes and nobody pleaded to be saved or screamed or masturbated or kicked at windows—even so, there were signs of mounting desperation in every face as the day wore on, and the arrival of five o'clock was like the cop's signal to unlock the big front door.

"Hi," he said, unlocking the door of his own home, released not only from the office but from the clangorous imprisonment of the subway.

"Hi, there," Janice said, and Tommy looked up from the television to acknowledge him with a mouthful of apple.

When he'd taken off his coat and tie he went to the place where the bourbon and the ice were kept, with Janice following him closely. "Make you a drink?" he asked her.

"Just a very small one. About a third of what you're having."

The phone rang in the middle of dinner, and when Janice came back from it she said Paul wanted to drop over for a drink later on. "You don't mind, do you?"

"Course not." And he guessed he didn't; but if it hadn't been for Tommy, solemnly slicing a pork chop across the table, he might have said he did. He knew what Borg would want tonight: he'd want to recommend a reputable psychiatrist, and Janice would sit nodding in wise approval, maybe even holding her husband's hand.

How had Borg known they were back from the country? But that was a stupid, easily answered question: Janice had called him today with news that John had acted "funny" all weekend and spent most of it in a drunken stupor. The two of them had been in cahoots on this thing from the start, after all. (It hadn't taken him long, walking the corridor at Bellevue, to figure out that there'd been nothing accidental about Borg's showing up in the Commodore bar that night.)

He didn't arrive until well after Tommy's bedtime; then he came in wearing an open shirt and a baggy sweater as if to prove there was no serious business at hand. All he wanted was a little Scotch, thanks—very light.

And the first part of their talk, as it had been for a year or more, was of politics. Hell, God knew anybody'd be better than Nixon, Wilder said, but even so he didn't quite trust Kennedy. A rich boy, a glamour boy, a senator who'd never once spoken out against McCarthy even after it was safe for anyone to do so, a candidate who'd bought the primaries and rigged the convention—and he wound up that discourse by proclaiming, as he'd often done before, that he himself was an unregenerate Stevenson man.

"Well, but John," Paul Borg said, "I think we have to agree that Stevenson was a Greek. Kennedy's a Roman. We need Romans in this country now." That was something Borg had said before too, and it was so neatly phrased that Wilder suspected he had read it somewhere.

On any other evening Janice would have said "Oh, exactly," as if the line were brand-new to her, and gone on to explain that she'd always sensed something a little soft and indecisive about Stevenson; but she kept her mouth shut and vanished into the kitchen to make coffee. There were more important things on which to agree with Paul Borg tonight.

Even after she was gone it took him quite a while to come out with the opening salvo. "John," he began, tamping his pipe with a careful forefinger (ordinarily he smoked cigarettes, but he reserved a pipe for moments like this; he probably used it with difficult clients, too). "John, have you given any thought to psychotherapy?" And the very word was enough to bring Janice softly back into the room, averting her face as she set a tray of trembling cups and saucers on the coffee table.

The question hung in the air and he made them wait for his answer, determined to keep his voice down. Tommy's bedroom was far away down a hall between two closed doors, but even so there must be no chance of his hearing this.

Given any thought to it? Yes, he had. Exactly once, on the last day in Bellevue when that greasy little clerk had made him say he would, as a condition of his release in Borg's custody. "So if you're speaking as my custodian, or whatever they call it, don't come to me. Go to him. Take Janice along too. I'm sure the three of you can work something out, even if you have to lock me up again first."

Janice was almost visibly fighting an urge to say "John,

that's not *fair*"; instead she sipped coffee to show that this, at any cost, would be a civilized discussion.

And Borg frowned through the billows of common sense that rose from his clenched pipe. They would get nowhere, he said, by harping on Bellevue. Neither he nor Janice had ever wanted him "locked up," as they'd both made clear time and again. For John to attack them now as some sort of conspirators was simply—

" 'Hostile,' right? 'Paranoid'?"

"Those are your words, not mine. Look: suppose we consider the events leading *up* to Bellevue. You had a nervous breakdown in Chicago; when you got back you were wholly irrational. And frankly—" he lowered his eyes "—well, this may be hindsight, but frankly I'd noticed a good many signs that something of the kind was building up over the past few months."

"Signs, huh? What signs?"

"Excessive drinking, for one; compulsive drinking. Irritability: you'd blow up over the slightest—over nothing. And moodiness; sulkiness. Sometimes Natalie and I'd be over here, or you'd be at our place, and you wouldn't say a word all evening."

Wilder almost said Maybe I was bored; instead he got a fresh drink and sat silent while Borg explained how much good a good psychiatrist might do for him. Oh, not one of the old-school, doctrinaire Freudians—and certainly not one of these new, underqualified "hip" people, either—but a sound, reputable therapist who'd see him twice a week and "work" with him.

A crisp little notebook was drawn from Borg's hip pocket, a page torn out and laid on the coffee table: Dr. Jules Blomberg, with offices in the East Sixties. This man had helped a client of Borg's to recover from an almost suicidal depression; he had helped an obese friend of that same client to lose a hundred pounds. And he was highly respected in the field: his papers were published in the best psychiatric journals; he'd lectured at many universities . . .

"And of course you've told him all about me, right? And set up an appointment?"

"I've told him a little about you, yes. The appointment is entirely your business."

Entirely his business. For some time there was no sound but the clicking of ice in his glass while he thought it over. What the hell. It might help; it might "work"; and if it didn't he could always quit.

"Okay," he said. "I'll see the guy." And he put both shoes on the coffee table to dramatize his capitulation.

But Janice was still tense, and Paul Borg made great flames as he tried to light his pipe for the third or fourth time. He didn't really know how to smoke the thing; maybe soon he'd stop trying. "There's just one hitch, John," he said at last. "Dr. Blomberg made it clear to me that he won't work with you unless you stop drinking."

"Well," he said, getting up. "There goes the ballgame. Dr. Blomberg is out of business. Dr. Blomberg is shit outa luck. So are you, buddy—" he pointed at Borg and then at his wife— "and so are you. I may be mentally ill and I may need 'help,' but I am not, never have been and never will be a drunk." And to prove it he made straight for the bourbon bottle and poured himself a big one. This was the closest he'd come to losing his temper all evening, but he didn't, cautioned not only by fear of waking Tommy but by a quick secret vision of Charlie bearing down on him in the corridor with his needle aloft ("All right, Mr. Wilder; I've warned you . . .").

". . . We've been friends for years, John," Borg was saying, "and it's often struck me that you have a low tolerance for alcohol. We've drunk together many times, matching each other drink for drink, and when I'd be just beginning to feel high you'd be—well, drunk."

"Matter of opinion. Prejudiced opinion. You do drink every day, right? Just like me?"

"Every day, yes. I don't drink at lunch but I always have a few after work; usually a few after dinner."

"Which means," Wilder said, "which means that along about three thirty or four you start craving it. You crave it so bad you can taste it, right?"

"No; it's not that way at all. I'm always tired at that time of day; sometimes by five o'clock I'm very nervous as well as tired. Then I have a few drinks and I'm not tired or nervous any more. Simple as that. Of course I need alcohol, John. The difference is, my system can handle it. I imagine it's purely a matter of body chemistry."

"How nice for you," Wilder said. "Isn't that swell."

Then they heard a high, shy call from Tommy's room. Janice hurried to him, while Wilder finished his drink in a gulp, and when she came back she said "He wants to see you, John."

"My God. He *can't* have heard anything. I haven't raised my voice once during this whole God-awful—"

"No, it's not that. He just woke up, and he says he wants to see you."

Going down the hall he found he wasn't steady on his

feet: he swayed and lurched against a wall with one shoulder.

Tommy was sitting up in bed with the light on, surrounded by Yankee pennants and Kennedy posters. His pajamas were rumpled, his straight hair stuck out in all directions and he looked younger than ten. He looked about six or seven.

"Well, hi," Wilder said, sitting on the bed. He sat close enough so they could hug, if that was what Tommy wanted to do, and it was. The warm feel of him and the sour, little-boy smell of him were almost enough to make him weep. "What's the matter, Tom? You just want a hug, or do you want to talk about something?"

For some seconds it seemed that he'd just wanted the hug; then he said "Daddy?"

"Yeah?"

"You went to Chicago for a week, right?"

"Right."

"And then your business kept you there for another week."

"Right."

"Well then, how come your suitcase's been in Mom's closet ever since a week ago last Saturday?"

"And what did you tell him?" Dr. Jules Blomberg inquired a few days later.

"What *could* I tell him?"

"Mm." Dr. Blomberg was his own age or younger, chubby and nearly bald; he wore pink-tinted glasses that magnified his eyes, and his office was very well appointed: rich-looking paintings, rich-looking abstract sculpture on low pedestals around the carpet. There was a psychiatric couch on which Wilder had refused to lie, and there were two deep leather armchairs in which they now sat facing each other, man to man. That was all he had learned so far about Dr. Blomberg except that he didn't take notes and had a habit of saying "Mm."

"Oh, looking back now I guess I might've found a way to tell him, but at the time it seemed impossible. For one thing I'd had a good deal to drink and my head was— I don't know. Anyway I just held onto him and said—I said it was a tough question but I promised him I'd answer it soon, and I guess I went into some spiel about how I never broke promises. I knew I had to get out of there fast before I started bawling all over him, so I tucked him in and turned out his light and I think he went to sleep. But the point is, doctor, that's when I decided to come to you."

"Mm. And to stop drinking."

"Right. That too."

And Dr. Blomberg spent the next twenty-five minutes, earning twenty-five dollars, on that. First he offered his professional endorsement of Alcoholics Anonymous as the most reliable, most enlightened and best means of dealing with the problem; then he dialed an avocado-colored telephone and asked for Mr. Costello.

". . . Fine, thanks, and you, sir? Good. Mr. Costello, I have a new patient here who wants to join the Program, and I wondered if you'd care to be his sponsor. . . . Well, I don't want to inconvenience you, but I'd say the sooner the better. Tomorrow; possibly this evening, if you're free. . . . No, actually, I think it might be preferable not to visit his home—there's a young child involved—I thought perhaps you might meet him alone for a cup of coffee. . . ."

A mercilessly bright coffee shop lay around the corner from this office (next door to a dark bar where Wilder had downed two quick ones to brace himself for confronting Blomberg and where he'd planned to repair for a few more as soon as Blomberg set him free); it was arranged that Mr. Costello would be there at the end of this session; then Blomberg earned a few more dollars in apologies and thanks: ". . . I hate to bring you out on such short notice, sir; I certainly appreciate it . . ." and in a silence allowing Mr. Costello to insist it was no trouble; he was happy to oblige.

With the phone in its cradle at last and Blomberg still glowing from the pleasantries, he checked his watch, found there wasn't time to open a new line of questioning and went back to a point he'd missed earlier in the interview about the nature of Wilder's job with *The American Scientist*: what exactly had Wilder meant by the term "classification specialist"?

"Oh. Well, see, most space salesmen go out after any kind of advertising they can find. I was hired away from another magazine because I brought in two new product lines the *Scientist* had never approached before—foreign cars and high-quality liquor. Both very lucrative."

"Mm. So you're the 'specialist' in those two 'classifications,' I see. And I imagine the liquor end of it must involve a good deal of drinking as part of your—work."

"No, it's not that simple, doctor. The liquor industry's very solemn about 'moderation.' I mean, that week in Chicago was a distillers' convention and of course there were parties, but that wasn't the trouble: I did all the heavy drinking on my own."

"Yes. Well, I'm afraid our time is up, Mr. Wilder."

The coffee shop was nearly empty, as if everyone on the block preferred the bar for which he still yearned, and he didn't have to wait long before his sponsor strode in with a briefcase.

"John Wilder? Bill Costello." He was ruddy and dapper, with sparse white hair as neat as Harry Truman's and a big smile of very clean false teeth, and his handshake seemed determined to prove what laying off the booze could do for a man's grip. "I want to congratulate you," he said when he was settled across from Wilder with both pin-striped elbows on the plastic table. "Not only on your decision for AA but for putting yourself in Dr. Blomberg's care. This town's loaded with psychiatrists and I know I don't have to tell you most of 'em are quacks. They'll treat people like you and me for years, ignoring our problem, letting us drink ourselves into the madhouse or the grave. Black, please," he said to the waitress. "Dr. Blomberg's one of your rare, very rare exceptions. I think the world of that young man."

"You a former patient of his?"

"Me? Oh, no; I'm afraid I'm too old to've had that privilege. I imagine Jules Blomberg was still a student when I—when I first joined the Program. Well. Down to business. When did you have your last drink, John?"

"About an hour ago, waiting to see the doctor."

"One for the road, huh?" And Bill Costello began heaping more sugar into his coffee than Wilder had ever seen anyone do. " 'One for the road.' Ah, God, how often we say that, people like us. Then next day we open up the paper: TOT SLAIN BY DRUNK DRIVER, and we think, hell, nothing like that could ever happen to me. Right?"

"How long've you been— I mean when did you have your last drink?"

"Nine years ago next month. October sixteenth, Nineteen Fifty-one. Oh, don't get me wrong, John, I'm not boasting. I'm deeply grateful for my sobriety, but it's nothing to boast about. People offer me a drink at parties and I ask for a Coke or some damn thing. If they press me I say I don't drink, and if they press me harder I say I'm an alcoholic. Not an 'ex-alcoholic' or a 'reformed alcoholic,' because you see there's no such thing. In AA we never promise anything, to ourselves or each other, except that we'll stay sober for one more day. Twenty-four hours. That's why it's so important to attend a meeting every night if you can, when you're starting out. But hell, John, I can't explain the Program all at once; you'll discover it yourself. Let me just leave a few things with you." And out of the briefcase came a handful of bright brochures (one entitled "Who, *me?*") to be spread on the table. "These are just to put in your pocket. This is more important: this is your directory of meetings all over the city. Dates, times and addresses. You'll find four or five to choose from every night—high-school gyms, church basements, loft buildings—all kinds of places." Then his false teeth flashed in a grin of invitation and challenge. "Feel like hitting one tonight? With me?"

And Wilder stuttered through an apologetic lie about having guests for dinner.

"Tomorrow night then? Or no, wait; damn. *I'm* tied up tomorrow night."

"That's okay. I'll go to one alone."

"Good. That's a good sign in itself. Many beginners are shy about walking into that first meeting alone. Well, we'll hit a few together later on. And here," he said, probing in the briefcase again. "This isn't a gift, John, only a loan. I don't care how long you keep it but I want it back; it's a dearly prized possession. Once you get into it you'll see why, and you'll want to buy a copy of your own. This is what we call the Big Book—our definitive text." It was as black as a Bible, and heavier. "Don't try to read it all at once; take it a chapter at a time. Let it soak in. One more thing. You'll see I've written my home and office numbers on the back of your directory. Now in theory, your sponsor's always available on the phone for times when you feel you're slipping, got to have a drink, can't control yourself; he's the guy who comes over or meets you somewhere and talks with you. Trouble is in my case I'm out of town a lot, so let's leave it this way: whenever I leave town I'll notify Dr. Blomberg and give him another number you can use, another sponsor, and of course I'll inform that man too. Fair enough? Well. It's been a pleasure." He spilled an overly generous amount of change on the table and led the way out to the street. "You headed downtown? I'll walk you over to Lex. What line of work you in, John?"

"I sell advertising. What do you do?"

"Oh, I guess you'd say I'm in show business. Television."

"You an actor?"

"No, the writing end. Did Hollywood screenplays for a good many years; before that I did radio. Now I sort of divide my time between here and the Coast. I'm one of the three story editors on 'Let's Ask Daddy.' "

"Well, I've certainly heard of that show, but I'm afraid I've never—"

"You're very fortunate." There was another vigorous handshake and another gleam of dentures under the streetlights. "I wouldn't want my worst enemy to watch the son of a bitch. Good luck, John!" And Bill Costello hurried away.

Wilder chose his first meeting because it wasn't far from home and didn't start until well after Tommy was asleep. But it was held in a church basement—he had uneasy memories of churches—and at first he didn't know how to be less conspicuous: hanging around the sidewalk as the other members arrived, or going inside to study the two rumbling coffee urns and the two home-made cakes (chocolate and coconut) along the rear wall.

"Most of you know me," said a man at the rostrum at last, while Wilder squirmed in the back row of folding chairs, "but I see some new faces tonight so I'll go through the old routine. My name's Herb and I'm an alcoholic."

And there was an almost thunderous response of "Hi, Herb!"

"I think we'll have a fine meeting tonight—two very fine speakers—but first I'd like to call on Warren here to read the Seven Principles."

"My name's Warren and I'm an alcoholic."

"Hi, Warren!"

The Seven Principles seemed to go on forever as the air grew dense with cigarette smoke and loud with coughing, and then a homely girl with a barely audible voice ("Hi, Mary!") was called upon to read the Twelve Steps.

"Our first speaker is no stranger here," Herb said, "but he's so modest a man that I'm sure he won't introduce himself properly. Bob's a highly successful management consultant—so successful in fact that I just heard today, and I didn't hear it from him, that he's been elected president of the Management Consultants' Association of New York. He always gives a stimulating, provocative talk, and—well, I'll leave the rest of it up to him."

Bob sprang for the rostrum like a man who runs a mile before breakfast every day, adjusted the perfect tailoring on his meaty torso, proclaimed himself an alcoholic and could scarcely wait for the cries of "Hi, Bob!" to dwindle before he launched his attack.

"I know 'management consultant' may sound nice and solid," he said, "but there was a time not too long ago when I couldn't manage myself—couldn't even consult myself without a triple Scotch in my hand, and we all know what those kind of consultations amount to. Oh, I guess I had it pretty bad in the war, picked up a few scratches—Guadalcanal, Tarawa, Iwo Jima—but hell, that's no excuse: millions of guys had it bad in the war. Anyway when I got out of the Marines I made a poor adjustment to civilian life—and I don't have to tell you good people what I mean by that. Went to business school and flunked right out because of my drinking; got a couple of jobs and lost 'em because of my drinking. Then I lost—lost my wife because of my drinking. Wonderful woman; stuck it out as long as she could for the sake of our little girl; finally just couldn't—couldn't stick it out any longer." And after that, he said with an appropriate tremor in his voice, he had touched bottom.

But the rest of Bob's story was all uphill: he had joined the Program with the help of a wonderful sponsor; soon he was back in school and doing well, holding down a job on the side to help support his child; after graduation a number of lucky breaks had helped him toward his present career. His former wife had married a fine man—a very lucky man—his daughter had made a wonderful adjustment and become a lovely teen-ager with whom he had a wonderful relationship; he himself had married again to—well, to the most wonderful girl in the world.

"Oh, I can count my blessings, sure," he concluded. "I count 'em all the time; but deep down I know there's only been one truly wonderful thing in my life, and that's my association with wonderful people like you—this wonderful organization of AA, this wonderful, wonderful fellowship. Thank you."

And he got a wonderful round of applause.

Their final speaker, Herb said, was a very gracious lady, a busy housewife and mother with many social and charitable obligations who nonetheless found time to drive all the way in from Westport several nights a week for AA; her presence was always a pleasure and he was sure they'd enjoy her remarks.

She was in her middle forties and pretty in a square-jawed way, very trim and fashionable in her full, sweeping clothes. "I'm Eleanor," she said, "and I'm a very, very grateful alcoholic."

She told of how in the worst of her drinking years she'd had to fix not one but three martinis for herself at five o'clock each day: one in the kitchen to help her through the preparation of dinner, one beside the hall telephone in case it rang—"I was terrified, simply *terrified* of talking on the phone without a drink"—and one near the children's bathroom in readiness for her supervision of their baths. Then of course there had always been wine with dinner and brandy afterwards, until she'd come to realize she was a slave to alcohol. And in the happy, post-Program part of her recital she made frequent use of the phrase "my sobriety."

"Eight'll getcha five that broad's never been drunk in her life," said the man beside Wilder, nudging his ribs and breathing whiskey fumes in his face. "Fucking society broad; matron of honor. Drives in from Westport in her Lincoln fucking Continental. Gets her kicks this way. Wait'll you see her serve that fucking cake."

But Wilder didn't wait for that. There was a passing around of baskets to collect dollar bills, an announcement listing members in various hospitals who would certainly appreciate cards and flowers; then everyone rose for an intonation of the Lord's Prayer and he was free.

He found the darkest bar in the neighborhood and drank until he was certain Janice would be long asleep —certain too, as he sank into a taxicab, that if the morning's paper read TOT SLAIN BY DRUNK DRIVER it wouldn't be his fault.

"Before we begin," Dr. Blomberg said at their next session, "I talked with Mr. Costello today. He's been called out to Los Angeles, doesn't know how long he'll be gone, but he asked me to give you this name and number in case you—"

"Yeah, yeah, okay; thanks."

"Have you been attending the meetings?"

"Two. The first was lousy—" he tried at some length and with no apparent success to explain that— "but the second was better, up in the West Seventies. They had it in an abandoned movie theatre; I sort of liked that.

Had an ex-cop who'd been fired off the force for drinking, said he was a security guard in a bank now but knew
he'd lose that too if he went back on the bottle; then
there was a girl who'd been a prostitute until her sponsor
helped her find work as a hairdresser. . . ."

"And you haven't been drinking?"

"No." That was a lie—even after the second, better
meeting he had sneaked three warm bourbons in the
kitchen before going to bed—but it seemed a lie worth
telling, at prices like this. "And I'd really rather talk
about other things, doctor. I mean I always thought you
were supposed to tell a psychiatrist whatever was on
your mind. For instance, coming over here from work
today I was thinking about the books we have at home.
There must be four, five thousand books—I'm not exaggerating—and maybe twenty of them are mine. All the
rest are my wife's. Thing is, you see, I don't read. I'm a
very, very slow reader. Guess that's the main reason I've
spent most of my life watching movies. I must've seen
damn near every movie ever made since back around
Nineteen Thirty-six—but don't let me get started on the
movies; I'll get back to the movies soon enough, okay?
Anyway, a few years ago my wife got me into one of
these commercial speed-reading courses and I was hope-
less. I mean the other people were poor readers too but
they didn't seem ashamed of it the way I was. They all
made progress; I didn't. Dropped out of the course halfway through, lost about five hundred bucks. I guess it's
what you people call a block."

"Mm. And I imagine that must have made difficulties
for you in school."

School. The word made him squirm in his chair and

clutch his forehead before he remembered Spivack's caution against such gestures, but what the hell: he was paying this man. "School," he said. "You really want to dig into that whole can of worms? My half-assed childhood? My crazy parents and all that?"

"Your crazy parents?"

"Well, not crazy in *your* sense—nobody ever had to lock them up or anything—but they were crazy as hell. Called themselves 'business people' all through the Depression, which meant my father was employed as an accountant in one office building and my mother did secretarial work in another. As long as I can remember they'd be lecturing me about 'Management' and 'Free Enterprise' and 'Venture Capital.' And this was their dream: my mother had this set of secret recipes for some kind of candy—she'd gotten 'em from her own family, back in Nebraska—and they were convinced all they'd need was a little luck and a little Venture Capital to establish their own business. Marjorie Wilder's Chocolates. Very classy, very expensive; chocolates with snob appeal. And do you see where I was supposed to fit in? The only child? The son and heir? I'd learn the business from the ground up; they'd groom me to take over; I'd be the damn prince. By the time they retired we'd all be millionaires, and when they died they'd have a living memorial: Marjorie Wilder's Chocolates, Inc.; John C. Wilder, President. Do you see what I mean by crazy?"

"Not exactly."

"Had a feeling you wouldn't. Never mind. School. I started out in the city school system, which damn near humiliated my parents to death. They couldn't afford a private school, but they found something even better.

You know Grace Church? Episcopal church down on East Eleventh? Well, it's fairly well-known—used to be anyway—and one of the big things about it was the boys' choir. The church ran its own little school for boys: if you could sing you not only got free schooling, you got paid. Every kid in the choir got five bucks a week, the soloists got ten, and pretty soon I was the soprano soloist. Of course I never did well at schoolwork, but in that school it didn't matter: they let me get by because I was such a hotshot in church. Not just every week, but in the big Christmas and Easter services when people came from all over to hear the *Magnificat*, or the *Messiah*. I'd stand there in the middle of the front row, about a head shorter than anybody else, and take off on these long, intricate solo parts, and God damn it I could *feel* all the women out there going apeshit over me. Do you get the picture? Little Mickey Rooney with the voice of an angel? Jesus Christ."

"I'm afraid our time is up, Mr. Wilder."

Their time was up time and again, twice a week, leaving him to stumble for Lexington Avenue with a headful of things he wished he'd said, whispering to himself all the way home on the subway; and Blomberg's first question at the next session was always the same: Had he been keeping up with his meetings?

". . . Yeah, yeah. Went to a new one last night, down in the Village. There was a young girl, started drinking at Sarah Lawrence; had an affair with one of her teachers and when he dropped her she tried to kill herself, wound up in Bellevue. Funny: after all these meetings she's the only other ex-Bellevue patient I've met—or heard, rather." He didn't tell of how he'd tried to pick the girl up after the meeting, with Varick Street in mind (she'd been a slender, bedraggled girl with big suffering eyes), or of how she'd almost physically recoiled from his suggestion that they might "get a cup of coffee somewhere" and hurried away down the sidewalk alone.

"But look, doctor; let's get back to where we were, okay?"

School consumed another therapeutic hour, with digressions back and forth in time: ". . . Ah, I was always kind of a dud in that school, soloist or not. One thing, I was a pious little bastard. It wasn't only the singing I loved; I loved the whole damned formal-religion scene—the rituals, the vestments, the prayers, the stained-glass windows—and I think I must've been just about the only kid in school who did. There was a lot of blowing farts in the choir loft, whispering dirty jokes and passing around dirty pictures, sometimes passing around half-pints of whiskey, daring you to take a nip. What I'm getting at, those other kids were *on* to everything: they had the kind of healthy skepticism it took me years to learn. Old Wanamaker's Department Store used to hire us every afternoon during Christmas season, to sing carols, and of course nobody complained because it meant a few more bucks for each of us, but can you imagine how much real money must've changed hands between the God damned store and the God damned church? What kind of horseshit is that?

". . . A lot of the kids were out of luck when their voices changed—some kids' voices didn't change 'right' for choral work, and even if they did, there was only a small section for tenors and baritones; they couldn't keep everybody. My voice changed right—not solo quality, but good enough—so they made a tenor out of me and let me stay through the twelfth grade; then I went into the army. Have we got any time left?"

"A few minutes."

"Because if I get going on the army it'll take forever, and it's not that important anyway—not nearly as important as what came afterwards. Let me just tell you one thing. At the induction center they gave us all an IQ test. Didn't call it that, called it the Army General Classification Test, but everybody knew what the deal was. You had to score a hundred and ten to qualify for officers' training—or any other halfway decent job, for that matter—and my score was a hundred points. So I asked if I could take it again, and some clerk said I could apply for it at my 'next post,' which turned out to be a basic training camp in North Carolina. And I did. There were only half a dozen of us taking it that time, and there was kind of a nice, easygoing lieutenant in charge: he let us watch while he corrected the papers, and when he came to mine he said I'd scored a hundred and nine. Then he said, 'Curious thing; you didn't get a single question wrong, but you only did about half of them.' I said something like 'Well, but, sir, if I got them all right, doesn't that indicate—" And he said, 'It indicates a hundred and nine. You must be a very slow reader, that's all.' "

And it was a week or two later that he had a fight with Janice—or a quarrel that came closer to a fight than anything since long before Bellevue.

It didn't happen until after dinner, after the dishes were washed and Tommy sent to bed. He was sitting on the sofa looking over the acres of books and wondering how anyone, with any kind of IQ, could possibly read so much, when she came and sat beside him.

"John, do you know something? I've been very proud of you these past—however long it's been." And she nestled closer to him on the cushions. "Enormously proud."

"Yeah, well, let's hold off on the enormous pride for a while. It hasn't been all that long."

"But if you could only see the changes in you. You *look* so much better; you seem to have so much more self-confidence, so much more spirit. You're a different person."

"Then why do you figure Tommy still acts funny around me? I don't think he's looked me straight in the eye since—you know, our little bedside chat about the suitcase."

"Oh, John, are you still brooding about that? That's ancient history. I talked it over with him weeks ago."

"You *what?* God damn it, Janice, I promised him *I'd* tell him, and I *told* you that. You had no God damn *business*—" He was on his feet in a spasm of anger, and she raced to close the hall door in the old ritual of precaution against Tommy's hearing them at their worst. "—No God damn *business* violating that promise."

"You've *got* to keep your voice down," she said, and he did, first clamping his jaws and breathing hard through his nose—the Bellevue method of self-control—but he liked the ring of his last line so much that he said it again, very low: "You had no business violating that promise."

"I didn't see it as a 'violation.' I thought you'd be relieved."

"You thought I'd be relieved." He tried to make that

sound contemptible and emphasized it by ~~pacing~~ the floor with shoulders hunched and fists tight in his pockets; even so, he had to admit she had a point. He *was* relieved, but he was damned if he'd let her know it.

She was back on the sofa now, not curled up but sitting straight, in her civilized-discussion posture.

". . . I asked him if he knew what a nervous breakdown was and he said he guessed so, but I could tell he didn't. So I said sometimes people worked so hard and got so tired that their nerves couldn't take the strain and they had to go to a hospital and rest. And he did seem to understand. You mustn't forget he's nearly eleven, John. And I said—"

"Yeah, yeah, yeah—oh, Jesus, I can picture it. You said 'Isn't it wonderful how Daddy doesn't get fall-down drunk any more?' "

"John, I never even mentioned your—"

"Well, thanks," he said. "Thanks for nothing." He grabbed his coat and raincoat and headed for the door, where he stood dramatically with one hand on the knob. "I'm going out. Maybe to a meeting, maybe to get smashed. If I'm not back by morning you'd better call the cops—or call Paul Borg; same thing. In the meantime you can take your Enormous Pride and shove it up your—shove it up your—"

He let the door click shut behind him before finishing that sentence; then he was out on the street and walking fast, downtown, with no idea of where he was going. Somewhere around Twenty-third he stopped for a drink —just one—and studied Bill Costello's directory for a meeting that might still be open. There was one on West Houston Street.

It took place in a fourth-floor loft, and its leader was quick to explain what made it different from most other meetings. "We don't schedule any formal speakers here," he said. "We're impromptu. We call on anybody in the room for a few minutes' talk; if they don't feel like talking we respect their privacy. I see a young fella over here on my left been with us a few times before, looks like he might like to say a few words; trouble is he looks all out of breath. How about it, Carl?"

A compact, tight-faced boy who couldn't have been more than twenty went forward, said his name was Carl and that he was an alcoholic.

"Hi, Carl!"

"And you're right, Tony, I am out of breath. Got on the wrong train in Brooklyn; had to get off down at Broadway and Delancey Street and I—I ran all the way."

"Whyn't you take it easy a second, Carl?" Tony said. "Get your wind back."

"Okay." Then he said "Guess the reason I keep getting lost in the subways is I'm not a native New Yorker. I'm from Kansas. Led a very sheltered childhood out there; what I mean is, I spent most of it in state correctional institutions. Wasn't bad; I always had three meals a day, always had clean clothes and a clean place to sleep and plenty of smokes, and I learned my trade. I'm a barber. Then I got out, and that's when I started drinking. Oh, if it was just me it wouldn't matter; I make good money; I'm a good barber even when I'm half crocked; but it's not just me. Past year or so, eleven months, I've been living with this girl in Brooklyn. And the thing is—the thing is, it's not working out. I'm not— She's not— It's not working out at all." He was silent for a few seconds.

"Hell, I know I can't bullshit you people. I won't claim I've quit drinking because it's not true." And here his voice could scarcely be heard. "I'm scared, you see. I'm scared she'll leave me. That's why I come to these meetings. That's why, when I take the wrong train like tonight, why I figure it's worth running all the way—worth it because if nothing else, if nothing else, I can be with people like you for an hour—just an *hour*—and be sober. Thank you."

There was plenty of applause but Carl didn't acknowledge it; he went quickly back to his chair and used it in a way he'd probably learned in the correctional institutions: sit stiff, keep both hands on your knees, look straight ahead and never smile, especially after any chance that you've said something dumb, or smart, unless you want somebody to think you're some kind of a fruit.

"I'd like to address my remarks to Carl," said the next speaker, a wobbling old man with few teeth. "I want to say 'Carl, I don't care how many wrong trains you take. I don't care how much running you have to do. Just keep coming, boy; keep coming. You're on the right road.' "

There were four or five other speakers, and then Tony took over. "We've got something special to conclude our meeting tonight," he said. "We've got a birthday. Now, personally, I've always thought most AA birthdays are kind of silly: you see them give some guy a cake with six, eight, twelve candles to prove how many years he's been dry, they tell his last name in honor of the occasion and he makes his little speech, and you sit there thinking What does *this* guy need AA for? He just tryna show off, or what? But a *first* birthday, that's different. That's

something else. That's an achievement. I mean those
first twelve months—well, hell, you know what I mean."
He nodded toward a curtained-off portion of the loft and
out came a pink man, all smiles, bearing a pink cake with
a single candle whose wavering flame he shielded with
his hand. Then Tony said "Will Mr. Sylvester Cummings
please come forward?"

A gaunt middle-aged Negro got up and went to the
rostrum, wearing a cheap blue suit and trailed by cheers
and whistles. He shook hands with Tony and thanked the
man who gave him the cake platter, but when some of
the audience broke into a ragged chorus of "Hap-py
birth-day to—" he held up one hand and said "No, no,
please; never mind the birthday song. I mean I appreciate it, but that's a song for children. I'm forty-seven years
old. Even my own children aren't children any more;
they're grown and gone." He stood looking down at his
cake for some time. "It doesn't seem possible," he said.
"A whole year. Only thing I know for certain, I never
would've made it without your help—without Tony here
and all you other people. I think back to the way I was
—way I was for more years than I want to think about
—and sometimes all I can remember is how I'd wake up
every morning on my knees with my arms wrapped
around that old toilet bowl, puking my guts out, and I'd
say to myself 'Sylvester, you are praying. You are wor-
shiping at the only altar in which you have ever truly
believed.' "

That won him a laugh, but he didn't smile. "I've never
been a very religious man, you see. Even here at these
meetings, when it's time for the Lord's Prayer, I just kind
of move my mouth a little and hope nobody's noticing.

Matter of fact I don't enjoy cake very much either—maybe some of you people can help me out on this one." He looked down at it again in a long, meditative pause. "But I have come to believe something, this past year. I've come to believe that I would rather—I would rather light one candle than curse the darkness." Then he blew the candle out, and there was a standing ovation.

It was enough to send Wilder home without stopping for even so much as a beer, enough to make him wake his wife and tell her he was sorry.

"Oh, I know, dear," she said. "I know . . ."

He had insisted he wouldn't spend much time on the army with Dr. Blomberg, and he didn't. The army had convinced him he wasn't very smart and jolted all the religion out of him; he'd seen action only at the end of the war in Europe and spent his whole final year in the mildewed "Tent Cities" of France, where there'd been nothing to do, between painfully infrequent three-day passes, but go to the movies every night. "I told you we'd get back to the movies."

"Mm."

"Funny thing: in civilian movie-houses people'd sit still for any kind of trash—you'd never hear anybody laugh out loud in a love scene or anything like that—but in the army there was nothing magic about the big silver screen any more, and we all got to be very vocal, brutal movie critics. We could spot a fake plot or a fake 'message' a mile away; we'd stomp and laugh and yell obscenities at anything cheap or trite or hoked-up or sentimental, and I remember thinking Jesus, these guys are like me: we've *all* been raised on movies, and we're just now beginning to figure out what frauds most of them are. And here's what I'm getting at, doctor: that's when I decided I wanted to make movies. *Good* movies. Oh, I knew I couldn't be a director—that'd take more talent than anybody with an IQ of a hundred and nine could claim—but a producer: the man who gets the idea, raises the money, hires the talent, puts the whole thing together. That's what I wanted.

"Course, I couldn't tell my parents, or thought I couldn't. They were still in the old apartment when I got home, working at their old jobs, and they both looked old as hell—they must've been in their middle fifties—but the damned chocolate business was bigger than ever in their heads. My father spent all his free time hustling up Venture Capital, and the funny part is he did well. Everybody was talking about a postwar boom: just the right time for a good, well-marketed luxury product to catch on. He took me along with him to meet some banker. 'This is my son John. Twenty years old; infantry veteran just back from Europe; went through the Bulge and all that. Going to Yale next month; he'll be in on the business from the start.'

"When we got out of there I said 'Dad, could you please lay off the Bulge? You know I didn't go through the Bulge.'

"He said 'They gave you the star for it, didn't they?'

"And the point is, Doctor, I'd told him time and again, time and again they gave the damn star to everybody within a hundred *miles* of the Bulge. So I said 'Look: it may not matter to you but it matters to me. Can't you see that?'

"And the little bastard just walked along—he *was* little, even smaller than me, with a face like a walnut and this old-timey, pearl-grey hat pulled down hard over his eyes—just walked along and said I had a lot to learn about the business world. Jesus.

"But I did go to Yale; that was the college they'd picked for me, and they'd been careful to send me the application forms the minute the war was over so I'd beat the big rush of GI Bill students. I still don't understand how I got in and I was scared shitless of flunking out. The reading assignments almost killed me—I'd be up reading all night while everybody else was out drinking and screwing around—but I made it through freshman year, and by then my parents were in business. They had a little factory up in Stamford with about six employees; they'd paid some designer a lot of money for the most elegant-looking package you ever saw; they were turning out honest-to-God chocolates every day and they had my own summer's work cut out for me: I was the assistant to an older guy who took 'the line' around to wholesalers all over New York.

" 'Taste one—just taste one,' the older guy'd say. 'Be our guest.' And I'd sit there smiling like a clown in my J. Press suit, wondering what the hell I was going to do with the rest of my life.

"Well, it didn't last long; my sophomore year was a disaster. Barely made it through the first semester, and along about April I sort of gave up. Went to the movies all the time, quit studying, quit trying, and I flunked out that June.

"And my God, talk about family tragedies! They seemed to think I'd done it on purpose, just to thwart them. Started bringing home armloads of other college catalogues, and I'd throw 'em away. Oh, I've always regretted that—there must've been plenty of colleges with remedial reading programs—but the thought of *any* college made me sick; besides, I knew they only wanted me to graduate for the sake of Marjorie Wilder's fucking Chocolates. Quarrels, recriminations, fights, tears— Finally I said 'I don't owe you people *anything*,' and I took off.

"Got a room in the city and answered a help-wanted ad for an outfit called Films for Industry: 'Learn the ropes of motion-picture production.' Paid me thirty-five a week to carry lights and drag cables around the floor and get sandwiches for the actors and the camera crew, and I mean that might've been okay if they'd been making halfway decent movies, even industrial movies, but they weren't. I remember one they made for Meade Record-keeping Systems; the title was *It Must Be Somewhere*—twenty minutes of unfunny slapstick about what happens in the office when an important paper gets lost. Bosses blowing their tops, secretaries crying, file cabinets dumped out on the floor; then the man from Meade comes in and saves the day. Finds the paper, says 'Record-keeping is my business' and goes into his sales pitch. The End.

"And the worst part, all those Films for Industry people were happy as clams—none of them ever thought of getting into real movies, even the girls. I took one girl out to lunch, tried to get her talking about movies and she looked at me like I was some dopey little kid: 'You mean *consumer* films? *Feature* films?' Didn't consider herself an actress at all; couldn't have cared less. Then it turned out she was shacked up with one of the Films for Industry executives; soon as his divorce came through she'd quit working and they'd settle down in Forest Hills.

". . . Oh, if I'd had any guts I'd have hitchhiked out to Hollywood and hung around the studios until somebody hired me as a grip or even a mail clerk—if I'd done that I might even have *become* a producer by now—but I didn't. Maybe I wasn't ready to make that big a break with my parents; I don't know. Anyway I didn't.

"Then somebody told me the *Herald Tribune* was taking on space salesmen, paying good money, not too fussy about college degrees. So I said I'd had three years at Yale instead of two, and that's how I got started in this racket. That's how I met Janice too—she worked there. We got married within a year and then we had our boy. By that time I was working for a trade journal, *Chain Store Age;* then I moved over to a magazine called *Vanguard* and then to *The American Scientist,* and somewhere along the line the whole movie-producer idea evaporated. Oh, don't worry, doctor, I'm not saying marriage tied me down; you won't catch me blaming my wife for everything I can't blame on my parents or any neurotic horseshit like that. The ambition just went away, that's all. It's come back now and then over the years—usually when I've been drinking, I guess—but it's gone. Nobody's fault but mine. You want to hear what happened to my parents?"

"Mm." And the doctor inspected his watch.

"Well, we had a halfhearted reconciliation after the baby was born, but in the meantime they'd found what I suppose you guys would call a surrogate son: another Ivy League type, only this one had his diploma, and he really did take over the business and build it up, just the way they'd always thought I would. They were rich as hell by the time they retired. My father died four years ago and my mother's in a nursing home now—she had a brain hemorrhage and she's pretty much a vegetable —but son of a bitch, you can't walk into any supermarket in America today without bumping into this big-assed revolving rack: Marjorie Wilder's Chocolates. Six bucks a box. How about *that?*"

"Mm. Yes. Well, I'm afraid our time is—"

"Not so fast, Doctor."

"Mm?" Blomberg blinked up through his pink-tinted glasses.

"You know something? You're the only dead-silent bullshit artist I've ever met. I tell you the whole God damned story of my life; you sit there saying absolutely nothing and hauling in a hundred a week of my money, and you know what that's called? That's larceny."

They were both on their feet. "I have another patient waiting, Mr. Wilder."

"Let 'im wait. You've kept *me* waiting often enough. I've got one question: When the hell are *you* gonna start talking? When's all this famous 'work' and 'help' and 'therapy' supposed to begin? Huh?"

"Mr. Wilder, I don't know what's brought on this hostility, but perhaps it's something we can discuss Thursday."

Then a line of Spivack's in Bellevue seemed appropriate: "Yeah, well, don't hold your breath."

"Do you plan to cancel your Thursday appointment?"

"It might just be," Wilder said, trembling at the door, "that 'our time is up' in more fucking ways than one."

"Do you want to terminate your association with me?"

"Suppose we let you sweat that one out. I'd like to picture you all alone here twice a week, watching all my money float away. So long, pink-eyes."

And jolting home on the subway he kept thinking of embellishments he might have put on that final speech: he might have said ". . . all alone here twice a week with your finger in your mouth, or up your ass—depending, of course, on whether you're an oral- or an anal-fixation type . . ." But then he began to wonder if Blomberg might pick up that avocado-green, snot-green phone and call Paul Borg with the news of his outburst. Well, hell. What if he did?

"Dear?" Janice said when they were alone that night, and at first he thought it might be about Blomberg and Borg, but it wasn't. "I've been looking through some of the AA leaflets— That doesn't upset you, does it?"

"Course not."

"The thing is, they say it's often helpful for a member's wife or husband to go along to the meetings, and I was wondering if— I mean I'd really like to. Especially the one you told me about, where the man said he'd rather light one candle than curse the darkness."

"Well, I don't know, I—okay. Sure."

They were climbing the stairs to the loft before it struck him that he might well be called on to speak tonight; and toward the end of the meeting Tony's index finger swung straight at his face.

"I see a man back there's been with us a few times lately; want to say a few words, sir?"

Blood beat in his ears all the way to the rostrum, and the voice that addressed the group through hanging veils of smoke didn't sound like his own at all. "My name's John and I'm an alcoholic."

"Hi, John!"

"I haven't been in the Program very long, but I've gone to meetings all over town and this one's the best I've found. Trouble is, it's the first time I've been asked to talk and that's a little embarrassing because my wife's here with me as a guest tonight—but what the hell, she's seen me make a fool of myself plenty of times before."

There was some laughter—not much—and he wondered if it might be bad manners in this group even to hint at being securely married, or to bring any kind of "guest."

"I'm a salesman, and I guess I always thought heavy drinking was part of a salesman's life. Well, that idea went down the drain a while back when I was locked up for a week in Bellevue . . ." He didn't know how to finish: he heard himself saying "still scared" and "grateful" and "with your help" until he found his way through a clumsy final sentence that allowed him to say "Thank you." He couldn't tell if the clapping was tepid or hearty or even if it lasted until he was back in his chair, where Janice made a display of squeezing his hand.

"You were wonderful," she said when they were out on the street again.

"The hell I was. All that self-pitying shit about Bellevue; all that false humility. I felt like an idiot."

"I thought you did very well. Besides, what does it matter? This isn't show business, after all."

He almost stopped on the sidewalk to turn her around and shout that it *was* show business—the whole God damn "Program" was show business, from Bill Costello to Sylvester Cummings; that psychotherapy was show business too, with an inattentive, pink-eyed audience of one—but this was no night for another quarrel.

"Oh, let's just walk a while," she was saying. "I love this old part of town; I don't think I've been down here for years and years. Remember all the walks we used to take around here before we were married?"

"Yup."

"Houston and Canal and Delancey, and we'd go to the Fulton Fish Market early in the morning, and we'd walk across the Brooklyn Bridge."

"Mm."

"That's odd," she said at an intersection. "This ought to be Seventh Avenue, but the sign says something else; I can't quite make it out."

"I think it's Varick Street. Turns into Seventh Avenue a few blocks uptown."

"You really are remarkable, John," and she clung to his arm in an affectionate, almost flirtatious way as they turned the corner. "You know *all* the streets."

Well, no; not all; but he did happen to know a few. And well within a block of the secret cellar he saw lamplight flooding up from its clean, closed Venetian blind. Whatever Paul Borg was doing down there tonight, with whatever girl, he sure as hell wasn't cursing the darkness.

"Seen the *Times* yet?" George Taylor inquired, easing one haunch onto Wilder's desk. "Bad news."

Like everything else concerning work these days it took a little while to sink in. He heard Taylor say "McCabe's lost the Northeast account" and watched his mouth

labor through many other words of supporting information. He said "Damn" because it seemed appropriate,
but then he had to hang his head, pretending to think it
over while he tried to puzzle out what Taylor had told
him. His brains seemed filled with sand.

Northeast Distillers was a giant of the liquor industry;
through the giant advertising agency of McCabe-Derrickson they had bought the full-color back cover of *The
American Scientist* every month for years, providing
one of the mainstays of Wilder's income, so it was indeed
bad news. "And what's the new agency again? Hartwell
and who?"

" 'Hartwell and Partners.' I never heard of 'em.
Prob'ly about six months old, one of these damn little
'creative' shops. Anyway you better get on the horn, try
to set up a presentation." And Taylor slid heavily off the
desk with the look of a bewildered old man. "I just don't
get it—a staid, conservative outfit like Northeast pulling
a switch like this. Whole thing's crazy," he said as he
turned away. "Seems like now Kennedy's in, everybody
wants to be some kind of a swinger."

There was some confusion at the Hartwell and Partners switchboard when he asked for the Northeast account executive; he talked with several impatient voices
before he found the man, whose name was Frank Lacy
and who sounded less than thirty years old.

"A 'presentation'?" Frank Lacy said as if the very word
had gone out of style—and maybe it had. "Well, I don't
see why not, Mr. Wilder. Things are fairly hectic around
here now, but I think we can fit you in. Hold on a sec.
How about Wednesday at ten?"

And so he found his way to the thirty-ninth floor of a

steel-and-glass tower, lugging the briefcase that contained his presentation in a sweaty hand.

WE HATE TO PRY

That was the heading of the big cardboard flip chart he propped on the central table of the meeting room, after making his own nervous opening remarks, and beneath it ran the words:

> That's why *The American Scientist* never asks its readers what they drink, how much they drink or when they drink it. It's all right to ask whether they hunt, fish, play tennis or golf, but a man's communion with his favorite tipple is a private matter. . . .

His audience consisted of five or six young men and three or four girls, all semi-collapsed in deep sofas and chairs; they didn't look bored but they were hardly spellbound, and that prompted him to risk a little extemporaneous talk. "I'm supposed to read this thing aloud to you," he said, "and I think I'm even supposed to underscore each line with my finger, but I'll spare you that. I mean the *Scientist* is a great magazine but I've never figured out where they hire the people who write this flip-chart stuff; at least I don't think I could get my mouth around 'a man's communion with his favorite tipple.' "

It wasn't a big laugh, and like Sylvester Cummings he didn't spoil it by smiling, but it was good-natured enough to make him feel at ease, even a little jaunty, as he paged through the rest of the chart.

Still, it seemed only reasonable that the 600,000 *American Scientist* readers would be as excellent a market for alcoholic beverages as they are for expensive cars, cameras, stereo components and European travel.

To find out, we performed a simple exercise in logic. First, a profile was developed of the alcoholic-beverage industry's prime consumer. *The American Scientist* reader was then compared to him. Here, feature by feature, are the results of that comparison:

And on the final page, in twin columns, the prime consumer and the magazine's reader turned out to be identical in every way. That page took longer to read than the others, which gave him time to glance over the pictures on the walls—much like Dr. Blomberg's pictures except that one seemed to be a framed comic strip —and at the people, especially the girls. One wore her tan hair like Jackie Kennedy's and had a face that made his heart turn over, but his several seconds of lust dissolved when he saw her long, slender legs: she'd be too damned tall.

"Well, so much for the flip chart," he said. "I have a few other things here to leave with you. This heavy one—" he felt like Bill Costello handing over the Big Book— "is a very thorough demographic survey called *The Subscriber Self-Portrait;* I hope you'll have time to look it over. And I'd like to sum up with a few points about our average reader. He's forty years old. He earns more than twenty thousand a year, and his work is so highly technical that you and I could never understand it. But he doesn't read the magazine at work; he reads it at home, and he spends four hours over each issue. I don't know what you people do when you're spending four hours at home with a magazine, but I—well, hell, I guess I commune with my favorite tipple."

It was time to get offstage. "As you know, Northeast Distillers already has six of our back covers. The other six are still available, and I think you'd be making a good decision, as soon as possible, to pick them up. Thanks very much." He shook hands with Frank Lacy and several others; then he got out fast and made for the reception room.

"That was nice," said a girl walking beside him. It was the girl with the face and the long legs, and the top of her head came only to his ear.

"Well," he said, "thanks. I always dread these damn things."

"That's what made it nice. I mean I could tell you hated it, but you did it well anyway. I think everyone was impressed." They were out in the reception room now, alone except for the receptionist who sat cuddled over her phone and murmuring seductively in what couldn't have been a business call. "Have you seen our terrace?" the girl said. "It's really the only nice thing about this place."

One panel of a glass wall slid open and she led him out onto a wide, windswept prairie of white pebbles. There were a few wrought-iron tables and chairs and a few stone benches among potted shrubs, but she took him straight to the low balustrade for a naked view of the city. To look out was spectacular; to look down was almost enough to scare the life out of him.

"We spent most of our time out here all summer," she was saying, "but I like it even better now." She didn't even seem to mind that the cold wind was spoiling her Jackie Kennedy hair, and he was already half in love with the proud, slim way she paced the pebbles—she moved like a student of modern dance—and with her big brown eyes and vivid mouth.

"Been working here long?"

"Just since I got out of school last June. I thought it might be fun because you get to do a little of everything, but it's—I don't know. *You* know." And she wrinkled her nose in disdain. "It's still *ad*vertising."

He asked her name—Pamela Hendricks—and when he'd tucked the whipping necktie back into his coat and tried to smooth his own flying hair he asked her out to lunch, which seemed to take her wholly by surprise.

"Well, no, actually, I'm afraid I'm—" And the brightness vanished so quickly from her eyes that he didn't dare say How about tomorrow? She was probably Frank Lacy's mistress anyway (Frank Lacy was a hulking, rock-jawed, big-shouldered son of a bitch, and he remembered now that they'd sat thigh to thigh during the presentation); she might well have brought him out here on the terrace only in some girlish attempt to make Frank Lacy jealous.

"Well. Maybe I could call you some other time."

"All right."

Then they were back in the reception room shaking hands, and he dropped thirty-nine floors in the elevator with a sense of falling back to reality.

Less than a week later he walked into his office to answer a ringing phone and heard, "John Wilder? Frank Lacy, Hartwell and Partners. Look: are those six back covers still available?"

"They sure are."

"Good. We want to pick them up; I'm sending over a contract this afternoon."

"Well, that's—that's fine."

"Great!" George Taylor said. "By Jesus, John, I knew you'd pull it off, if anybody could. Damn, I'd treat you to lunch if I wasn't tied up."

And the word "lunch" rode happily back with him to his own desk, where he called Hartwell and Partners and asked for Pamela Hendricks.

"Oh," she said. "Hi, there. Congratulations."

"How'd you hear about that?"

"Oh, well; word gets around." Which probably meant Frank Lacy had mentioned it as she lay stroking his massive chest in bed.

"I was just wondering if you'd have lunch with me today."

"Well that's very nice, but actually I'm afraid I'm—"

And this time he cut her off in mid-sentence with all the authority of a man who has nothing to lose: "Okay. How about meeting me after work, then. For a drink."

There was a slight pause. "All right. I'd love to."

But two other calls had to be made.

". . . Janice, there's this guy on the Jaguar account flying in from London this afternoon; George wants me to take him out to dinner. No big deal; I'll probably be done with him by ten, then I'll hit one of the meetings . . . Okay . . . See you in the morning."

The second call wasn't quite so easy. "Mr. Paul Borg, please . . . Paul? John. Listen: I just want to know if you're going down to Varick Street tonight. . . . Okay, good. Is it clean? Sheets clean? Towels clean? . . . What do you mean, how'm I doing? I'm doing fine. How're *you* doing? . . ."

He took her to the Plaza in the hope of impressing her, but she'd evidently been there many times before.

The first drink tasted so good that he let her do most of the talking while he savored it, sitting beside her and watching her profile. The tip of her small nose bobbed very slightly up and down at each syllable beginning with *p, b* or *m,* and that seemed a lovely thing for a girl's nose to do.

She talked about her school, a small experimental college in Vermont called Marlowe, of which he'd never heard—"I mean it's sort of like Bennington only more so; *and* coeducational"—and about her father in Boston and her older brother who was an "absolute genius" at the piano, and he began to realize she was a rich girl; maybe even a very rich girl.

"What does your father do?"

"Oh, he's a banker. An investment banker. Anyway . . ."

And over the second or third drink she explained why she was never free for lunch: "I was—well, 'seeing' Frank all summer—Frank Lacy—until his marriage counsellor advised him to break it off, and he did. But we still have lunch together every day to sort of prove we're friends. I know that sounds silly."

"And you're still crazy about him."

She shook her head and pressed her lips tight. "No. Not really; not at all any more. I mean it seems to me that a man who lets a marriage counsellor make his decisions for him isn't—well, isn't much of a man. You're married, aren't you?"

"Yeah; yeah, I sure am."

"Well, would *you* let some marriage counsellor talk you into— Oh, never mind. It's too complicated."

During the prime-rib dinner, with wine, she complained that most of the other people at Marlowe had been "so terrifically creative—oh, I don't mean 'creative' in the twerpy advertising sense; don't get me wrong—" and she aimed her knife straight at his throat to make sure he didn't. She meant poetry and painting and sculpture and music and dance; she meant theatre—"Everything from Sophocles to what's-his-name, you know, Beckett—all that stuff. I was always the world's dopiest, no-talent square. Still am, in fact."

By the time the coffee and brandy arrived her talk had subsided and she'd begun to look at him as if through a mist of romance; then at last he had his arm close around her in a taxicab.

"*What* street?" she said. "Where's that?"

"Just a little place I think you might like."

"You're sweet, John." And she offered up her mouth for the ritual first kiss, allowing his hand to cradle one breast as they began the long ride down Seventh Avenue.

She was great. At least that was the word that kept spilling from his mouth as they clung and rolled and locked and thrusted in the bed beneath the sidewalk, with the Seventh Avenue subway rumbling under the floor: "Oh, you're great . . . oh, baby, you're . . . oh, Jesus God, you're great . . . You're great . . ." She said nothing, but her gasps and moans and her long high cry at the end were enough to suggest that he'd been—well, not too bad himself.

They lay silent for a long time afterwards while he

pondered the remarkable truth that he was thirty-six years old and had never known this much pleasure with a woman before. He almost said it: You know something? I'm thirty-six years old and that's absolutely the best I've ever—but he checked himself. She might laugh at such a confession, or pity him, after all her damned "creative" boys at Marlowe and a whole summer of romping with Frank Lacy. Instead he said "Pamela? How old are you?"

"I'll be twenty-one in February."

She disentangled herself, got up and walked naked across the linoleum, reminding him of the girl on the raft that weekend after Bellevue. How could any girl his size have legs like that?

"That first door's just the toilet," he called after her. "The sink's in the kitchen."

"Oh," she called back, "I see. Like a French apartment."

So she'd been to France too—probably all over Europe, on long vacations since childhood—and as he padded to the liquor cabinet he allowed his head to fill with maddening images: Pamela shyly opening those legs for some oily nobleman at a champagne breakfast in the Bois de Bologne; Pamela delirious and clawing the back of some grunting Spanish peasant in dirty straw; Pamela sprawled and breathing *"Te amo"* to some Italian racing driver on an Adriatic beach . . .

But soon she was back with him. He had made a couple of drinks and pulled on his pants; she was wearing an old raincoat of Paul Borg's that she'd found in the closet, and they sat close together on the edge of the bed. "This *is* a cozy little place," she said. "I hardly noticed it when we came in because I was so—you know, horny—" And it was all he could do to keep from saying Horny? Honest to God? For *me?* "—but it's really sort of nice."

"Well, it's not much of an apartment, but it serves its — I mean, I like it too." He touched the rim of his tinkling glass to hers. "So. I guess this is what might be called a man's communion with his favorite tipple."

"Mm," she said like Dr. Blomberg, and so he learned that weak jokes didn't go over very big with Pamela Hendricks. Twenty years old or not, she required something funny to make her laugh. Another thing: never once that night did she say "What's your wife like?" or ask if he had children, or make sly inquiries about how many girls he'd brought down here, and that alone set her apart from the others.

After a while she began pensively stalking the floor in Borg's raincoat and went back to her old and apparently favorite topic: the dilemma of being the world's dopiest, no-talent square.

". . . One funny thing, though," she said while he fixed himself a new drink, "I know I can't act and I don't photograph well, and I certainly can't write and wouldn't know what to do if somebody handed me a camera, but I've always had this feeling I'd be good at making movies. Good movies."

His drink was made, but he let an extra shot of whiskey slide in over the ice cubes before he looked up into her wide, dead-serious eyes.

"Me too," he said.

4

The air is very thin in the mountains of Vermont, and nothing there seems real to a city man. The massed trees are overwhelming, the browns and greens of the earth are unbelievably rich, and there is too much sky.

"Right around this next turn," Pamela Hendricks said. "You'll see a sign."

He was driving a yellow Avis Rent A Car so massive and fluid that it seemed to drive itself, with the back seat full of luggage and bottles of bourbon. "It's the funniest thing," he told her. "None of this seems real. I can't believe it's really happening."

"Well, you'd better start believing," she said, "because it is. Slow down a little now, or we'll miss the sign. No, wait; there it is—see?"

And the sign read MARLOWE COLLEGE, 5 MI.

It was late summer again, and the past half year had been the most jubilant time of his life. After the first few winter weeks, on nights when he was supposed to be at

AA meetings, he had stopped taking her to Varick Street; instead they used her own "luxury" apartment in the East Eighties, for which her father paid the rent. He would ride uptown in fright that she wouldn't answer the door—or, worse still, that another and bigger man might answer it for her—but she was always there alone, sometimes still in her street clothes, sometimes fresh from her bath and wrapped in a loose terry-cloth robe, sometimes in a nightgown whose only purpose was to be slipped off and dropped weightlessly to the floor as they made for the bed.

At first a great deal of their talk was of movies, and on one of their most memorable nights he related the whole scenario of *The Champ,* starring Wallace Beery and Jackie Cooper, which he'd seen when he was seven years old.

"God, what a memory," she said, and when he came to the end she almost wept.

"Oh, it wasn't the first movie I'd ever seen," he told her. "In those days you had to have a good many movies under your belt by the time you were seven, but it was the first that made a real impact on me. It knocked me out. That final scene, with old Beery dead of a heart attack after regaining the championship and the kid's parents trying to hustle him out of the dressing room, and the kid saying 'I want the Champ! I want the Champ!'—that was too much. I didn't cry because it was very important not to cry at that age, but I walked out of that theatre with my throat on fire and as soon as I got in bed I cried like a little bastard."

He told her of other movies he'd liked before she was born, but not all of them pleased her. Some she'd seen on television and said were trash, others she'd seen at the Museum of Modern Art and called pretentious. When he described *Gunga Din* as "maybe the best *boy's* movie ever made" she squirmed in boredom. "And you mean after Sam Jaffe gets killed they hold a special parade and pin a medal for him on the regimental flag, and they get some actor dressed up like Rudyard Kipling to recite his poem? Even if I were a *boy* I'd have laughed at that."

"You wouldn't have laughed when they showed Sam Jaffe's ghost coming up through the poem, wearing a full-dress British uniform and making a British salute."

"I think I might have vomited."

Another time she dwelt at some length on the mystery of why great novels—even good novels—were so seldom made into halfway decent movies. "I mean they've done all right with Dickens, especially the English, but I guess that's because his writing is so visual in the first place."

"Mm."

"But when you think of all the dismal failures: *Madame Bovary* with what's-his-name's wife, Jennifer something or other . . ."

"Mm," he kept saying of each one she mentioned, and "Yeah," though he'd read almost none of the books. He was damned if he was going to let her find out about his reading problem.

". . . And when you think what those Hollywood people did with *From Here to Eternity!*"

"Yeah." The truth was that he'd liked that picture and might have read the book on the strength of it, if it hadn't been nearly a thousand pages long.

"And did you ever see the mess they made of *The Great Gatsby?* With Alan Ladd?"

Now, wait a minute. Alan Ladd had taught him not

only how to comb his hair but how to carry his shoulders and how to walk, and how a short man could look at a girl in such a way as to leave no doubt of his carnal intentions.

"It was an outright *betrayal* of the book," she said. "They made it into some cheap little gangster flick."

"Well, hell, movies aren't books; they're two different forms, that's all. Besides, you'll have to admit Alan Ladd was pretty good in *Shane.*"

"Oh my God. *Shane.* Like *High Noon.* Adult Westerns. You know what an adult Western is? It's a contradiction in terms."

"Okay, look. What's the single best American movie you've ever seen?"

"The single best? I don't know. Probably *Cit—*"

"Right. *Citizen Kane.* And can you imagine what kind of a novel that would've been? A piece of schlock. A half-assed, sensational book by some all-thumbs Harold Robbins about the life of William Randolph Hearst. See what I mean?"

She bit her lip, nodding slowly, and for the first time that night her face glowed with admiration.

"That's what the Europeans have known for years," he hurried on. "Movies are movies—though I must say some of your European favorites have been screwing up that concept lately: your Fellinis and your Antonionis and whatever artsy-craftsy fool it was who made *Hiroshima, Mon Amour,* and your—your sacrosanct Ingmar Bergman."

Her teeth released her lip and her eyes narrowed, ready to argue again. "What's the matter with Bergman?"

"Partly just that—he's sacrosanct. Any New York

movie critic with the guts to call Bergman overrated
would be fired on the spot. But the main thing about him
is worse."

"What's that?"

"He doesn't have any sense of humor. Think about it.
The man doesn't have any sense of humor."

She thought about it, stroking his chest, and announced that she guessed he was right.

But their first real quarrel had nothing to do with
movies. It happened shortly after the abortive invasion
of Cuba, which very soon became known in the press as
the Bay of Pigs.

"Whaddya think of your Wonder Boy now, baby?" he
demanded, having stalked into the apartment, made
himself a drink and sat down to relish it.

"He was badly advised." She was fully dressed and
walking the carpet with her arms folded across her
breasts. "It wasn't his fault."

"Who do you think *ordered* those poor raggedy-assed
bastards to go in there and get wiped out? Huh? And
then *lying* about it! Making a patsy out of Adlai Stevenson in front of the world. It's the most inept, arrogant, cowardly—"

"Look, John. If you're going to rant and rave I don't
want to—"

"Who's ranting and raving? I'm talking politics, that's
all."

"No you're not. You think you are, but you're not. You
know why you don't like Kennedy? Because he's tall."

"Ah, come on."

"It's true, though. He's tall and handsome and a war
hero and he's got a beautiful wife as *well* as a reputation

as a cocksman— He's everything you're not, and you can't stand it. It's loathsome. I don't think I want you to stay here tonight."

She might as well have kneed him in the groin, but he tried a boyish, conciliatory smile, swirling his ice cubes. "Is it okay if I finish my drink?"

"I'd rather you didn't. You look as though you've been drinking all day. Why don't you just get up and leave before you make an even bigger fool of yourself?"

At the door he wondered whether to say "Can I call you?" but that would make it all too easy for her to say no. Instead he slung his raincoat jauntily over one shoulder and said "Well. See you in the funny-papers." On the elevator it occurred to him that "See you in the funny-papers" was something people had said in the thirties; she'd probably never heard it, and it must have struck her as drunken gibberish, if she'd been listening at all.

The first bar he came to was loud and Irish, festooned not only with shamrocks and the green cardboard lettering ERIN GO BRAGH but with a framed photograph of President Kennedy from the waist up, making him look very tall indeed. Six or eight years ago the portrait might well have been of Senator Joseph McCarthy. He left after a couple of quick ones and found a dark, mercifully apolitical lounge of deep leather and black mirrors, where the only sounds were the tinkle of heavy glassware and a muted jukebox. What the hell was he going to do? Calling her was out of the question, if only because he'd had so much to drink now that he'd only mess it up worse.

"I've lost my baby," he whispered into his glass, and might have begun to weep except that this kind of bar would tolerate no crying drunks. He had to make plans.

He wouldn't call her for two weeks—well, one week. Then, assuming she'd welcome him, he would arrive at her door with a bashful, cold-sober smile that hardly any girl could resist. When she offered him a drink he'd say "No thanks; not just yet," and with any kind of luck he'd have her back.

The funny part was that the week seemed to pass quickly. The office was the worst—every time his phone rang he thought it might be Pamela—but it was endurable, and so was life at home. On his meeting nights he went to movies instead of bars, or movies before bars, and he tried to drink nothing but beer. On the final day of the week he was all anxiety: he dropped two dimes on the floor of the phone booth before managing to get one into the slot, and his finger trembled in the dial.

"Oh," she said.

"Look: can I—would it be okay if I come over to-night?"

"Well, sure. Come on up whenever you want. I mean —you know—whenever you can."

And he did, complete with a bouquet of roses which made her laugh.

"Why didn't you call for so long?"

"I thought you were sore at me."

"That was *last* week."

He didn't ask if she had "seen" or "dated" anyone else all week, and once they were in bed it no longer seemed to matter.

And it wasn't very many nights later, during one of his rambling autobiographical monologues, that he told her about Bellevue. He tried to make it light and brief but she wouldn't let him: she pressed for more and more details, sitting up against the pillows and chain-smoking, and when he falteringly came to the end she said "God. Have you ever thought of what a *movie* that would make?"

He hadn't, and he didn't start thinking of it until he'd gotten up for two cold beers. "I don't see it," he said. "It'd be like some *New York Post* exposé on the Terrible Conditions in City Mental Health Facilities."

"No it wouldn't," she insisted. "Not if it were done right; it wouldn't be like that at all. Think of the mood; the characters; the situations. It could be—well, I know this is a cliché, but it could be the world in microcosm. And you may be one of the very few patients they've ever had who can remember it all so vividly, because you were stone-cold sane the whole time. You know something, John? Just from the way you tell it, I'll bet you've really been thinking of the whole thing in cinematic terms all along. Even while you were going *through* it."

"Well, I don't know. Yeah; come to think of it I guess I have, in a way."

"Of course you have. It's an absolute natural for the screen. And hasn't it occurred to you that you might be the only man in America who could do it right?"

"How do you mean, 'do' it? No money; no talent."

"But you said you always wanted to be the man who raised the money and *hired* the talent. Isn't that true?"

"Well, sure, baby, but let's be realistic. I'm only a salesman, after all, and I've got a family to support, and I—"

"John, I refuse to let you throw this beautiful idea away just because you're feeling dumb and middle-class tonight. You be quiet and drink your beer; let me think."

And soon the brave beginnings of her plan began to emerge: it might just be possible, she said, to make this

film on a very, very low budget. First of all, the script
would be no problem. There had been a wonderfully
talented writer at Marlowe College named Jerry—Jerry
Porter. He'd sold a story to the *Atlantic* while still in
school, but then decided he'd rather work "in film" and
had done some marvelous scripts, one of which had been
optioned and nearly bought by a good producer. She
would call him tonight—she was sure he'd be interested
—and if John would arrange to meet him they could get
started on the screenplay right away. And Jerry had a
friend named Julian Feld, another Marlowe graduate
three or four years his senior, who was a director—"a
magician with the camera." Julian had spent a summer in
France studying with Truffaut; he'd worked as a second-
unit man in Hollywood and made some civil rights docu-
mentaries in the South, but the last she'd heard he was
back here in New York with time on his hands. Both Jerry
and Julian had money of their own—they came from
enormously rich families—and might even help out with
the financing of the venture; at the very least they'd be
willing to work on spec. So would another young Marlowe man she knew—an artist and stage designer who
would do the set—and so would most of the actors. God,
there had been more fine actors at Marlowe than he could
imagine.

"Wait a second, sweetheart. You can't have a bunch of
fresh-faced college kids playing Bellevue characters.
What about all the Negroes and Puerto Ricans?"

"I've already thought of that. Julian can round them
up. He knows scads of them."

"You mean some of his best friends are Negroes and
Puerto Ricans."

But she seemed not even to hear him as she hurried

on to a triumphant conclusion: if the script and the casting and rehearsals were done by midsummer, they could all go up to Marlowe and do the actual shooting there, in one of the great Marlowe barns. Think of the money they'd save! They'd have to get the dean's permission, of course, but this was just the kind of thing Dean Walcott loved—an experimental film created on campus.

"What time is it?" she demanded. "Oh, good, it's still early. I'll call Jerry right now."

Jerry Porter turned out to be a slight young man with a nervous boyish face and a handlebar moustache that picked up suds when he drank beer, and he was indeed interested. Wilder met with him at regular intervals over a period of five or six weeks, telling him everything he could remember about Bellevue—about the look and sound and feel of the place, about Charlie and Spivack and all the others. Jerry frowned and listened and took notes and asked questions, and when the screenplay began to take shape he introduced Wilder to the director, Julian Feld.

"I think you've got the makings of a good little film here, Mr. Wilder," Julian said, just as Pamela had promised he would. "I'd like to work with you." He was squat and moody-looking, given to wearing work shirts with so many buttons unfastened as to suggest that a dark pelt ran from his nostrils to his ankles, and he lived in an East Village loft that soon became the stage for casting and preliminary rehearsals.

"Isn't it wonderful," Pamela said, "how everything's working out?"

"Hold all my calls, honey," George Taylor said. "Now. What can I do for you, John?"

"A favor. Look: I know my vacation is set for July and I want to take it then, but I want two more weeks at the end of August. I want you to fake up a business trip for me."

All the joviality drained from Taylor's face; he looked as if they scarcely knew each other. "Fake up a business trip?"

"Hell, George, you know I'm way over my quota. I don't have to tell you how much money I've brought into the magazine over the past couple of years. And the thing is—the thing is I've got a girl."

That was all it took. What did she look like? How old was she? How had he met her? "Well, now, let's see," he said at last, getting down to business. "A couple of weeks in August? Just between the two of us I imagine that might be within the—you know, the realm of possibility."

He had dreaded his real vacation, the one in "the country," until Janice declared it would be only sensible for him to drive back to town four or five nights a week for his meetings. Sitting on the raft with her toward the end of their last afternoon, he came out as casually as possible with his lie about August.

"Two whole weeks in Boston?" she inquired. "He's never sent you to Boston for that long before."

"He isn't 'sending' me, Janice; it's something we worked out together. Matter of fact it was mostly my idea. We're having a lot of trouble with the Northeast Distillers' account, you see . . ." Talking, he looked down at the heavy spread of her thigh on the wet boards and then into the top of her bathing suit. How could he ever have been so young and callow as to believe that this was the woman for him? For life?

"Hey, watch, Mom," Tommy was calling. "Watch this." He loped across the raft (he was skinny, but on the tall side and filling out; at least he would never be a shrimp like his father), took three or four awkward bounds on the springboard, flung himself into the air and came down all arms and legs in a great splash.

"Wonderful, dear," Janice called when his soaked head appeared again, and Wilder said "Pretty good one, Tom.

". . . There's been a change of management up there," he went on, "and there's a good chance they might drop McCabe-Derrickson and go with one of these new, small agencies—in which case they might very well drop the *Scientist*. The first week is just the distillers' convention, and I'll spend that just sort of glad-handing around as usual, but the second week's the important one: that's when I'll have to do everything I can to persuade Northeast not to change agencies—or, if they do change, persuade them to keep on buying space in the *Scientist*."

"I'm afraid I'm not following this. I've never really understood your business."

"Well, to put it simply, if they drop the magazine it'll mean a loss in personal income to me of something over six thousand a year."

"Six thousand a *year?*"

She understood that, all right, and after a long and respectful silence she had only one admonition: he would be careful, wouldn't he? Would he try to keep up with his meetings?

"Oh, hell, yes. They've probably got as much of an AA organization in Boston as here. Don't worry about that."

*   *   *

"As you see it doesn't *look* much like a campus," Pamela said. "It looks more like an old New England farming village or something, which is pretty funny when you consider it's the single most expensive college in America. When my father asked why it looks so poor, they said it's because most of the money goes into faculty —the faculty's enormously well paid."

"Oh."

"These are some of the classroom buildings and the dorms," she told him as he eased the car between two rows of white clapboard structures. "It gets prettier farther on, when we come to the Commons and the—wait! Stop! There's Peter!" She sprang from the car and ran to embrace a scrawny boy wearing faded Levis and a new beard, which he fingered self-consciously as she made the introductions.

". . . Peter's the marvelous designer I told you about. This is John Wilder."

Wilder expected the boy to hold out a loose hand and say "Hey, man," or to squint past him at the car and murmur "Nice set of wheels"—he looked like that kind of kid—but instead he shook hands firmly and said "How do you do, sir," just as the youth of Wilder's own generation had been taught to do.

"Where are the others?" Pamela said. "Is everybody here? Are Jerry and Julian here?"

"They're all over in P barn, Pammy; can I have a lift?"

"P barn is Peabody barn, you see," she explained as the boy pressed shyly into the front seat, "and C barn is Carlton—that's where you've built the set, isn't it, Peter? —and L barn is—"

"They run the whole school in barns?"

"Don't be silly; I've *shown* you the classroom buildings and the dorms. The barns are simply for—well, ac*tiv*ities."

Jerry and Julian sat in the big double door of P barn as if waiting to have their picture taken for the film section of a national magazine, but they got quickly to their feet as Wilder's car pulled up.

"Come on inside," Julian said, and they let Pamela and Wilder go first into what seemed like a primitive wooden cathedral. Most of its great space was in shadow, but there were mote-filled shafts of sun slanting down from high, small windows to make yellow rectangles on the floor. The scent of marijuana hung in the heavier, more solemn smell of ancient lumber, and Wilder had to wait until his eyes grew accustomed to the dimness before he made out clusters of men sitting on bedrolls and knapsacks against the walls. He recognized the actors from Julian's loft, and he guessed the people he didn't know were cameramen and technicians.

"Well," said the big Negro who'd been hired to play Charlie. "Here's the man." And there were courteous little greetings from some of the others: "Hi, Mr. Wilder. Hi there, Miss Hendricks . . ."

Somebody handed Wilder a Styrofoam cup of red wine and he said "Thanks, that's fine, but wait—we've got better stuff in the car."

Out in the late afternoon sunshine again, under the deep rustle of lofty trees, he found he was trembling. He got the whiskey from the car, but on the way back he had to stop a few feet short of the barn door because he wanted to get his emotional bearings, to strengthen his soft knees and slow down the beating of his heart. He was totally free for the first time in more years than he could remember. He was standing on a lawn of the single most expensive college in America. He was about to return to the girl he loved and to a barnful of men for whom he was "the man." It was a little too much for the mind and senses to absorb all at once.

"Great!" somebody said of the whiskey, and somebody else said "Trouble is we got no ice."

"Who needs ice?"

"There's ice in the snack bar at Commons," Pamela said.

"Commons is locked up, Pam. Refectory's locked too."

"Where're we going to *eat*, then?"

"Have to go down the road to Dirty Ed's, I guess, or else blow a bundle and go to the Old Colonial."

She looked crestfallen, but only for a second. "Well, never mind that now. Nobody's hungry yet. Listen, Julian: you had your final rehearsal today, right? And you start shooting tomorrow?"

"Right."

"Well then I think this might be the time for one last run-through of the script," she said, walking out into the middle of the floor to address them all, and Wilder noticed something aggressive in the fit of her tight white slacks. For a moment she seemed like a bossy little rich girl telling the other children how to play. He was in love with her, but he had discovered there were times when she wasn't very likable. "Jerry can read the camera directions," she was saying, "and the actors can read their parts. That way we can all—"

At least three of the men groaned, and the others

showed by their faces that they thought it was a very poor idea.

"No," Wilder said, "come on, Pamela; these guys've been working all day."

She turned on him with bright eyes. "Well, can't we at least have a meeting?"

"How do you mean, a 'meeting'?"

"Get some chairs," she said, "and sit everybody down, with Julian in charge, and have a *discussion*. That way, if anybody has any problems, we can get them settled now. I mean this is our last chance—we're *shooting* tomorrow."

And probably because she looked so helpless—or because she was the only woman there—they all complied. Lights were turned on, folding chairs were drawn from some recess in the barn and set up in a ragged half-circle, and a kind of "meeting" came to order.

"Okay," Julian said. "Has anybody got any problems or anything?"

Nobody did, which caused embarrassed smiles around the group, until the man playing Charlie got to his feet. "Something's been bugging me about my part all along," he said, "and I've just now figured out what it is. Charlie's the only Negro in the cast—with the exception of the little faggot kid—the only Negro in the cast who speaks what white people call Perfect English. All the others talk like stereotype down-home niggers, and I object to that. On racial grounds."

Julian turned to Jerry for an answer, and Jerry looked confused. "Well, Clay," he said, blinking and tucking his forelock behind one ear with nervous fingers, "it strikes me that Charlie speaks pretty much the same way you do."

"Shee-it. Look, man, I'm an actor. That's my trade. I had to go to school and *study* this Perfect English. I've played *Othello* with white kids who had to learn British accents for the same reason. That's not the point. The point is, this cat Charlie's a *nurse*. Where'd *he* study, and what for? What's *his* excuse?"

"Well," Jerry said, "maybe Mr. Wilder can help us there."

And Wilder was scared. All the Negroes in the barn were looking at him. "First of all, Clay—I'm afraid I don't remember your last name—"

"Oh, you're afraid? Well, I'm afraid I don't remember your *first* name, Mr. Wilder."

"John."

"Braddock."

"First of all, Mr. Braddock, I don't agree that Charlie speaks Perfect English. He speaks neutral English, or rather neutral American—the kind of accent telephone operators and radio announcers use. Sure he's only a nurse, but he's been in charge of all these lunatics every day for a good many years, and maybe he's developed that manner of speech as the best way of—you know—maintaining authority. Does that make any sense?"

"Some," Clay Braddock said. "Yeah, that makes some sense."

And when the talk had moved on to other things Pamela hugged Wilder's arm—a little too vigorously, he thought—and whispered "That was wonderful. You know what you did? You just saved practically the whole movie."

"I don't have a problem," said the man playing Spivack—or "Klinger" as he was called in the script. "Far from it; I'm in love with my part. I just want to take this opportunity to thank you, Mr. Wilder. I never did get a chance to thank you properly in New York. It's an absolutely *ex*quisite part, and it's perfect for me." He was all in white, as if ready for tennis—white shirt and shorts, white socks and sneakers. "I don't mean just professionally, though it's certainly that too, but in a personal sense. I've been in analysis for three years, you see—deep analysis—and I can't imagine a more cathartic experience. Klinger could be my breakthrough: this caustic, sarcastic, egomaniacal creature who loathes the very word 'psychiatrist'—oh, and by the way I think it's marvelous that we never do find out what brought him to the ward in the first place—and the subtle suggestion of incestuous feelings for his sister; it's all just perfect. Perfect."

"Well, that's fine," Wilder said, not looking at him. "But I think it's Jerry you ought to thank."

"Oh, I have, I have—both for writing the part so beautifully and for hiring me. It's just that I feel an enormous gratitude to you, too, because it was you who *conceived* the role. Oh, you look embarrassed. Have I embarrassed you?"

"I move the meeting be adjourned," Julian said, and there was a great scraping of chairs.

Wilder found a place in the shadows where he and Pamela could sit and drink warm whiskey, but it wasn't long before Julian came over, bringing Jerry and Peter behind him.

"You people want to see the set?" he asked. "Peter's worked his ass off on it; thought you might at least want to look it over."

All five of them, in two cars, rode out across the darkening campus to C barn, where Julian flicked on many lights. At first all Wilder could see was a maze of raw wallboard, but Julian was quick to guide them through the first opening. "If you'll come this way you'll see what we've done—tried to do anyway. We're shooting in black and white, of course, so the colors don't matter. Here's your corridor. I know you'll say it's too short, but don't worry. A camera can make thirty feet look like sixty if you use it right. Same goes for the bunks. We've only got eight bunks, but I can give an illusion of five or six times that many. Peter got the bunks from this home for retarded kids they're tearing down upstate; then he put hinges on 'em and went to a scrap-metal yard for the chains and the grids. Look." He slammed two bunks against the wall, clamped them, and drew the grid across them. "That look right? Sound right?"

"It's fine; fine."

"And here's your padded cells. The padding was another of Peter's inspirations; borrowed it from the gym here at school. Look all right?"

"Looks fine." But Pamela and Peter weren't there, and he had begun to wonder where they were.

"And here's one of your windows. You stand here, I'll go around and light it, then you tell me if the light's right."

It was; either an early grey morning or a late grey afternoon.

". . . and as for your mess hall, if you'll just come through here . . ."

"Fine," he kept saying. "Where'd you get the benches?"

"Peter borrowed 'em from the library. And here's

your front door, with the cop's stool, and here's Charlie's KEEP OUT door . . ."

It was all fine, but where was Pamela?

". . . Oh, and here," Julian said. "Come over this way. Here's your Jerk-off City."

It was a perfect replica of that loathsome alcove; and there they were, Pamela and Peter, sitting cross-legged on a single dirty mattress and sharing a joint.

"What's the deal?" he asked her. "Don't you want to see the set?"

"I'm too tired," she said. "Besides, I don't have to see it—I know Peter's done everything beautifully."

"Yeah, well, that's true. He has."

"And anyway I'm starving. Can't we please go have dinner now?"

Wilder drove for what seemed many miles to a restaurant where tough, expensive steaks were served by waiters dressed in the tight knickerbockers and white stockings of Revolutionary times.

". . . Oh, hey, Pam," Jerry said with his mouth full. "I forgot to tell you. Guess who's on campus?"

"Who?"

"God."

"No!"

"Yup. Old God the Father himself. Went to England for the summer, got bored and came home early. He's holed up in his old study. I told him about the picture; he said he'd like to meet John and all that. Said he'd especially like to see you again."

"Did he really? Oh, I'd *love* to see him. You think it's too late?"

"I don't think he'd mind. I'll call him first."

Wilder finally managed to swallow a stringy piece of meat that had threatened to gag him. "Will somebody tell me what's going on? Who's 'God,' for God's sake?"

"Oh, he's just the most wonderful, wonderful man," Pamela explained. "He's probably the most serene and learned and beautiful person I've ever known. He's a philosophy professor. His name's Nathan Epstein, and he's a widower, and he's about—I don't know; sixty? We used to call him 'God' and 'God the Father' because we adored him so much. You'll see why."

"Did he know you called him 'God'?"

"Oh, of course not; he'd have been terribly embarrassed. That was just a silly undergraduate thing of ours."

"Wouldn't be too sure of that, Pam," Peter said. "It wasn't only our class that called him that. I imagine the kids've been doing it ever since he first came here—ten, twelve years ago."

And Jerry came back from the phone to announce that Mr. Epstein would be happy to see them in half an hour.

His house on the outskirts of the campus was very small, the picture of a lonely scholar's retreat, and when he opened the door it turned out that he was small too —about Wilder's size. His thick white hair was disheveled and he wore a sweater so old and raddled that it seemed ready to fall off his back, but his face did look wise—like some commercial artist's vision of a Supreme Court justice.

"Pamela!" he said, opening his arms for an embrace in which she melted. "My little Nietzsche scholar. Have I ever told you," he asked the others over her shoulder, "that this young lady wrote one of the best term papers on Nietzsche I've ever read? And Jerry; Julian; Peter—"

he managed to shake hands without releasing his grip on Pamela— "How nice of you to come. And you're Mr. Wilde, right? Or is it Wilder?"

"Wilder. Good to meet you, Mr. Epstein."

Only then did he let Pamela out of his arms, and she seemed reluctant to leave. "I've heard so much about your film project, and I must say it sounds fascinating. Won't you all come into the other room? We'll have some coffee and a little brandy."

The other room was his library, or study. All four walls were packed with books—more books even than Janice owned, and more impressive because only a few of them had bright jackets: the rest were old and dark. There was a desk, too, with piles of manuscript and a portable typewriter and a rack of well-used pipes (unlike Paul Borg, Mr. Epstein knew how to smoke a pipe), and there were enough chairs for everyone to sit down while he went about the business of the brandy bottle and the glasses. Rooms like this, and men like this, always gave Wilder a fresh sense of pain and loss at having flunked out of college.

"Well, Jerry," Epstein was saying, "I'm sure screenwriting is a challenge, but I do hope you'll get back to fiction before long. That *Atlantic* story was really striking. And Peter: I must say I'm a bit disappointed in you, designing a film set when you could be off somewhere painting. Joe Barrett told me— Well, never mind what he told me; surely you must know what a talented painter you are."

"I'll get back to it, Mr. Epstein; it won't go away. I just got hooked on this movie. Julian talked me into it."

"Yes, well, I imagine our friend Julian could talk anyone into anything. And you, sir," he said, approaching Wilder with the brandy bottle. "Would you care to tell me something about your—your film? I understand it's set in a public psychiatric ward. Bellevue, is it?"

"That's right. I had all this material on my hands, you see, and I've always liked movies; this Bellevue stuff seemed right for a good experimental movie, that's all."

"Mm. Are you a psychologist, Mr. Wilder?"

Only then was it clear that Epstein didn't know the truth. The kids hadn't told him; and why should they? Why should anyone tell anyone? But almost before he knew what he was doing, he told the truth himself: "No. Actually, I was a patient in Bellevue."

"Oh?"

"Oh, just for a week," he hurried on, "and that was just because of the Labor Day weekend, but I—" Appalled at his own voice, he wondered why he couldn't have said he was a social worker or a hospital executive. Would the kids have cared? Why was he spilling his guts instead? Did he think it might make him more interesting in Epstein's eyes? But what was "interesting" about having been a mental patient? "—anyway, I was locked up there," he concluded, and he wondered if Pamela and the others were embarrassed for him.

"My goodness," Epstein said. "And now you're trying to turn that unfortunate episode into a work of art. I think that's very—interesting." Then one of the pipes was drawn out of the rack, and while tamping it he said "Julian? Do you think I might drop over and watch the filming?"

"Sure. Be a pleasure, Mr. Epstein. I'll get you a copy of the script, too."

Epstein said that would be fine, and for the next half hour, while he smoked and fondled and flourished his pipe, the talk excluded Wilder altogether. It was all reminiscence—the old professor chuckling over happy days with four favorite students—until the time came for everyone to rise and move toward the door.

"Well, Mr. Wilder," he said then, "if you want to make a good film I think you've come to the right place. There's something rare about Marlowe, something—oh, stimulating, invigorating—I discovered it when I first came here and decided I'd never work anywhere else. There's an intensely creative atmosphere up here that I've never been able to define or explain. I don't mean to sound fanciful, but Marlowe casts a spell—" and here he broke off for a self-deprecating laugh. "Oh, I know if I tried telling this to some of my New York friends they'd say 'spell, schmell,' but even so, I think it's true."

All the way home to their dormitory room he let Pamela do the talking ("Isn't he wonderful? . . ."), and he drove with his jaws clenched tight because he was weak with the need for a drink. He made himself a good one as soon as their door was shut, and even before she finished hanging up her clothes and taking a shower he'd begun to get a little drunk. He wanted to ask if she *had* been embarrassed when he told Epstein he was a patient; he wanted to discuss his strange compulsion to let people know the worst about himself—this confusion of what was weak and ugly in himself with what was "interesting"—but he couldn't find the words to begin. And the more he drank, the more that topic receded in his mind until it was replaced by irrational, sickening images of jealousy.

"Aren't you ever coming to bed?" she called from between the sheets.

"In a while." By this time he had stripped down to his shorts and he was pacing the cold floor with a glass in his hand, returning again and again to the bottle on the table. "Got a couple of questions first," he said. "What *were* you and Peter doing there in Jerk-off City tonight?"

"What? John, I don't even know what you're—"

"Yes you do. You and that dreamy-eyed little bullshit painter, bullshit designer, both of you smoking pot and feeling each other up— How many times you make it with *him* in the old days? Huh?"

"I'm not listening to any of this."

"Yes you are, sweetheart. And how about Jerry? Isn't he just the sweet, sensitive young writer though? And how about Julian? What the hell d'ya think—you're *fooling* me with all these kids? Ah, you may fool me with the kids, baby, but I've got your number with the old professor. Yeah, yeah, 'My little Nietzsche scholar.' God the Father my ass! How many times did *that* dirty old bastard get into your pants? Huh? Huh?"

That was when he tripped over something (a wastebasket? a suitcase?) and the cruel weight of the floor clobbered his shoulder. Then she was up and helping him to his feet—it wasn't easy; it took all their combined strength—and they staggered and fumbled their way into bed together.

"Oh, John," she said, "you're a drunken, hateful, foul-mouthed bastard and you're half crazy, but I love you."

And what could he do after that—all passion spent, all jealousy dissolved—what could he do but murmur "Oh, baby," and fall heavily asleep in her arms?

5

". . . I don't *care!* I don't *care!* Can't you idiots understand? I don't *care!* I *want* my father to see me like this!"

"All right, Henry; easy now . . ."

"Don't call me *Henry*, you dumb black bastard—call
me Doctor or I'll break every fucking bone in your—"

"You ain't gonna break nothin', Doctor . . ."

"Cut!" Julian said. "Okay, hold it right there. What's
the trouble, John?"

"No real trouble," Wilder said, "it's just that I think the
orderlies ought to be rougher on Klinger. They don't like
him; he's a troublemaker; he calls them spades and jiga-
boos, and they're tired anyway from working the night
shift. I want to see them *really* grab him and yell at him
and muscle him around before they shoot him out."

"Oh, *yes*," said the man playing Klinger. "Yes, that's
absolutely right."

Mr. Epstein dropped in toward the end of the third
afternoon and tiptoed to where Wilder and Pamela

stood on the apron of the set, holding a forefinger to his lips. He watched the actors for a while, watched the cameras and the sound apparatus and the lights and the trailing cables and wires, and at Julian's next cut he said, "Could the three of us step outside?"

He led them out onto the rich, sunlit grass. "I've read the script and I think it's splendid," he said, "and I have every confidence in Julian's direction, assuming the actors and technicians are competent. But I must say, Mr. Wilder—and I certainly don't mean to embarrass you—I must say I think you're the most admirable man in this venture." He paused there, letting the silence fill with afternoon wind in the trees. "To endure an experience like that, to observe it all so acutely despite the wretched emotional state you must have been in, and then in all humility to recapture it, to project it, to find order in the very chaos of it—I find that remarkable."

No man had ever spoken to Wilder quite that way; it was enough to make his throat swell and his eyes sting. "Thank you, sir," he said, and Pamela squeezed his arm to emphasize the compliment.

"Didn't I tell you he was special?" she said to Epstein.

When Epstein walked away, going home, he wanted to follow him—he wanted to join him in that wonderful library for further talk about order and chaos—but Pamela led him back to the barn instead. By the time they got there the day's work was done and most of the company was relaxing with cups of wine and excited talk about the movie.

". . . I see Charlie as a kind of Christ figure," a young man was saying. "He's immensely strong and immensely gentle; he *does* try to 'save' the men, and he—"

"No, no, no," another man said. "*Klinger*'s the Christ figure—the *crucified* Christ . . . ."

"Balls," Julian said. "Since when does every movie have to have a Christ figure in it? This is a movie about a madhouse and it's gonna stay that way. If anybody wants to read more into it they're welcome to—that's *their* business. Maybe it's society in microcosm—I might buy that—but I'm not even gonna shove *that* down their throats. Christ's sake, let the story speak for itself."

"Man," Clay Braddock said, "you said a mouthful."

And John Wilder—the most admirable man in the venture—sat sipping his whiskey and smiling at everyone, enjoying it all. To find order in chaos—why, of course; that was what he'd wanted all his life.

". . . Your father? Your father didn't believe you either?"

"Well see, he got it from the other kids' fathers. He says 'Ralph, I want you to tell me exactly what happened up behind that sign.' So I tell him and he says 'That's not the way *I* heard it,' and I says 'I *swear!* I *swear!*' He just sits there and looks at me like I'm some kind of—some kind of—I don't know. And ever since then, ever since then—"

"Wait— Excuse me, Julian."

"Cut! What's the matter, John?"

"Just that I think this scene might be done a little more subtly. The way it stands now we all believe Ralph's story —it's a pitiful story of brutality and misunderstanding, and that's okay as far as it goes. But what if we played it so nobody'd be quite sure whether to believe it or not? I don't want to make Ralph a liar—nothing that blatant

—but I want him to be a very complicated, troubled kid. He's told it this way so many times that maybe even *he* isn't sure if it's true any more. I want the audience to sort of read between the lines here. I guess what I'm after is a little whaddyacallit, a little ambiguity in the scene. Does anybody see what I mean?"

Julian did—"Right, John"—and the boy playing Ralph did too, after thinking it over. He and the Negro boy had been recruited from the High School of Music and Art; they were two of the best actors in the cast, and when they played the scene again it was just what Wilder had hoped for.

". . . Man. I mean, that is one tough story. Hey, listen, though; I got an idea. Let's play a game. Let's play pictures. You know how to play pictures, Ralph? . . ."

Pamela was waiting for him, out of sound range, and she said "Oh, that was perfect."

"Well, I don't know about 'perfect,' but I think it's better."

"All your ideas are so good," she said. "You really do have a natural talent for this."

"Want to take a walk?" It was a warm afternoon on the sixth or seventh day of shooting. What he had in mind was to take her out across a meadow and into some woodland that might have a fragrant, mossy clearing where they could rest, and where she might tell him more about his natural talent.

"A walk?" she said. "Oh, not now; I don't want to miss a minute of this."

A little later Julian called for a ten-minute break, and it seemed as good a time as any to suggest an idea that had been taking shape in his mind for days.

"Look," he said. "I know how you feel about Christ symbolism, Julian, but Spivack—or Klinger—does tell about a man who thinks he's the Second Coming; says he puts on a show once in a while. And if we're going to mention the man, why don't we ever get to meet him? If he puts on a show, why don't we see it?"

"Mm," Julian said. "What would he do?" Everyone was listening now.

"I don't know. He might recite the Sermon on the Mount at the top of his lungs until they shoot him out, or he might—well, try to crucify himself. That'd be better, because it's more visual. Get a slim young guy, have him strip down to a loincloth kind of thing, have him climb up on the back of a bench against the wall and—you know—go into the crucifixion pose, until the orderlies have to come and haul him down. See what I'm getting at?"

They all waited for Julian to speak first, and he took his time, frowning. "I don't know, John," he said at last. "Might be a little obvious."

"Oh, I don't think so at all," the man playing Klinger said. "It'd be marvelous if it were done right."

"As a matter of fact," Jerry said, "I did think of something like that when I was doing the script; trouble was I couldn't figure out where to put it in."

"Think of it in visual terms," one of the actors said. "The audience has been locked into the ward all this time seeing nothing but ugliness and squalor, and then suddenly—wham!—here's this classical image of the—"

"And the irony!" someone else said. "A crucifixion in a madhouse. I think it's tremendous. Tremendous."

Julian paced the floor a few steps one way and a

few steps another. "I don't like it," he said. "It's cornball."

"*Corn*ball!" Pamela cried. "Oh, Julian, you're missing the whole *point*. It's the most beautiful idea anybody's had yet. It could serve as the objective correlative for the whole—"

"Ah, objective correlative my ass. I'm sorry, Pam, but I don't see it, that's all."

Other strident voices were raised against him; when it was clear that the majority opinion would hold, that Julian would give in, Wilder stole away from the set. He had made his suggestion and he felt no need to defend it; now he wanted solitude and he wanted to be outdoors.

He took a cupful of whiskey along, but after the first few sips he found he didn't want it; he set it carefully on the grass beside the barn and started walking.

He had never seen such beautiful country, but it wasn't the landscape alone that increased the pump of his heart as he walked; it was the dizzying rise of his self-esteem in this past incredible week. Epstein saying he was the most admirable man in the venture; Julian deferring to him time and again; Pamela saying "Oh, that was perfect" and "It's the most beautiful idea anybody's had yet"—all this and more crowded his head. He had been born for this, for finding order in chaos, and all the wasted years had been a mistake. John Wilder was coming into his own at last—*this* was reality—and he trembled with a pride and pleasure he hadn't known since he was eleven years old and the soprano soloist at Grace Church.

Glo-o-o-o-ria in excelsis De-e-o . . .

To find order in chaos; to find order in chaos. He felt exalted as he trod the grass; he felt tall.

The earth was spongy underfoot and there were hummocks that made him stumble; the stumbling jogged him rhythmically along until a little chant or jingle began to sound in his ears. Even when he stopped and steadied himself with his arm around the trunk of a tree it persisted:

When you meet a man who's spent a half a
    lifetime
In a life he doesn't like or understand
When you find him hugging trees and
    collapsing at the knees
That'll be the

He let go of the tree—it left a spoor of sap on his shirtsleeve—and walked again, beginning to feel as if hundreds of needles were gently pricking his flesh. His vision was distorted too: colorless flecks hung and danced before his eyes; and still the doggerel went on, as real as if someone—Epstein?—were whispering the words beside him:

If he wants to find an order in his chaos
If he wants to put his passion on the screen
If he comes to me in time and says

"Hi, Mr. Wilder," said one of the minor Marlowe actors on his way to the set.
"Hi. Hey, wait—wait."
The boy stopped and gave him a long, odd look.
"Can you tell me how to get to Mr. Epstein's house?"
"Sure. You're headed in the right direction. See that dirt road? Leads you right up to it—it's only a couple of hundred yards. You okay, Mr. Wilder? You look—"

"How do I look?"

"I don't know." And the boy lowered his eyes like a girl. "No special way, I guess; I just—never mind. By the way, I think it's a great film, Mr. Wilder. Really great."

He was headed in the right direction—anyone could walk a couple of hundred yards, even with knees like jelly—and now the words were clearly in Epstein's voice:

If he comes to me in time and says da da da da
  dime
That'll be the

He didn't want to look up because he knew the sky had turned from blue to red and yellow, and he didn't want to look back because Pamela and all the young men were gathered there under the massed trees to urge him on—keep going, John; keep going—so he looked down at his own walking feet. These were the feet that had taken him through years and years of error and falsehood; now they were treading the dirt of the right road at last—the true road, the high, lonely road of self-discovery. . . .

"Well, Mr. *Wilde*r," Epstein said, opening his white door.

He stepped inside and slumped against the vestibule wall, barely able to stand. He stared into Epstein's calm, wise face and Epstein peered at him closely, encouragingly, as if he'd been waiting for this very confrontation for years.

Go on, John, the young people behind him were saying; go on. Say it.

But he was paralyzed with indecision. If he said what seemed so clearly to be expected it might be all over. He would be himself, but he might be—

"Yes, sir?"

Then he said it: "Brother, can you spare a dime?"

And Epstein didn't seem at all surprised. "A dime? Why, certainly; I'll be happy to oblige. Won't you come in while I—"

"No—no, thanks. I'll wait here."

Epstein went into his study for a moment and then he came back. "One thin but very shiny dime," he said, and he looked straight into Wilder's eyes as he gave it to him; then, smiling, he held out his right hand for a ceremonial handshake.

If the dime hadn't done it the handshake would, and Wilder hesitated again. Go on, John; let it happen.

Epstein's smile had given way to a troubled look, but his hand was still there and Wilder shook it.

"You're—all right, aren't you, Mr. Wilder?"

"Yes. I'm all right." He had taken the man's hand at last, and because there should have been a thunderclap of recognition he provided one, or at least a sound deep in his throat like the tolling of a great bronze bell.

Epstein looked puzzled. "I'm afraid I don't— Can I get you a glass of cold water? We have wonderful fresh spring water here."

"No. No water. Nothing." He couldn't move from his slumped position against the wall until he'd made a moist fist around the dime and sunk it deep into the pocket of his wrinkled summer slacks. He was being tested and he hadn't yet passed the test. There was more to this; there had to be more. "Thank you," he said. His mouth was almost too dry for speaking. "I'm sorry if I—"

He turned and walked down the short path to the road, feeling Epstein's eyes on his back.

He was careful to go back the way he had come, holding the coin tight against his pocketful of loose change. There had to be more to this, and all at once the weather changed as if to confirm it. The sky darkened quickly as he walked, or stumbled; then there was a quick brilliant tree of lightning and a roll and crash of thunder of exactly the kind he'd expected on shaking Epstein's hand. The earthbound trees flew violently in the sudden, wet wind, all their leaves turned inside out and pale, and the rain came in a cold pelting that drove him to the nearest shelter—a telephone booth set in a cement block on the grass beside the road. Now he knew the purpose of the dime, and he knew that Epstein knew it too.

When you see a fellow waiting in a phone booth
With a dime he doesn't quite know how to use . . .

The overhead light came on when he shut the folding door, but he had to rest on the little bench and wait for his heart to slow down and his throbbing head to clear. Then very carefully he pressed the dime into the tinkling slot.

That'll be the second coming
That'll be the second coming
That'll be the second coming of . . .

He was dialing, careful to stop after seven precisely measured digits, and he listened to ten rings before he hung up and let the coin fall through the machine. Wrong; but if he tried again it might be right. Wait, Epstein's voice counseled him. Wait and have courage, John. There is time. He shut his eyes and seven vivid numerals appeared behind the closed lids; he dialed them quickly but carefully, and on the seventh ring there was a click.

"Hello?" a woman's voice said.

"Hello. Is this— Are you my mother?"

"I'm afraid you have the wrong number."

"No I don't. Please stay on the phone. Listen. I'm doing the best I can to put all this together and I've only got one dime, you see."

"Young man?"

"Yes. I'm still here but my time is running out. Please just wait."

"Well, I'd like to help you but I'm afraid you have the wrong—"

"Please. Just wait. I know you think I'm crazy but I'm not. I'm very, very serious and this is important. Wait. I'll get the right question in a minute."

"Young man?"

"Yes. I'm here. Please don't hang up."

She did, and the dime was lost, but that didn't matter: he had plenty of dimes. The only important thing was to keep trying, to try again and again until . . .

There was a rapping on the glass pane and he looked around to find a young girl standing there. The rain must have stopped because her hair and her clothes were dry; she was trying to open the door of the booth and he had to get up from the seat to help her.

"John? Do you know how long you've been *in* there?"

"No."

"And you haven't even been *talking;* just putting in money and dialing and—oh John, are you all right?"

"And who are you? Are you some kind of half-assed Mary Magdalene?"

"Am I *what?*"

"Wait a minute." He closed his eyes and pinched the bridge of his nose with thumb and forefinger. "Who are you, then? Are you Ginny Baldwin?" Ginny Baldwin was the first girl he had ever loved; if she said yes to this it might at least mean he was seventeen again, with his whole life ahead of him and all his terrible mistakes unmade.

"John, will you stop this? You *know* me, for God's sake."

"No, I don't. What time is it?"

"It's almost six."

"You mean six in the morning or six in the—"

"John, if you're kidding I'll never forgive you for this. You're either kidding or you're—oh, God. Come along with me; we're going home."

And he allowed himself to be led away across the grass. "Then you mean it was all a delusion," he said, trying to keep up with her.

"What did you say?"

"I said none of it was real."

"None of *what* was real?"

"Never mind."

"John, do you know who I am now? Do you know where you are and everything?"

"No, I—no."

"Well, listen carefully. I'm Pamela Hendricks. It's August Nineteen Sixty-one and we're at Marlowe College in Vermont."

"Vermont?" That was when he started to cry, because

what she said did have the ring of reality; and if this was real and all the rest was a dream, then he'd made a colossal fool of himself and everyone at Marlowe College knew it, or would know it soon. He could feel their stares on him as he walked and tried to hide his tears with his knuckles—stares of contempt and ridicule from the very people whose encouragement he'd felt on the road and in Epstein's doorway; Epstein would be laughing at him too.

Back in the wood-smelling dormitory room she acted like an efficient nurse. First she told him to take off all his clothes and get into bed; then she came and sat beside him in a creaking bedside chair.

"John," she said after he'd stopped crying, and it could have been noon or midnight, "are you awake?"

"Yes."

"If I leave you alone for a few minutes, will you promise not to leave this room?"

"Yes. Now promise *me* something."

"All right, dear." She was stroking his brow with cool fingers, like a young mother trying to tell if her child has a fever.

"Whatever happens, promise you won't let them take me away."

"Oh, of course. I promise, baby. I won't let anybody take you anywhere."

Hours seemed to pass after that—was he awake or asleep?—until there was a light knock at the door and Epstein's voice said "Mr. Wilder?"

"Wait a second." He sprang for the closet, got his pants and pulled them around his nakedness before he let the man in. "What can I—do for you?" he said.

"Nothing at all, thanks." Epstein sat down in a chair against the wall. "Frankly, Mr. Wilder, I only came over because I'm concerned about you."

"Oh, you are, huh? Well that's pretty funny, because I'm concerned about *you*. I mean I may be an impostor, but you're worse. Do you know that all the kids in this college call you God? That they call you God the Father?"

Epstein's little chuckle was infuriating. "Oh, now; in the first place I don't believe that for a minute, and secondly I don't see what it has to do with—"

"Oh, you don't, huh? It has everything to do with everything. Listen. Listen to me. Don't philosophy professors ever listen, or do they just talk? First of all, there've been altogether too many religious jokes flying around this campus these past—however long it's been. 'God the Father, God the Son, God the Holy Terror'— stuff like that. Tell me you haven't heard 'em and I'll call you a liar. I'll call you a few other things while I'm at it, Epstein. I'll call you a sanctimonious old fraud and I don't care *how* many books you have in your famous library; if I knew you better I think I'd be able to call you a dirty old man too. Kind of like it up here, don'tcha? Oh, 'Marlowe casts a spell,' all right—all these sweet little girls coming back every fall just dying to impress the old teacher any way they can— Ah, I've got your number, Epstein. Wait. Let me finish. . . ."

And he did finish, though it took him a long time. At one point Epstein said "I'm afraid I'll have to leave now," and the door clicked shut behind him, but Wilder went on talking to the empty room—first smoking all the available cigarettes and trying in vain to find the liquor, then going to the sink and cupping up many handfuls of cold water to his mouth like a man dying of thirst. He called Epstein every ugly name he could think of, he blamed Epstein for everything that had gone wrong in his own life and asked Epstein to defend himself against these charges, and he went on talking until he collapsed in bed again.

Sometime later there were voices outside the door. He heard Epstein talking and Pamela's voice in tears, and the low, courteous voices of two or three men he didn't recognize.

When a pair of strong arms helped him to stand at last it seemed an act of great kindness; so did the hypodermic needle sunk into one buttock. After that he was somehow fully dressed again and a number of people were helping him into the back seat of a big automobile, and after that there was nothing but silence as the car bore him away. He wept a little as he rode; then he gave in to heavy waves of sleep as deep as drowning.

The first thing he knew, on waking, was that he wasn't at Marlowe College any more. All the smells were different here, and the woman who sat beside him wasn't Pamela. She was old, with blue-white hair, wearing a nurse's uniform and reading a paperback novel.

"Miss?"

She laid her book aside and inspected her watch before answering. "Yes, sir?"

"Can you tell me where I am?"

"Elizabeth Fanning Hospital."

"Where's that?"

"Middlebury, Vermont. How're you feeling today, Mr. Wilder?"

"I feel—I can't move my—"

"Don't move that arm, sir, you'll upset the I.V." And she got up quickly to make sure he didn't move it again. His hand was taped to a gauze-wrapped board from which a length of clear plastic tubing rose to what must have been an intravenous feeding bottle above his head. The aluminum crib-sides of the bed were up, as if someone had been afraid he might fall out.

"What happened to me?"

"I really don't know, sir; I'm only the morning shift, you see. Try and relax now: I just want to make a note of when you woke up. Then I'll check your temp and your blood pressure and whatnot, do a few little things like that. I don't think we're going to need that old I.V. much longer; we'll see what Doctor has to say about that. I think we're well past the worst of it, anyway, Mr. Wilder; I have a feeling you'll be up and around in no time."

"What's that stack of papers?"

"Oh, those are just your nursing bills. You've been on twenty-four-hour nursing care, you see, private nursing, and the bills do mount up, but I wouldn't worry about that now. You have Blue Cross, don't you?"

"I guess so."

"Well, then, you see? I'll tell you one thing, Mr. Wilder: far as I'm concerned you've been a model patient. Course I'm only on mornings and I can't speak for the other girls, but what little I've seen you've been grand. Just grand. Not a speck of trouble, morning after morning. You talked quite a lot, but that made it interesting."

"I did? What did I talk about?"

"Oh, all kinds of things. I couldn't always follow it, but it was *int*eresting. . . ."

He must have fallen asleep to the sound of her voice, because when he opened his eyes another nurse—much younger and wearing glasses—was standing in the room.

"You have a visitor, Mr. Wilder."

And there she was, as fresh and beautiful as ever, wearing a bright summer dress and so eager to clasp his hand as she sat down that some of the private nursing bills spilled from the bedstand.

"*Oh*, you look so much better," she said, and then she did her best to bring him up to date. First of all, the shooting was finished—wasn't that wonderful? All that remained was for Julian to get a little exterior footage of Bellevue back in town, and then to edit the film—that would take time, of course—and make arrangements to have it scored (personally, she thought it would be more effective *without* music, but Julian wanted recorders and guitars), and they'd have an honest-to-God movie "in the can." "But everybody's been terribly concerned about you," she concluded. "It was all I could do to keep them *all* from coming over here."

"Tell me something. I mean I still haven't put it all straight in my head." He knew better than to ask the next question but he asked it anyway, to test her. "Why am I here? What exactly did happen to me?"

"You really don't know?" She lowered her voice. "You had a nervous breakdown, baby. A whopper." And he listened very closely while she gave her version of it, to find out how much she knew about the Christ delusion. Apparently she knew nothing at all, nor had she guessed anything.

". . . and the last thing you said when I left to try and find Jerry or Julian or *some*body, the last thing you said was 'Don't let them take me away.' Do you remember that?"

He said he did, very dimly, and he continued to listen as carefully as any police investigator, as carefully as any psychiatrist, as her light, pretty voice hurried on.

". . . and when I got back I found Mr. *Ep*stein sitting on the steps outside our door, smoking his pipe and looking as calm as an old—I don't know, an old priest or something. He said he'd called Elizabeth Fanning here and asked them to send over some people to get you. I said 'But that's the one thing I *promised* him—' and he put his arm around me and said 'Pamela, my responsibility is more important than your promise.' Wasn't that sweet?"

"Very sweet."

"And he said he knew you were a good, sensitive man but that these things just happened sometimes, to the best of us, and the older I grew the better I'd understand."

"You sure that's all he said about me? 'Good' and 'sensitive'?"

"Oh, I guess he used a few other words too—all very complimentary. He really likes you a lot, John; you mustn't worry about that. Oh, and one funny thing: when the hospital people were taking you out to the car you pulled yourself up very straight as if you were going to make a speech, and you said 'I have never depended on the kindness of strangers.' "

"Did I really say that?"

"Yes; why?"

"Because it's from a play. It was a woman's last line in *A Streetcar Named Desire*, only it's a whaddyacallit—a paraphrase. In the play the woman says it when the people from the asylum come to get her, only she says 'I have always depended on the kindness of strangers.'"

"You really are something, John. That's exactly what Mr. Epstein said he thought it was, only he wasn't sure —and he's the most learned, well-read person I know."

By dinnertime that night he was sitting up and eating from a tray; the next day they gave him slippers and let him sit in a chair when Pamela came; and at the end of visiting hour they let him walk her slowly down the hall.

"Just a moment, Mr. Wilder! You can't go any farther than that. I'm sorry, but this is a locked ward, you see."

It must have been the next morning when the psychiatrist came to his room—a very young man whose striped boxer shorts showed plainly through the translucent white nylon of his uniform. "How're you doing?" he asked.

"Okay, I guess; but listen, doctor. I have more questions than you can possibly answer all at once. Have you ever dealt with a man who thought he was Christ? Because that's—that's what happened to me. At the peak of my—you know, my breakdown—I thought I was turning into some kind of messiah, a second coming of Christ."

"Mm." The doctor eased one haunch onto the windowsill and began playing with the cord of the Venetian blind.

"And I mean I know that's pretty bad—that's *crazy*— and I know you're going to recommend I see a psychiatrist back in New York, but that's out." He was short of breath, his mouth was dry, and he felt his features contorting into a tight, pugnacious grimace, as if his lifelong combination of Mickey Rooney and Alan Ladd had become a death-bed James Cagney. "The thing is, I can't be psychoanalyzed, doctor. I've tried it and I know. It just doesn't take with me. Oh, maybe it's my fault, but whether it's my fault or not isn't the point. The point is it simply doesn't *work*. Can you understand that?"

"I think so." The doctor was examining the Venetian blind cord as if it were an uncommonly interesting piece of string. "As a matter of fact, Mr. Wilder, I don't put too much stock in that kind of treatment myself, but that's because I'm prejudiced. I was trained by one of the pioneers in a new school of psychiatry. Drug therapy. Chemicals. Pills. Oh, our common tranquilizers were only the beginning, back in the fifties. Now we have a wide range of medications—antidepressants, psychic energizers, antipsychotics—drugs to take you up or bring you down in any number of subtle, medically controlled ways; and the field is getting more sophisticated every day. . . ."

Had Wilder ever heard of Myron T. Brink? Well, he certainly might have if he paid attention to *Time* magazine, on whose cover Dr. Brink's picture had recently appeared. This was the man he had mentioned earlier, the drug-therapy man who'd been such an inspiration to him as a student. Brink now spent much of his time as a world traveler, taking his new kind of psychiatry to foreign nations—just last month he'd been decorated by the Republic of South Africa for his work in greatly reducing that country's mental-patient population, and that was only the latest in many such honors—but he still maintained a small private practice in New York, on the Upper East Side. When he was away his patients were served by one or another of his three-man staff, all competent men. And one minor advantage in working with Dr. Brink was that his fees were very reasonable. Was Wilder interested?

". . . Of course I can't promise that he'll take your case," the doctor concluded, "but we can try. I'll write to him today. Now. You want to tell me something about yourself, Mr. Wilder? Apart from the fact that you thought you were Christ, I mean?"

Could this amiable youth really be a psychiatrist, of whatever school? That was what Wilder kept asking himself as his voice gained strength and confidence in answering the simple questions. It was all a little too good to be true, like coming up to Marlowe with Pamela, and like Pamela herself. Maybe, after all these years, his luck really had begun to change. And why not? Wasn't it about time? Hadn't he served a long enough apprenticeship among the losers of the world?

"Guess what?" Pamela said breathlessly one morning. "You're being discharged this afternoon. Good thing I brought all your stuff, isn't it? I've been bringing all our luggage every day, just in case."

"How we going home? In the car?"

"Heavens, no; that would take forever. It's a rented car, remember? We'll take it over to Middlebury airport and fly home. Come on and walk in the hall with me, or maybe they'll let us go downstairs and walk on the grounds. Have I told you what a beautiful day it is? It's an absolutely *gorgeous* day."

Only then, with the news of this gorgeous day, did he

think of his wife. He had promised to be home from Boston in two weeks, and now it had been nearly three.

It was still early when they got to the airport—Tommy would be in school—and he shut himself into a phone booth with a sense of being a small, guilty boy.

". . . Janice? Listen, I'll be home in a couple of hours; I'm at the Boston airport now. The thing is, I've been sick; I've been hospitalized, and I couldn't call till now."

"It's all right," she said. "We didn't expect you."

"What do you mean, you didn't expect me?"

"Don't you think Tommy and I have learned not to expect very much of you?"

Sweat was sliding down his ribs under his summer suit. "I don't think that's fair. Doesn't it matter to you that I've been in the hospital?"

"Yes; I hope you're better now. You must be, or they wouldn't have let you out."

"Janice, I—"

"All right, John. We'll see you when you get here."

6

"*Oh*, yes," said Myron T. Brink. "You're the man I heard about from my young friend up in Vermont, right? Well. Let's look at the record." He was muscular, grey-haired and well-tailored, reclining in a black leather lounge chair with a file folder open on his lap. Neat piles of similar folders lay closed on the carpet beside him, right and left, as if the whole task of being a world-renowned psychiatrist were a matter of orderly paperwork. "All right, Mr. Wilder," he said at last. "I think we can do business together. Just let me ask a few routine questions first; then I'll prescribe some medication and send you on your way. Fair enough?"

Wilder went home that day with four pill vials rattling in his coat pocket, and he was stowing them in the medicine cabinet before he realized that he couldn't possibly keep them here: he would have to keep them in his desk at the office, or up at Pamela's place. Looking at each label in the bright bathroom light, he tried to memorize the names of the damned things. Brink had assured him that the names didn't matter—they were silly names dreamed up in pharmaceutical houses—but they were as baffling as words in a foreign language. How could he ever tell Hilafon from Haldol, or Plithium from Plutol? One was a tranquilizer, he knew, and one was an antidepressant, and still another was what Brink had called an antipsychotic, good for someone recovering from a breakdown, but if Brink had explained each prescription before handing it over the message was lost on him now. And if the names were confusing, what about the dosages? "100 mg, three times daily," one label read, and another: "8 mg, one capsule at bedtime." Could an absent-minded man be expected to keep track of all this?

"Dinner's ready," Janice called; so he knew it was time to stop worrying and wash his hands.

"We're having Tommy's favorite tonight," she said when he was settled at the table. "My own very special meat loaf, baked potato with sour cream, and a simple tossed salad. It used to be one of your favorites too, John. Is it still?"

"Sure is. Especially the meat loaf. You suppose I could have another slice?"

"Why, certainly, kind sir," she said. "I'm very flattered. I know what your real favorite is, though, and if you're very good we might have it on Sunday."

"What's that?"

"Roast beef, of course. Good roast beef with Yorkshire pudding and Brussels sprouts. How could you forget?"

"Right. That'll be fine, Janice; I'm looking forward to it already."

Was this really happening? Was she sitting there forking meat loaf into her mouth and dabbing at her lips with a napkin, and was Tommy really there across the table? How could any family as unhappy as this put on such a show every night, and how long could it last?

"How'd school go today, Tom?"

"Okay, I guess," the boy said around his chewing, and he swallowed. "It's only the second week, though."

"Like your new teachers?"

"They're okay. I like Mr. Caldwell the best; he teaches math and he's funny. He's really a funny guy, iike a TV comic or something. And the older guys told us he never stops; he keeps it up all year."

"Well, good. Here's hoping *you* keep it up all year."

"Keep what up, Dad?"

"Your grades. What'd you think I meant? Aren't you the boy who finished up last year with a straight B average?"

"I don't know; I guess so."

"Almost a straight B-*plus* average," Janice said, and the three of them went on that way all through dinner.

"We having dessert, Mom?"

"We certainly are. Which would you rather have— butter-pecan ice cream or coconut cake?"

It was incredible.

"You're an escapist, Wilder." That was what his old Latin teacher had said back at Grace Church School, and he remembered it now as he escaped uptown on the subway, ostensibly bound for an AA meeting but really to visit his mistress. "You're an escapist pure and simple. I watch you drag your poor tired body into this classroom every day and then bolt for the door like an athlete when the bell rings, and I know. What's the matter with you, boy? You want to be an escapist all your life?"

"I guess not, sir."

"What? Speak up, I can't hear you. That's another thing, another sure sign of the escapist character. You can make enough noise when you want to—*I've* heard you do those big soprano solos in the choir—but whenever it suits your purpose you're quiet as a snail. I want you to open your mouth now, as wide as you do down in church, and tell me what you just said."

"I said I guess not, sir."

"Guess not what?"

"Want to be an escapist all my life."

"Then you'd better shape up. You know what they say in the Navy?" Wilder had long forgotten the old man's name but he would never forget this lecture, or the faint scent of halitosis that hung around the old man's desk, or the way his wrinkled hands trembled or the fact that he used a paper clip for a tie clasp. "You know what they say in the Navy? They say 'Shape up or ship out.' And that applies to you, boy, as long as you're in my classroom and as long as this funny little school pays my salary. Is that clear?"

Well, he had never really shaped up—the world had spared him that—but he'd never really been made to ship out either, unless he wanted to count his flunking out of Yale. There had always been some middle course and he'd always taken it; and now, as the loud dismal cars of the IRT pulled away from Grand Central and there was nothing to do but wait and watch the Bellevue-like faces of passengers across the aisle, he guessed the old Latin teacher had been right after all: he had grown up an escapist; he would be an escapist all his life.

But by the time the train set him free at Pamela's stop

he had put the whole dark issue out of his mind. This was no night for tortured introspection.

"Hi there," she said. "Feel like a drink?"

"I guess not tonight; I'll cool it."

"You? Turn down a drink? Really?"

Really. And it was all because Dr. Brink had worried him today by saying, at the very end of the interview, "You drink much, Mr. Wilder? Well, as long as you're on this one—" here he'd held up one of the prescriptions, but by the time Wilder was out on the street he couldn't remember which— "I'd lay off the drinking altogether if I were you. This is your antipsychotic, you see, and it doesn't mix with alcohol. Just remember that; doesn't mix at all."

"Saw my new doctor today," he said when they were nestled deep in her blue sofa and he'd drawn her close enough to let her head rest on his chest.

"Oh? What's he like?"

"Very busy. I guess he has to fit his private patients in between jet flights to South Africa, or China, or wherever the hell he goes. No, he's nice enough. And it's great to deal with someone who doesn't expect you to *talk* all the time; I can't tell you how great that is."

"Mm."

Was she just sleepy, or was this the beginning of what he'd feared since Elizabeth Fanning Hospital—that she might soon grow tired of hearing about his delicate mental health? There was no point in taking any chances, so he shut up. "How was your day?"

"Oh, all right, I guess; same old stuff at the office, with Frank Lacy *mooning* at me all day. God, how I've come to despise that man. Why doesn't he just fire me and be done with it?"

"You could always quit."

"No, I won't do that. It's not a bad job, and it'd be a terrible bore having to look for a new one. Besides, the job keeps my father happy. Oh, John, I almost forgot—*Julian* called today."

"Has he started cutting the picture yet?"

"No, and from the way he talked I have an awful feeling he's going to put it off. We'll have to keep after him. He wanted to know how you were, of course, and he asked us both to come to a party at his place next week. Jerry'll be there, of course, and Peter, and some of the other Marlowe crowd. You won't mind, will you?"

"Course not. They're nice kids."

There was a long, increasingly heavy silence before she said "John? You know something? I wish you'd quit referring to my friends as 'kids.' They're all full grown, after all. Did you like being called a kid when you were that age? After being in the army and everything?"

In the end he agreed to have a drink with her ("Make it light," he said, like Paul Borg), because it seemed the only way of restoring some romance to the evening. It even seemed, though he hardly dared to admit it to himself, that having a drink was his only guarantee of success with her in bed. What was the matter with him tonight?

"God, that was something," she said when they'd exhausted themselves. "And you know what, John? I waited for this all day long in that terrible office. Just this."

"Mm. Me too." But he lay staring in the dark for a long

time—he might as well have been in bed with Janice—
wanting to creep away and fix himself another drink. Oh,
just a *very* light one, doctor; I promise; the lightest drink
you ever saw. Could it really matter much, after all, on
his very first night with the pills working in his blood-
stream?

"Honey?" she called. "Where are you? Where're you
going? Is it time to go home?"

"Not yet; I'll come back before I leave."

Out in the semidarkness of the living room he went
straight to her gleaming little bar, and then to the
kitchen for fresh ice. There, he told himself, like a
mother soothing her child. There . . . there . . . there . . .

The view of the city from Pamela's living room was
extraordinary, every bit as grand as from the white-peb-
bled terrace at her office, and watching the subtle play
of light and dark out there gave him something to do as
he sipped and breathed, sipped and breathed. He took
his time, though, because it was very important to make
this ceremony last.

Julian's loft might have served, if stripped of all deco-
ration and darkened for business, as another setting for
the celebration of Sylvester Cummings's single candle;
but on the night of his party its multicolored brilliance
hurt the eye, its enormously amplified music rocked and
rolled from the walls and it was packed deep with a
laughing, jostling crowd in which, at first glance, no face
looked a day over twenty-five.

"Pammy!" Julian yelled from the makeshift doorway
of his bedroom. "And John! Great to see you, man! You're
looking great! Feeling better?"

"Feeling fine, thanks."

Julian seemed a little drunk, or high, as he took their raincoats and flung them on top of the heap on his bed —or maybe it was just that being a host intoxicated him. "Jerry 'n' I figured it was *us* that put you in the hospital up there," he said, "as much as anything else—all of us, I mean. That was a pretty frantic couple of weeks. Fun, though, wasn't it? I mean it *would*'ve been fun, if you hadn't gotten sick."

"Yeah; yeah, it was fun."

"Julian," Pamela said, "this may not be the time to bring it up, but when *are* you going to finish the picture?"

"Pammy, I told you on the phone. I've got so damn many things going now I honestly don't know *when* I'll get to it—and the point is, these other things pay money. Got to have *some* money, don't I? Don't worry, though; 'Bellevue' has a very high priority in my plans. But what're we talking shop for? This is a party! I want you two to go out there and have fun tonight. Move around! Relax! I know you don't light up, John, but there's plenty of wine, cold beer in the tub, and you'll find some hard stuff over in the corner near Chester Pratt. Okay?"

"Okay, Julian."

They found a place to sit on the floor close to the beer tub, and it wasn't long before Jerry came over and sank beside Pamela. He rolled a joint and shared it with her, and for a little while they talked quietly between themselves.

". . . I don't think I *want* to meet him if he's that awful-looking skinny man," she was saying. "Is he always this drunk?"

"He's amazing. I never saw anybody put away so much booze in my life. I've seen him five or six times now, and he's been bombed out of his mind every time. Even the night I went out to Princeton for his reading."

"When do you suppose he ever gets his work done?"

"Beats me. Sure does get it done, though. Christ, what a book."

"How'd you get to know him, Jerry? You didn't say."

"Wrote him a letter, that's all; told him I'd like to do a film adaptation, and he wrote back."

"Who's this?" Wilder asked.

"Chester Pratt," she said. "He wrote *Burn All Your Cities*, and he's standing over there."

"Come on," Jerry said, getting to his feet and reaching down for her hand. "I might as well introduce you. Isn't every day you get to meet an important writer."

For once Wilder was not intimidated by a tall man—even a celebrated one, even when Pamela said she was "so happy" to meet him and called him "sir." The important writer was tall, all right, but thin to the point of frailty, and his drink-distorted face was that of a weak, sad boy more than a man.

"What kind of a book is *Burn All Your Cities?*" he asked her when they were back beside the beer tub.

"I thought it was a fine novel; now I'm not so sure. Have you ever seen such a wreck?"

". . . Pammy! Oh, Pammy, it's *mar*velous to see you!"

"Pam!"

A breathless cluster of Marlowe girls descended on her now—girls she hadn't seen since graduation, girls of all shapes and sizes in all varieties of dressy and casual clothes, all with their smiling "dates" in tow—and although she managed to be pleasant enough she was clearly no match for their enthusiasm.

". . . and Ruth, Grace, Polly; this is John Wilder."

They were delighted to meet him; they had heard so much about him; and as soon as they'd gone she said "John? Do I seem as young as that to you?"

"No."

"Good. And you know something? You were right. They *are* kids. Not just the girls; the boys too. Julian with his swinging pad and his strobe lights and his amplified rock; Jerry giving us the inside dope on his Important Writer—you notice how he's been over there sucking *around* the man all night? Let's go home."

"It isn't even ten yet."

"I know, but this is awful. I don't care if I never see *any* of these people again. And I'm glad it's early; that gives us more time to ourselves."

Janice was asleep when he got home, as usual, and before going to bed himself he lingered in the living room to prowl along her bookshelves for *Burn All Your Cities*. There it was, close to the floor, in a bright yellow jacket with red lettering. Pratt's photograph on the back was scarcely recognizable: it must have been taken when he was sober.

It was nearly a month before his next visit to Dr. Brink, and by then the only thing to do was lie a little about his drinking.

". . . Oh, I've had a little since I saw you last, yes," he said while the doctor scribbled something in his folder. "Not much; a few very light ones here and there." The way the doctor seemed able to listen and write at the same time was unnerving.

"Well, I don't imagine a few very light ones'll kill you, Mr. Wilder." He was still writing, glancing up only occasionally as if to make sure his patient was still there. "How've you been otherwise? Feeling any better?"

"Feeling fine. That whole breakdown business up in Vermont seems like ancient history now; hard to believe it ever happened."

"Good; that's the spirit."

"Doctor?"

"Mm?"

"I don't mean to be nosy, but can you really listen and write at the same time?"

That earned him a light, dry chuckle. "Don't worry about the writing; the writing's just routine. When you've been in this field as long as I have you learn a few things." He put the folder aside and got up. "Now I'm going to play doctor for a minute. Mind taking off your jacket and rolling up your left sleeve? I want to try something." He advanced on Wilder, seized his wrist in a powerful grip and began flexing his arm vigorously at the elbow, up and down. "No, no, you're all tense. Just relax; go limp. There, that's better. Good, that's fine. . . . Good." He went back to his chair, made a quick notation and closed the folder.

"I think you're doing very well, Mr. Wilder. As you'll see, I'm taking you off Haldol today—that's the antipsychotic—so you can relax a little on the drinking. Not too much, of course; you've still got to be careful because none of these medications are meant to be taken with alcohol. Just remember one drink will have about the same effect as two for you from now on, okay? If you were a hard-core alcoholic it might be different, but I don't think you are. Hard-core alcoholics don't hold down highly paid jobs with distinguished magazines. Incidentally, some day when we have more time I wish you'd tell me more about *The American Scientist.*"

"Do you read it?" He was so relieved about the drinking question, as he put on his coat again, that an exchange of harmless pleasantries about his job seemed just the thing. He even forgot to ask what the arm-flexing had been all about.

"Oh, I've been a subscriber for years. Started taking it originally because my wife liked the covers and the art-work—she's an artist herself—and then I got hooked on it. Even wrote an article for them once last year. It's surprising: for a commercial magazine they do maintain a very high level of scientific integrity."

"What issue was your article in, Doctor? I'll look it up."

"Oh, don't bother. August issue, I think. I don't mean to rush you, Mr. Wilder, but this is one of my busy days." And he rose to shake hands, walking Wilder to the door in readiness for his next patient.

Later that week Wilder found a copy of the August issue on his desk—he had asked one of the girls to pull it from the file—and there it was, as big as life in the table of contents: "The New Psychiatry, by Myron T. Brink, M.D." There wasn't time to read it in the office, but he took it home and promised himself to read it soon. In the end the magazine somehow found its way to Pamela's apartment, and when he asked her about it at Christmas-time, long after it had ceased to matter very much, she said she guessed she'd thrown it away.

*   *   *

All at once it was spring again, and Julian still hadn't edited the film, let alone arranged to have it "scored" for recorders and guitars. For all they knew he hadn't even taken his exterior footage of the streets around Bellevue. And he no longer made the excuse of having to work for money; all he could talk about these days was his deep involvement with Jerry's adaptation of *Burn All Your Cities*, which he said might well be the professional breakthrough for them both.

"I could *slit* him," Pamela said after one more futile phone call from her apartment, one night when Wilder was there. "He seems to feel he doesn't even have to apologize to us any more. I thought directors were only supposed to be arrogant and callous *after* they got famous."

"What I don't see," Wilder said, "is how Pratt would let a couple of kids do his book in the first place. I mean if it's such a great novel he must've had offers from *real* movie people."

"No, I don't imagine he has. The book wasn't a big seller, and it's a very downbeat story. Besides, he must find it flattering to have eager young men dancing attendance on him this way, talking about his Integrity all the time. Anyway, Pratt's beside the point. It's Julian. You know what I think? I think he's decided he doesn't really *like* 'Bellevue,' and he's just too cowardly to say so."

"Well," he said, "there's not a hell of a lot we can do about it, is there."

"All we can do is ride *herd* on him. I'm going to call him night and day until I wear him down, and I think you ought to call him too, from the office—will you promise to do that?"

He did—or at least he tried: he got three busy signals at Julian's number, and he was about to try again when his phone rang.

"John?" Janice said. "I'm sorry to bother you at work but this is important. Could we meet somewhere for lunch today?"

"I'm afraid not, dear. George wants me to—"

"All right; wait. Let me think."

"Is everything all right? Is Tommy all right?"

"Well, that's the thing, you see; it's something *about* Tommy."

"What? What is it?"

"It's not a thing we can discuss over the phone."

So there was nothing to do but sit there while she waited and thought. Somewhere in the outer office one of the girls shrieked with laughter over the clatter of typewriters, and another said "Oh, Mr. Taylor, you're terrible!" He wanted to get up and shut the door, but the phone wire was too short.

"Janice? You still there?"

"Yes. I'm thinking. Oh, wait—we can discuss it tonight. I just realized you don't have a meeting tonight. I know: we'll tell Tom we're going to a movie, and then we'll go to that nice new coffee shop around the corner, what's it called? You know the one. It's all red and black, and they serve good pastry. We can talk there in comfort as long as we want."

For the rest of that day, all through his boring business lunch and his long afternoon of business calls, he was as preoccupied as a conscientious family man. But it wasn't Tommy that kept his mind far away from the job, it was Janice. What in God's name was he ever going to do about Janice? He couldn't get over how pitiful she'd sounded on the phone—talking of nice new coffee shops all red and black, where they served good pastry and where two tired parents, however badly estranged, might go and discuss something painfully close to their hearts "in comfort."

"Oh, this'll be such fun," she said at dinner that night. "I don't think I've been out to a movie in ages and ages."

"Sure you have, Mom," Tommy said. "You went to a movie last week."

"That isn't what I mean," she told him quickly. "I mean going out to a movie with your father. It'll be like a real old-fashioned date for us, won't it, John?"

"Sure will."

"Do you want to call up the Borgs, dear, and see if they're free? If they are we could make it a foursome; that might be even nicer."

Was she kidding? What was he supposed to say to that? He glanced uneasily at his son before answering. "Isn't Paul out of town this week?"

"Oh, that's right, he is. Of course we could call Natalie—I imagine she'd love to get out—but somehow a threesome isn't nearly so much fun, is it?" And when he stole a quick look at her he found one of her eyes wrinkled shut in an elaborate wink of conspiracy. The funny part was that Tommy wasn't even paying attention.

"May I be excused, Mom?"

"Of course you may."

Because the night was warm she wore a summer dress—the same blue-and-brown, breast-enhancing dress she'd worn to visit him in Bellevue, the dress she always called his favorite—but because it might turn chilly later she carried a wide, light stole over one arm. That stole, too, was a heartbreaker. He had given it to her as a birthday present years ago, after seeing one just like it slung from the shoulders of a pretty girl at the office. But the girl at the office had known how to wear the thing, as a sort of elegant loose shawl, and Janice hadn't. From the moment she'd rushed from her birthday celebration to pose with it at the hall mirror ("Oh, I *love* this, John . . ."), he knew she would never learn to wear it—it looped and dangled from her elbows like a rope—and every time she tried only made it worse.

"We're going now, Tommy," she sang now from the vestibule. "Be sure and get to bed the minute that program's over. No fooling around tonight, okay?"

"What was the point of all that about the Borgs?" he asked her in the elevator.

"I don't know; I just felt I had to keep talking about something, so he wouldn't see how anxious I am."

The coffee shop was very much like the one uptown where Bill Costello had dramatized the value of Alcoholics Anonymous for him, but this turned out to be an even more dramatic evening.

"Oh, let me see," she said to the harried young Puerto Rican waiter. "I think I'll have some of your lovely cherry cheesecake, and coffee with lots of cream. Are you sure the pastry's fresh tonight?"

The waiter could only stand there with his order pad, sweating and looking confused.

"One cherry cheesecake, two coffees," Wilder told him.

"God," she said before the waiter was out of earshot,

"doesn't *any*body speak English in this town any more?"

"Sh-sh."

"I know. I keep forgetting how much New York has changed. Everything's changed. All right. Let me start at the beginning. Last Friday there was a phone call from the school. All his grades are down and he's failing two subjects. They're going to hold him back, John. He's not going on into seventh grade with the rest of his class; at this rate he may *never* get to college—and that's only the beginning." She fumbled in her handbag for Kleenex, pulled out a cluster of the stuff and blew her nose. "I'm sorry," she said. "I knew I'd cry." And there was nothing to do but reach across the damp plastic table and hold her hand.

"Look, Janice; this is nothing to get upset about. Kids go through phases, that's all. He can go to summer school. You should've seen my grades when *I* was that age."

"Yes, and you were a great success at Yale, weren't you? You've had a wonderful, distinguished career, haven't you? Oh, you earn good money, I'm not saying that, but since when has the measure of a man been— oh, I'm sorry; I'm sorry; don't let me get this way. It's just that I've been so—"

"Okay; okay."

"I've been so lonely, John, and there's never anyone to talk to. I'd be in analysis myself if I thought it would do any good. Oh, thank you *so* much, waiter, this is lovely. Oh, and look, it *is* fresh too—it must've been baked just this morning—thank you; that'll be all for the moment."

"Missus? Something else?"

"No, I only said—" She closed her eyes and whispered "God, God" through clenched teeth.

"That's all for now," Wilder said, and the waiter retreated with a wavering smile.

"But that's only the beginning," she said. "That was *last* week, and it was only the principal's office. Yesterday there was another call, and this time it was the guidance counsellor."

"The what?"

"Guidance counsellor. All the schools have them now. He wouldn't say a word on the phone; he said I'd have to go in, and I did. I thought he'd just want to talk about the grades, and it was partly that, but the rest of it is much, much worse. He said—oh, John, he said Tommy's emotionally disturbed and he thinks we ought to have him see a psychiatrist. Right away."

Wilder had learned once, in some elementary science course either at Grace Church or at Yale, that the reason for a retractable scrotum in all male mammals is to protect the reproductory organs in hazardous or distressful situations: sharp blades of jungle grass, say, will brush against a running animal's thighs, and the testicles will automatically withdraw to the base of the trunk. He wasn't sure if he had it right—did he have anything right that he'd ever learned in school?—but the basic idea seemed sound, and in any case it was happening to him now: his balls were rising, right there in the coffee shop.

"What does he mean, emotionally disturbed?"

"He exhibits hostile, antisocial behavior," she said. "He doesn't have any friends. Twice this term—or maybe it was three times—he's pulled chairs out from other boys just as the other boys were sitting down, and one of those boys had to have X rays taken of his spine."

She had been slicing her cherry cheesecake into neat, moist sections; now she raised one piece to her bared teeth but it crumbled and part of it fell on her dress, and it seemed to be this small disaster as much as the spinal X rays that reduced her, once again, to tears.

"A *child* psychiatrist, you mean?" Pamela said. "Isn't that a little extreme?"

"I thought so too, at first. Went in and talked to the guidance counsellor myself, tried to have a few hearty, man-to-man talks with Tommy, but I finally had to give up. There's no denying it: he *is* kind of withdrawn and sullen. Janice says I ought to spend more time at home, and I guess she's probably right."

"Oh, you guess she's right, do you? Well, I think it's emotional blackmail."

"How do you mean?"

"Oh, John, you're too much. Do you really think she *still* doesn't know you have a girl? After all this time?" She sat up quickly in bed—not to stand and fight, as he'd feared, but only to make sure her cigarette wasn't burning the sheet. "Sometimes you're the most sensitive, intelligent man in the world, and sometimes you're as dense and naïve as a—I don't know. *Cert*ainly she knows. If she hasn't asked you about me point-blank it's just part of her strategy."

"Okay, I'm naïve," he said. "I guess the really naïve thing was thinking I could talk this over with you."

"I don't know; it seems to be a thing married men do. God knows Frank Lacy spent enough time pouring out *his* dreary little domestic problems."

This was bad. If she started comparing him with Frank Lacy he might not survive the night. He got out of bed and put on the terry-cloth robe she had bought him for Christmas, and the feel of the robe alone was enough to brighten him. "Let's change the subject," he said. "In fact let's not talk about anything at all. Let's sing."

"Sing?"

"Sure. If there's one thing I know better than old-time movies it's old-time songs. Didn't I ever tell you that? Wait. We've got to do this right." At the bathroom mirror he doused and combed his hair and made sure the lapels of the robe were straight, and then he was ready. "You ready?" he called. "Turn on the light, then, and get this." Only when he'd heard the click of the light switch did he throw open the bathroom door and advance on her with a tricky little dance step, in full song:

Columbus discovered America
Hudson discovered New York
Benjamin Franklin discovered the spark
That Edison discovered would light up the dark
Marconi discovered the wireless telegraph
Across the ocean blue
But the greatest discovery
Was when you discovered me
And I discovered you

"But that's *marvelous*," she said when she'd finished laughing and clapping her hands. Throughout the performance she had sat up in bed and hugged her knees like a little girl, and now her face was radiant. "You even sing well. I mean you don't just carry a tune, you really *sing*."

"Sure." At least she wasn't close enough to feel the rapid beating of his heart. "I wasn't a choirboy for nothing."

"Sort of a light, funny Eddie Fisher," she said, "or a heavier Fred Astaire. Listen. Go back in there and come out again. Sing me another."

"Nope. The secret of any entertainer is knowing when to stop. Anyway it's time to—you know. Go home."

"Oh, please. Will you promise to sing another one next time?"

"Sure. I got a million of 'em."

He sat heavily on the edge of the bed, staring at his empty shoes, and the shape of his back must have been eloquent because her arms came tenderly around him from behind and her fingers played with the hair of his chest.

"Poor baby," she said. "I know you're feeling terrible about your boy."

"No, it's not that. It's just—hell, you know. Going home, is all." Because going home meant riding for miles on the IRT with the city's lost and beaten night people, with nothing to do but remember nights long ago when a plain, pleasant girl named Janice Brady had said she loved the Brooklyn Bridge and the Staten Island Ferry, and because "Columbus Discovered America" was the best of the many, many songs that had helped win Janice Brady's heart.

He did begin to spend more time at home—he told Janice he would cut down to two or three AA meetings a week, instead of five—and though it meant less time with Pamela it made him feel like a responsible father.

Twice he left work early to take Tommy to ball games (wasn't that the kind of thing responsible fathers did?), and both times, nursing an after-game beer in some clamorous eating place near the stadium, he tried to draw him out.

"How's summer school going, Tom?"

"I don't know; all right, I guess."

"Think you'll do a little better next year?"

"I don't know."

Once he asked him about the psychiatrist—"You getting along all right with Dr. Goldman?"—before he realized that this was an invasion of privacy, and he amended it quickly: "I mean, *you* know, you don't have to tell me about that if you don't want to," while Tommy soberly chewed his hot dog and kept his own counsel.

"Does he ever talk to you about the psychiatrist?" he asked Janice.

"Not a word—and I don't know if that's a good sign or a bad one. What do you think?"

Seeing Pamela only two or three nights a week did make a difference: every time, it seemed, she was full of news that had nothing to do with him.

"I had lunch with Chester Pratt today," she said one night, "or rather I had lunch with Jerry and he brought Chester Pratt along. He's really very nice when he's sober."

"Oh?"

"Jerry made something of an ass of himself, as you can imagine—trying to hog the conversation, calling him 'Chet' all the time—but when Pratt did get a word in edgewise I thought he was charming. Very intelligent and witty and—well, charming, that's all."

"He writing another book now?"

"No, that's the sad part. He says he can't afford to start a new book yet; he has too many debts. He owes money to his ex-wife, and he owes back taxes and I don't know what-all. He'll have to get some kind of job; it seems an awful shame."

"Why? Most people work for a living."

"I know; I just meant—*you* know. It's a shame because he's so terrifically talented. Of course you haven't read the book; you wouldn't understand."

"Well, if he's going to hold down a steady job he'd better go easy on the booze."

"Oh, that's silly; just because he was drunk at Julian's party that time doesn't mean—besides, you drink a lot, and you hold down a job."

"What kind of job is he looking for?"

"He said he might go back into public relations—he's done that before—or he might look for work in Hollywood. He said both prospects were equally bleak."

But Chester Pratt settled for neither of those things. Two or three weeks later Wilder was waiting in Dr. Brink's outer office, flipping through a copy of *Newsweek*, when he came across this item on the "Periscope" page:

Justice Department

After months of searching, the Attorney General has found a new speechwriter. He is 37-year-old novelist Chester Pratt *(Burn All Your Cities)*, who was recommended for the job by Harvard critic T. J. Whitehead, a Kennedy intimate.

"I know," Pamela said that night. "Jerry told me. Jerry said Pratt says he'll be the only man in the New Frontier who's in it for the money."

That was the first of several nights when she failed to respond to the urgency of his lovemaking—"I'm sorry, John, I guess I can't tonight"—and the following week she called him at the office to say she wasn't feeling well; she was coming down with the flu or something; she would call again as soon as she was better.

He could taste the end of the affair like bile as he went about his business routine and endured his time at home, and he tortured himself with wondering where he'd gone wrong. It now seemed clear that things had never been quite the same since his breakdown at Marlowe— and was that so surprising, after all? How could any healthy girl be expected to care for a mentally un-balanced man?

On two or three nights he really did go to AA meet-ings; other nights he drifted from bar to bar, or sat with Janice and did his level best to hold up his end of the endless conversation about their son. One night Tommy was so expansive at the dinner table, telling the plot of a television comedy he'd liked and interrupting himself with laughter, that Janice was heartened.

". . . Oh, I *am* beginning to see daylight in all this, aren't you?"

But the next night she was in darkness again: the first report card from summer school had come in, and Tommy was still failing the same two subjects.

When Pamela was well again her voice on the phone was more polite than eager, but even so the knowledge that he would see her tonight was bracing; it helped him sit quietly through a dinner with the Borgs.

". . . Maybe *you* could have a talk with him, Paul," Janice said the minute Tommy's door was shut for the night.

"Why me?"

"Because he loves and admires you so; he's always thought of you as a kind of uncle, ever since he was tiny."

"Well, that's nice to hear, Janice, but I think you're exaggerating. In any case I don't see much value in 'having a talk'; I agree with John there. Seems to me you're doing all you can; the only thing now is to wait and hope for the best."

"Paul's wonderful with children," Natalie Borg said. "I've always said he would've made a wonderful father, if only . . ."

There was nothing she relished more than a chance to talk about her youthful hysterectomy; and Wilder sat through it all sipping coffee and congratulating himself on his patience.

"If you people will excuse me," he said at last, "I have a meeting to attend."

All the way uptown he tried to decide what song he would sing tonight. He'd used up "You're the Top" and "I Get a Kick Out of You" and some of the other standards; besides, they weren't so effective because Pamela knew all the words. Only when he was in the elevator did the perfect song occur to him: an old and little-known Al Jolson number called "Where Did Robinson Crusoe Go with Friday on Saturday Night?" He almost giggled to himself, picturing the way he'd deliver it in the terry-cloth robe.

"There's something we have to discuss," she said, and from the way she said it he knew it wouldn't be a discussion at all. She had something to tell him—something he wouldn't like—and he had better shut up and sit down and listen. He did, nursing his whiskey as if it were the last drink in the world, while she walked around and around the room in her working clothes with her arms folded across her chest. "I'm moving," she said. "I'm quitting the job and I'm giving up the apartment and I'm leaving New York, probably for good. It does mean the end of things between you and me, and I'm sorry, but we always knew it couldn't go on forever, didn't we?"

"Yeah," he said, surprised that his voice was low and calm. "Yeah, I guess we always did know that." He wanted to spring to his feet in fury and say "Who's the man?" or to go down on his knees and throw his arms around her thighs and beg her to stay, but he did neither of those things because it seemed important to play the scene her way. And one small, irrational part of his mind suggested that if he did this well, if he was "civilized" and kept his emotions under control, she'd be so impressed that she might still change her mind. He took a careful sip of whiskey before he spoke again. "Where you going?"

"To Washington." She was sitting down now, tapping the ash from her cigarette, and she was clearly so relieved to have the worst of it over that she told a little too much. "I have a friend there who thinks I might qualify for a job in the Justice Department, and it's too good an opportunity to—"

"Wait a second. It's Chester Pratt."

"What if it is?"

The hell with being civilized; the hell with everything. He was on his feet and bearing down on her in a jealous rage. "How long have you been sleeping with that bastard? Huh? I asked you a simple question: how long?"

"John, I don't see any point in losing your temper. There's really—"

"How *long*, God damn it. Answer me!"

"It's not a question that deserves an answer."

And suddenly he passed from anger to an agony of self-abasement and pleading: "Oh, baby, don't go." He touched her shoulder with one hand. "Please don't go. I need you; I need you. . . ." He had done both the things he'd sworn not to do—he had shouted and he'd begged —and there was nothing left.

"I knew this would be difficult," she said, "but you can't bring back something that's over. We had some good times together, but it's—well, it's over, that's all."

All that mattered now was to get out of here before she asked him to leave, and he managed it in a kind of stupor that might have passed for dignity. "Okay," he said, moving for the door, and he stood with one hand on the knob for ten beats of his heart, giving her every chance to call him back, before he said "So long" and let himself out.

Then he was in the Irish bar with the tall picture of President Kennedy on the wall (and maybe Bobby was shorter, but it couldn't be denied that there was something very tall about all the Kennedys and all their men, and all their women). He was drinking double bourbons and staring into the mirror at his Alan Ladd haircut and his painfully familiar Mickey Rooney face, wondering how it would be possible to go on living.

7

He had no one to confide in but Brink.

"There's been a big change, doctor. I've lost my girl. She's gone to live with Bobby Kennedy's speechwriter."

"Well, that's upsetting, of course," the doctor said, writing quickly in his file folder. "Still, if nothing else it means your life is a good deal less complicated now, right? Look on the bright side."

There wasn't much to see on the bright side.

He was glad when Tommy labored through summer school with passing marks and rejoined his class in the seventh grade, and when his talk at dinner seemed to indicate that he did have friends, but he couldn't share in Janice's sense of triumph. If Tommy was a stranger to them now it was only the beginning: he was sure to grow more and more inscrutable as he moved into adolescence. Thirteen, fifteen, seventeen—they wouldn't be able to relax until he was twenty-one and getting out of college, and by then he'd be a man with little if any allegiance to home.

It was clear now that Julian would probably never finish the picture—when he tried to call him once the operator said his number was no longer in service—but it wasn't hard to put the whole thing out of his mind. It seemed preposterous that he had ever entertained the idea of producing a movie; with Pamela gone there was no longer any point in it, and he let it all drift away.

Early in the fall he had an affair with a girl who worked for one of his accounts, but she didn't please him because she wasn't at all like Pamela. She laughed all the time and talked through her laughter; her skin was rough and there were wrinkles in the backs of her thighs. She diverted him for three or four nights on Varick Street; after that he stopped calling her up.

He did very well at his job—before the end of the year he brought two new European car advertisers into the magazine; his earnings were almost twice those of any other salesman, and George Taylor called him "indispensable"—but it gave him no pleasure.

Not even talking politics could rouse him. Paul Borg spent at least one October evening insisting that Kennedy's handling of the crisis over the Cuban missile sites had been "masterly"—that when the Russian ships turned back it had "signified the end of the Cold War, for all history to see"—and Wilder didn't argue with him except to ask once, in a small voice that was quickly overruled by both their wives, what Borg thought might have happened if the ships hadn't turned back.

Then a month or two later Borg held forth at some length on his newfound admiration for the President's brother Bobby: he had "grown" as Attorney General and developed into a responsible leader in his own right. He would almost certainly emerge as a hero in the Civil Rights Movement—"Have you read some of his recent speeches?"—and there was every indication that in six years he would be a worthy successor to the Presidency.

"Oh, I think so too," Janice said. "Isn't it marvelous to think we're all in such good hands? And aren't they a beautiful family? All of them?"

If they would excuse him, Wilder said, he had a meeting to attend.

He did go to a few meetings—not only the one on West Houston but others uptown. Once he thought he spotted his old sponsor Bill Costello in the audience and approached him afterwards in the crowd around the coffee urns, but it was another white-haired man who turned out to be a gloomy Polish engineer.

On Christmas Eve he sat in the living room with Janice while she wrapped and tied the last few presents to be tucked under the spindly tree. Their Christmas trees seemed to get smaller and more apologetic-looking every year, but they always smelled the same—a green, pungent smell that took him back to early childhood. He was about to say Why didn't we get a bigger tree? but that might spoil the gentle, innocent mood of the evening. Instead he strolled along her bookshelves until he came to *Burn All Your Cities* and pulled it out. "This any good?" he asked.

"Oh, it got good reviews," she said, looking up from where she sat on the carpet and wiping a strand of hair away from her eyes, "but I thought it was a little—overwrought. Why?"

"No reason. I met him once, is all. The author."

"Oh? Where?"

"At an AA meeting. Apparently he had a drinking problem at one time."

"Did he give a talk?"

"No; I was just introduced to him."

"Well, you might enjoy it, John; I don't want to spoil it for you."

It touched him that she seemed to feel he might "enjoy" reading a whole book. "No," he said, "I don't think I'll bother with it. Didn't much like his looks, as a matter of fact."

"Don't, then. You've always had a sure instinct about people. That's probably one reason you're so good at your work."

"Oh, I don't know. In the kind of work I do almost anybody could make a living."

"Why do you always say that? I think what you do must be very difficult, and you do it extremely well." She got to her feet and turned off all the other lights in the room, letting the colored lights of the tree bathe everything in a soft pinkish glow. Then she sat curled up on the sofa and said "How does it look?"

"Fine," he said, and sat beside her. "It really looks fine, Janice." After a pause, feeling as shy as a boy, he said "You always do everything right at Christmastime."

"Shall I get some Christmas music on the radio?"

"No, don't bother. Let's just—sit here a while."

And almost before he knew it they were in each other's arms. Gasping and moaning, they were all over each other like a couple of crazed adolescents.

". . . Oh John," she said as he helped her into the bedroom, "it's been so long."

"No it hasn't; it just seems that way."

"That's what I mean. So long since we really—since we both *really*—oh, John . . ."

He thought of Pamela only fleetingly as they rolled and locked; then he put her out of his mind. All that was over. This was probably where he belonged.

Janice called it "our second honeymoon," which made him wince when she wasn't looking, and it lasted through the winter and well into the spring. Finding he could make love to her out of something other than a sense of duty was a pleasure in itself, and there were other pleasures: she talked less, or at least did less of the kind of talking whose only purpose was to fill silence, and many little things in her behavior seemed to suggest a renewal of self-esteem—almost a new serenity.

Then it was summer again, and he was nearly thirty-nine years old. When they went up to "the country" there were not one but three or four girls on the raft whose sweet young flesh was a daily torment, and on the kitchen shelves of the bungalow there wasn't even so much as a bottle of cooking sherry.

"Think I'll run into town for a meeting tonight," he announced while she was snapping string beans for dinner.

"Well," she said, "all right, but you've already been to three this week. You really think it's necessary?"

"Sometimes," he said, "you have to trust my judgment in these things."

Once in town he made straight for the bar at the Biltmore, where he drank until past midnight; then he went over to the downstairs bar of the Commodore—the place from which Paul Borg had taken him to Bellevue —and drank until closing time. When he crept unsteadily up into the hotel for a room he knew his voice wouldn't sound right if he called her, so he saved his lie until morning: he'd had trouble with the car; the mechanic had wanted to keep it overnight; he hadn't called earlier for fear of waking her. And she apparently believed him, though it often seemed, looking back later, that the end of the second honeymoon could be dated from that night.

Nothing happened all fall until late in November, when he and George Taylor were strolling back from lunch and found a crowd blocking the sidewalk in front of a television store. Several women were crying and one or two of the men looked ready to cry too, and it wasn't long before they learned that the President had been shot in the head. The cameras were panning over the shocked, grieving crowds in Dallas, and then they cut to Walter Cronkite soberly repeating the news.

"Guess I'd better get home, George."

"Right. I'm cutting out too."

And by the time he got home Kennedy was dead.

"It's one of the most frightful things in history," Janice said to the television set. Her eyes were red and blinking; she used one hand to wipe them with Kleenex and kept the other arm around Tommy, who'd been sent home early from school. "*Oh*, he was such a great man; and he was so *young*. He'd only just *begun* his career. . . ." Soon she would call Paul Borg, if she hadn't already, for confirmation in her mourning.

". . . shock that has shaken the nation and the entire Western world," Walter Cronkite was saying.

And through it all Wilder sat numb, saying very little, wondering what was the matter with him.

Later in the afternoon there were scenes of the Dallas police hustling a suspect named Oswald into jail—all you could see of him was that he was scrawny and wore a T-shirt—and of a righteous cop holding up a scope-sighted rifle to the cameras. Only then did Wilder realize what he felt, and it sent him into the kitchen for a secret nip of the whiskey Janice kept for guests. He felt sympathy for the assassin and he felt he understood the motives. Kennedy had been too young, too rich, too handsome and too lucky; he had embodied elegance and wit and finesse. His murderer had spoken for weakness, for neurasthenic darkness, for struggle without hope and for the self-defeating passions of ignorance, and John Wilder understood those forces all too well. He almost felt he'd pulled the trigger himself, and he was grateful to be here, trembling and safe in his own kitchen, two thousand miles away.

"It's a terrible thing," he said, rejoining his wife and son. "It's a terrible, terrible thing."

Everything changed in February.

He was sitting in the office, wondering whether to go out for a drink and kill the rest of the day—an indispensable man could afford to do things like that—when his phone rang and it was Pamela.

"My God," he said. "Where are you?"

She sounded shy, as if she hadn't been sure whether to call him or not. "I'm staying at the Plaza. I was wondering if you'd like to meet me here for a drink this afternoon."

She had changed a little—that was the first thing he noticed when he found her in the cocktail lounge. Her eyes and mouth were different—older, more "sophisticated"—and her very way of sitting in a chair and talking had taken on a new authority, but instead of dwelling on these things he concentrated on something he'd noticed long ago: that the tip of her nose bobbed slightly with each pronunciation of *p, b* or *m*. She was, she said, "finished" with Washington, and that seemed to imply that she was finished with Chester Pratt too.

". . . I mean it *was* pretty exciting, being in Justice," she said. "I worked in the Public Information office—I was right across the hall from the Attorney General—and I'll probably never have a more interesting job in my life. The trouble was mostly Chet's drinking—he really is a terrible soak, and he probably never would've been hired if Bob had known."

"Who's 'Bob'?"

"Kennedy. Nobody but the family calls him 'Bobby.' Anyway, he hired Chet in a hurry because he needed a speechwriter right away, and it was two or three months before his FBI report came through. It was full of stuff about his alcoholism, but by then Bob didn't have the heart to fire him, so he let him stay on. And Chet did try, I guess—he wrote some good speeches—but he seemed to feel that if he stayed sober all day he could go to hell with himself at night and on the weekends; that made it kind of rough on me. Then toward the end, just before the Assassination, the drink began to show on him: he looked like hell and he had the shakes—he'd have to sneak out across the street for quick shots of vodka to get him through the day. In an awful kind of way the Assassination was a break for him: when people started handing in their resignations it meant he could quit decently. That's when I quit too."

"Where is he now?"

"Here in town someplace, I guess. I honestly don't know, and I don't care. I broke off with him last month, before I went up to see my father. It seems like years ago now."

And no wonder, because the trip to see her father had changed her life. "I always forget how old he is," she said. "He's over sixty now, and sometimes he seems even older than that. I guess he's never really been happy since my mother died; anyway, he's always saying Mark and I are all he has in the world. Did I ever tell you about Mark?"

"Only that he was an absolute genius at the piano."

"Did I say that? Well, I guess it's true enough. He's been studying in Rome for four or five years, and last summer Daddy went over to visit him. I think he thought it was time for him to stop studying and start performing. And he found him— John, if I tell you this will you promise not to laugh or say something awful? You have to promise."

"Okay."

"He found him playing cocktail piano in a tourists' hotel; that's part of it, and the rest is worse. He's living with another man in an apartment that's all mirrors and black velvet. He's turned homosexual, you see."

"Oh."

"And I guess some other father might've been able to

take it, but not Daddy. He thinks in terms of Sodom and
Gomorrah. He says he doesn't want anything to *do* with
Mark any more, and I think he means it. Anyway, the
whole thing has made him sort of a super-father to me,
if you can understand that."

"I think I can."

"So when I went up there he said 'What do you want,
Pamela? What do you want in all the world?' I think he
was hoping I'd say marriage and a family, but I still don't
feel ready for that; maybe I never will. I thought it over
for a few days—I mean that's the kind of question you
have to think over—and then I told him I wanted something to do with filmmaking. I even told him a little
about you."

"About me?"

"Oh, not really anything *about* you, just that I'd been
—well, fond of a man who was interested in movies too,
and that we'd worked together on an experimental film
that hadn't been finished. And the point is, John, by this
time he was practically reaching for his checkbook. I
mean I *know* he has more money than he knows what
to do with, but I never expected anything like this. He
said 'Would you like to go to Hollywood?' I said there
were plenty of places besides Hollywood for making
movies, and he said there were other places than Detroit
for making cars, too; he said if a thing is worth doing it's
worth doing right. And John, he offered to finance me for
any amount up to fifty thousand dollars."

"That's quite a lot."

"I couldn't believe it." For a moment she looked like
a little rich girl boasting of her father's extravagant birthday gift. "But he said I wasn't a child any more and I

could be entrusted with responsibility, and he said 'If
you're going out there you don't want to be poor.' And
John—" She got out a cigarette and lit it with a gold
lighter that had probably been another of her father's
gifts; or maybe it had been a gift from Chester Pratt.
"—John, the thing is, I do want to go, but I don't want
to go alone. I want to go with you."

"Until Chester Pratt sobers up, you mean?"

"I knew you'd say something like that. How can I
convince you? Listen: I read over Jerry's screenplay of
'Bellevue' the other night and it made me cry, thinking
of you. Oh, listen—" She put her cigarette in the ashtray
and leaned close to hold his wrist in both tense hands,
and all at once he knew what had drawn him to her in
the beginning, even more than her perfect flesh; it was
her voice. "Listen. Why *not* come with me? Do you have
anything better to do with your life?"

"Janice," he said a few nights later, "there's something
I have to tell you."

He didn't look at her face until he'd gotten through
the hard part—he wanted a separation; he was going to
California; he had an opportunity to become a producer;
there was a girl—and when he did risk a glance at her
he found she looked blank: he couldn't tell if she was
being "civilized" about it or if she was stunned.

". . . And there's enough in the bank to last you and
Tommy nearly two years," he was saying, "not that you'll
need that much. With any kind of luck I'll be able to start
sending you money on a regular basis within a year,
maybe inside of six months, and of course I'll always . . ."

"So you've made up your mind," she said at last.

"Yes. I have."

"Then there's nothing I can say, is there?" She got up from her reading chair and walked a few steps away from him, holding her shoulders high. When she turned he expected her face to be ugly with rage, but it was almost pretty in a plain way. Her eyes were bright. "Oh, John," she said. "And I thought we were getting along so *well* together."

". . . And I'll be out there a long time," he said to his son the following night. "Maybe six months, maybe longer. But we'll keep in touch."

"Okay, Dad."

"And maybe when I get settled we can arrange for you to fly out for a visit. Would you like that?"

"Sure; that'd be fine."

"Might be fun for you, flying out to the Coast by yourself. And there's plenty to see in Los Angeles—lot of good baseball, for one thing."

"Okay, Dad."

"It's the biggest damn fool thing I ever heard of," George Taylor said. "You're not only leaving *me* in a hell of a mess, walking out on all your accounts, but you're behaving in a completely—a completely irresponsible way. Traipsing off to California with no more idea of— John, a man doesn't spend all these years building something and then kick it to pieces. What about Janice, for God's sake? What about your boy?"

"They're well provided for."

"That's not the point. The point is a man needs a *home*, for God's sake. You want your little girl, all right, fine, *have* your little girl, but don't—well, to put it coarsely, don't shit where you eat." His flushed face and pouting lips showed he was both sorry and glad he'd put it that way. "All right!" He held up one hand as if to ward off a blow. "All right; maybe that part of it's none of my business, but *this* part"—he jabbed the top of his desk with a stiff index finger— "this *is* my business. This is your whole career you're throwing away."

"I've never thought of it as a 'career,' George. The fact is I've never liked it."

And Taylor rolled his eyes to the ceiling. "Never liked it. Work your way to the top of your profession and then decide you've never— Ah, you make me tired. You're not acting like a man at all, you're acting like some crazy kid. Movies! What in the name of Christ do *you* know about movies?"

"Well, let's see," Dr. Brink said, turning the pages of a heavy book that looked like an encyclopedia. "Los Angeles. I don't know anyone out there I can recommend personally, but you can't go wrong with UCLA. Write down this name: Burton L. Rose. Must be a competent man if he's in charge of the unit." And he put the directory away.

"Now. As for your medication, I don't think any change is indicated; when you run short of pills you can get refills from Rose. If this were an ordinary business trip I'd let it go at that, but I'm a little concerned about the—uncertainty of your plans."

"So am I."

"You'll be running into situations you can't begin to

anticipate, and you may find yourself under a good deal of stress."

"That's what I'm worried about, doctor. I mean not worried, just apprehensive."

"Apprehensive, right," the doctor said, as if that were the word he'd been groping for, and he tapped his silver ballpoint pen against his teeth. Then he started scribbling on his prescription pad. "We don't want to take any chances. So here's what we'll do. I'm giving you three additional medications to be taken only in case you feel you're about to go over the edge. Just remember, these are for bad times only. Put a rubber band around them; keep them in a separate part of your suitcase. Consider them your emergency kit. Fair enough?"

"Fine. And listen, doctor; since I may not see you again, I want to thank you for all your—you know—all your help."

"Not at all," Brink said, rising to shake hands. "It's been a pleasure."

8

The Los Angeles airport was so bewildering that Pamela was almost in tears by the time he steered their rented car into the maze of Freeways.

"What do I look for?" he asked her as the enormous green-and-white signs loomed and passed overhead.

"Look for Sunset Boulevard," she said. "That'll at least be—look *out*, John—that'll at least be a place to start."

All he knew about this city, from two brief business conventions, was that it wasn't really a city at all. It went on for miles in all directions without ever becoming a city, and the part of it called Hollywood was the most elusive of all; but starting at Sunset Boulevard sounded better than starting at Hollywood and Vine.

"Good," she said when he'd navigated the exit and they were riding down the pleasant, palm-lined avenue. "Now if we just stay on this for a while it ought to turn into the Strip."

It did, and they checked into a motel not far from Cyrano's. Soon he was pouring whiskey over little motel ice cubes and she was kicking off her shoes on a king-size double bed. If nothing else, they were here.

"Cheers," he said.

"I guess the first thing we ought to do is find an apartment," she said, "even before we call Edgar Freeman. Don't you think?"

Edgar Freeman was their only "contact," a producer-director at Columbia Pictures whose uncle was an acquaintance of her father's. He had answered her letter with a cheerful note saying he'd be happy to see them for "lunch at the studio."

"Right," he said. "And listen, let's allow two days for finding an apartment. Three days tops."

It took them four, and the place they found wasn't very rewarding. It was on one of the streets running south off the Strip, and its only real advantage was in being on the ground floor, with a private entrance. The living room was decorated mostly in the colors of cantaloupe and honeydew; it was habitable, once they'd removed the large-eyed Keene reproductions from the walls, and the bedroom was better, but the whole place looked as impersonal and transient as a motel suite.

"Hell, it's only temporary," he said as they unloaded bedclothes and kitchenware and groceries from the car on the fifth day. "We'll find a better place once we know our way around. Besides, it's cheap and convenient and it's got a phone. That's all we need for now."

"I'm so glad we didn't get involved in a two-year lease," she said, "or anything like that."

He watched her while she called Edgar Freeman, watched her tense artificial smile when she said "I'm *so* glad you remember me . . ." and then the joyous dip of her head when she said "Today? Well, that would be marvelous, if you're sure you . . . All right, fine, then. . . . Twelve-thirty. . . . Fine, then, Mr. Freeman. . . ."

Then they were driving up to the parking lot outside the big, forbidding hulk of Columbia Pictures, and she was carrying a copy of the "Bellevue" script on her lap.

"Freeman?" said the uniformed man who sat just inside the door, screening all visitors. "Second floor, fourth door to your left." And the little metal sign there read "The Freeman Company."

"Just a moment," said a pretty young secretary who was evidently British, and in a moment out he came— a tall, slender man, elegantly dressed in the Eastern, Madison Avenue style, shooting his cuffs and smiling as if Pamela and Wilder were the two people he wanted most to see in the whole of his busy day.

"Come in, come in, sit down; I'll be with you in just a second," he said, and he ushered them into a big sunlit room where four or five other men were standing. He made the introductions so quickly that Wilder could remember none of the names, and then he returned to what had apparently been an interrupted conversation. There was nothing to do but sit in one of the deep sofas and wait.

"I think that's the answer, Edgar," one of the men was saying. "If we can't get any support here we'll take it to Japan."

"It's a long shot," Edgar Freeman said, "but it's worth a try. Let's get Sarah in here." He sat at his ample desk and pressed a button, and the young British girl came in.

". . . letter to Mr. E. C. Moyoto, Executive Producer,

Japanese World Films, Inc., Tokyo, Japan. Dear Mr. Moyoto: Remembering our pleasant conversation at the International Conference of Filmmakers last June, I hope you will be interested in the attached screenplay —*Okinawa*—and will agree with me that it's a splendid property for joint Japanese-American production. Paragraph."

"Beautiful," one of the men said.

"As you will see, the screenplay is based on extensive research into all aspects of the historic battle, from both sides, and some of its most moving and memorable moments are those depicting the heroism and sacrifice—no, scratch that, Sarah—depicting the humanity, heroism and sacrifice of the Japanese armed forces. I look forward to hearing from you soon. Sincerely yours, et cetera."

"Beautiful," the man said again. "That's a great letter, Edgar."

There was some other talk that Wilder couldn't follow; then the cluster of men left the office and Freeman stood up. "Sorry to keep you people waiting," he said. "Some mornings are like that. Ready for lunch?"

The executive dining room served no liquor—that was Wilder's first disappointment—and had no windows, but an Italian sex goddess sat two tables away from them and there were recognizable if lesser stars nearby.

"I ought to be celebrating today," Edgar Freeman said. "It's my fortieth birthday; sort of a milestone. I guess all it really means is that I can't call myself a young director any more. Have to move aside for the new generation."

"How many pictures have you made, Mr. Freeman?" Pamela asked him.

"Oh, let's see." And he studied a sauce-dipped shrimp on the tines of his cocktail fork while he thought it over. "Seventy-two. No, wait—seventy-four."

"Seventy-four *pictures?*"

"Oh, it's not a record. Comes close, though, for a man my age, especially since nearly all of them showed a profit. I did most of them for Bonanza International over the past twelve years. A lot of people bad-mouth B.I., but I enjoyed a very happy relationship with them."

"Wait a minute," she said. "Are they the people who do those teen-age beach pictures?"

"Beach pictures and bike pictures, right. Also horror pictures. B.I. was the first to understand and exploit that market, and they've done extraordinarily well. They're very sound, astute businessmen. Generally when you hear someone knocking B.I. in this town it turns out to be envy, pure and simple. An awful lot of people would like to know how they do it. I came over to Columbia because I thought it was time to get into a more ambitious kind of product, maybe catch up with my European reputation—I have quite a critical following in Europe, you see, especially in France, especially for my horror films—but so far I must say I'm not very pleased with this studio." He popped the last shrimp into his mouth and shoved the iced dish neatly to one side. "With certain of the ruling executives anyway. We can't seem to get together on *properties,*" he said. "We've developed three or four good scripts—what *I* consider good scripts—and none of them has generated much enthusiasm. First I gave them a really exciting Civil War Western."

"What's a Civil War Western?" Wilder asked.

"Northern cavalry, stockades, escaped Southern prisoners, Indians, chases, gunfights, a rape—thank you," he said to the waiter, accepting a plate of beef-and-kidney stew. "Then I gave them a good solid gangster script based on the St. Valentine's Day Massacre, and now I've given them a World War Two piece about Okinawa. It's like pulling teeth. If we don't agree on something soon I'll go over to another studio. Well; tell me about yourselves. What've you got there?" And he reached across the table to pluck "Bellevue" from beside Pamela's plate.

"I don't think you'd be interested in that," she said quickly. "It's an experimental short feature; we—some friends of ours—"

" 'Screenplay by Jerome Porter,' " he read aloud. "Is that the same Jerome Porter who wrote *Burn All Your Cities?*"

"Yes. I didn't know that was—"

"It hasn't been released yet," Edgar Freeman said, "but everybody's talking about it. The director's a young man named Julian Feld; apparently he's done quite a job."

"Oh? Well, actually, Julian directed this picture too; it was filmed, you see, back in the East, but it was never edited. We—"

"That so?" he said, thumbing the pages of the script. "Well. You travel in good company."

"Are they out here now?" she inquired. "Jerry and Julian?"

"Either here or in New York. They're probably working on new things; I imagine they'll be very busy young men from now on. How do you people feel about dessert? Rum cake or chocolate parfait?"

RICHARD YATES

"God!" Pamela said when they were out in the parking lot. "Beach pictures, bike pictures, horror pictures. So much for Mr. Edgar Freeman."

"Never mind. He's not the only man in Hollywood."

But he was the only one they knew, and that knowledge made their ride home a cheerless one. This was an appropriately desolate part of town—an Orange Julius stand, gas stations, a mammoth drugstore, the grubby white edifice of the Hollywood Palladium—and Wilder drove with great care because he wanted to get home safely, as soon as possible, and have a drink.

"Even if Jerry and Julian *are* here," Pamela said, walking around the apartment with a tinkling glass, "how do you suppose we'd ever get in touch with them? And even if we got in touch with them, what could they do?"

"I don't know, baby. We'll just have to—you know—play it by ear." He wasn't quite sure what he meant by that (Play *what* by ear? What did they have to "play"?) but it sounded like a good answer, and he trusted the whiskey to ease them both through the rest of the afternoon.

Burn All Your Cities opened in a great many theatres across the country the following week—they read about it in the *Los Angeles Times*—and there were very favorable reviews.

> In his first time out, young Julian Feld displays a formidable directing talent. Jerome Porter's muscular screenplay is a faithful rendering of the Chester Pratt novel, and Feld makes the most of it. Few viewers will come away from

Burn All Your Cities unmoved; many are sure
to find it one of the top cinematic experiences
of the year . . .

Pamela wrote letters to both of them, addressed in
care of the production company, and while waiting for
answers they explored the city. Beverly Hills looked
suitably rich, but the houses—at least those that could
be seen from the road—were too close together. The
Hollywood hills were prettier and some of them com-
manded nice views, but the canyons led too quickly
into the enormous suburban waste of the San Fernando
Valley. Downtown Los Angeles held no surprises and
seemed to promise that the best parts of town must lie
to the west, but when they drove out to the beaches
they found only sandy, weatherbeaten slums. Time and
again they came home weak with hunger and the need
for a drink, feeling oppressed. They had plenty of time
and plenty of money, but neither was much consola-
tion.

"Go home for a drink," Pamela said one afternoon.
"That's all we ever do. We go home for a drink, or three
or four, and then we try a new restaurant and have two
or three more, and then we go to bed. If only there were
*some*one to call; *some*one to go and see—just *any*one."

He might have reminded her that the whole crazy
idea of coming out here with no prospects had been hers,
but he didn't want to risk a quarrel. It was bad enough
being in this together; it would be unendurable if they
were at each other's throats.

"Take it easy, baby," he said. "Something's bound to
turn up."

A letter from Jerry came at last, with a New York postmark, and she tore it open with trembling fingers.

> Glad you're both in L.A. and hope to see you if I come out again. *Cities* was something of a hit, as you may have heard, and Julian and I are deep into other projects now. . . .
>
> I do know a man out there who might be interested in co-producing "Bellevue." He is very rich, a kind of gentleman producer, always on the lookout for what he calls artistic properties, and not a bad guy at all. His name is Carl Munchin and he lives in Malibu. I'll write him today and tell him about you two; you can take it from there . . .

And they were still counting the days before it would be safe to call Carl Munchin when Carl Munchin called them—the nicest thing that had happened to them in Los Angeles so far.

". . . Why don't you drop a copy of your script in the mail to me, Mr. Wilder?" he said. "Then I'll read it and get back to you."

That meant a few more days of waiting, and of being afraid to leave the apartment because the phone might ring, but Munchin did get back to them.

"I think it has possibilities," he said. "I knew it would be well written because Jerry Porter's a good writer, but I didn't expect the material to be so interesting in its own right. Listen: can you come out here this afternoon, so we can talk about it?"

He lived in a part of Malibu they could never have discovered on their hopeful visits to the shore—many miles north of the public beaches, in a big house that was well hidden from the road. The house itself was a wondrous blending of out- and indoor luxury: there was so much furniture on the broad patio that it seemed like a living room, and so much vegetation in the living room that it seemed like a patio. He was a big, tan, bald man with a small tan wife, and they wore matching safari jackets. Helen Munchin never took her eyes off her husband's face when he was talking, and she looked wholly absorbed. Only in the intervals of his speech did she allow her gaze to stray from him, and then it met the visitors' eyes in a way that said Isn't Carl wonderful? Aren't I the luckiest girl in the world?

". . . The way it stands now you've got a nice little art-house piece," he said. They were drinking gin and tonic on the patio while the sun set in the gleaming Pacific. "It could fill out the bill with some short foreign film. Probably get a few bookings in New York, maybe one or two in San Francisco, and forget the rest of the country. Might do better in Europe, but not much. Whereas what I have in mind would be a selling proposition as well as an art piece; I mean a commercially viable property. Let me fill you in. First of all, there's one central weakness in your script. Your protagonist—the man all this Bellevue business *happens* to—is never really characterized."

"We planned it that way," Wilder said. "We wanted him to be a sort of nameless observer, you see, a kind of Everyman."

"Impossible. You can't start with an Everyman." And Carl Munchin wagged his forefinger from side to side, smiling cannily, like a high-school English teacher about to make a trenchant point. "Only through the particular can you find the universal." He paused to let that sink in; then he got up and began pacing the flagstones in his clean desert boots. "I mean who *is* this guy?" he demanded. "What's he like when he's *not* in Bellevue? How does being in Bellevue change his life? I want a revised, shortened version of this script of yours to serve as part one, you see. Then I want to see a part two and a part three. You follow me?"

"I'm not sure," Wilder said. "What would happen in parts two and three?"

"We'll have to get ourselves a good writer and work it out. Just as a guideline I'd say build him up for another breakdown—a real breakdown—in part two, and then in part three let him have it. Pull out all the stops. Oh, if this were Nineteen Forty-five or Forty-six I'd say play it differently; put him in the hands of a brilliant psychiatrist, let part three be his struggle to a miraculous recovery— the analyst helps him remember some childhood experience that clears up all his problems—but people aren't buying that stuff any more. Today's audience is more sophisticated. I say let him go crazy. Wipe him out."

"Would he commit a crime?" Wilder said. "Like assassinating Kennedy or something?"

"That might work except everybody knows who assassinated Kennedy. Besides, I don't think he has to commit a crime. Just let him get so he can't live in civilized society any more. Make him a real paranoid schizophrenic. If our writer doesn't know how to handle that we'll send him out to Camarillo with a tape recorder."

"Where?"

"Camarillo. The state hospital. Go out there with a

tape recorder, listen to the way those people talk. Might pick up some good ideas."

"Mm," Wilder said. "Well. What do you think, Pamela?"

She took a neat sip of her drink before answering, and then she addressed Munchin. "I'm afraid I still don't see why something can't be done with the picture as it is," she said. "I don't know if John made this clear to you, Mr. Munchin, but it's already been filmed. It was never finished—never cut, that is—but it was filmed and directed by Julian Feld, the man who did *Burn All Your Cities*. And even if it *were* limited to an art-house distribution, isn't there a good chance that it might lead to other things? Bigger things?"

"Sure it might," Munchin said. "You'd always have that hope. But just for now we're talking about what's of interest to me, right?" He smiled engagingly, displaying many clean, strong teeth. "The three-part version is of interest to me. The short version is not."

She wouldn't let him go. "Well then, do you know anyone—or know *of* anyone—who might be interested?"

"Honey," he said, still smiling, "even if I did I wouldn't tell you."

She looked stung for a second, until Helen Munchin's happy laugh announced that he was only teasing, and over the pouring of fresh drinks he went back to his plan.

Put a man in Bellevue, let him go back to whatever problems sent him there, let those problems work on him until he's up to the breaking point and then watch him break—watch him go down beyond the reach of any psychiatric help—that, Carl Munchin said, was a story:

the kind of material a good writer could sink his teeth into. And getting a good writer would be no problem. "This town's crawling with writers. If we can't get Jerry Porter we'll go to an agent—I'm in touch with two or three of the top agencies—and we'll have a first-rate writer working for us in no time."

"Well, I don't know, Mr. Munchin," Wilder said. "We'll have to think about it and talk it over some more."

"Sure you will. You may not see the possibilities right away because you're married to this short version, this Bellevue section, but keep an open mind. I think we have the makings of a very distinguished motion picture here." And when he said "a very distinguished motion picture" his wife gave a little shudder of pleasure. Then she stood up to indicate that the cocktail hour was over.

"We'll get together on this again soon," Munchin said. "Meanwhile, can you leave a copy of that script with me? I'd like to show it to a few people, kind of sound them out. Well, it's been very enjoyable. Talk to you later."

". . . And we don't even know who the man *is*," Pamela said as they rode back along the Pacific Coast Highway. "Jerry says he's 'a kind of gentleman producer,' but what's *that*, for heaven's sake? Besides, I think his Big Idea is lousy, don't you?"

"I don't know. Still thinking about it."

"*Oh*, I'm so disappointed. I thought he'd want 'Belle-vue' in its own right, and here he takes off on this whole new tangent. John, do you realize where we'd be if only Julian had finished this picture long ago? We'd have come out here with a whole finished *thing* to sell—we'd have been able to deal with *distributors* instead of groping around among the Edgar Freemans and the Carl Munchins."

He told her to forget Edgar Freeman. He said Munchin was different. Munchin had said he'd show it to some people, and that could lead to almost anything. "I don't think it was a bad day's work, baby," he concluded, and as he steered down the highway he planned other ways to cheer her up: they would go to the best restaurant they'd found and drink just enough to restore the dwindling glow of Munchins' gin; then they'd order whatever looked best on the expensive menu, with wine, and through it all he'd make her see that Munchin's idea wasn't necessarily so lousy after all. . . .

"Yes it is," she insisted, turning the stem of her brandy glass between her fingers. "It's asinine. It suggests that anyone who's spent a week in Bellevue is destined for a life of madness. What kind of nonsense is that?"

He felt as if he were trying to convince her, once again, that *Gunga Din* was the best boy's movie ever made. "I don't think it suggests that," he said, "or at least it wouldn't have to, if we got a good writer. Oh, I'll agree Munchin was pretty silly today, but he was talking off the top of his head. A good writer could particularize the man, make him a flesh-and-blood character with problems uniquely his own. Then the story of his downfall would follow its own logic. Don't you see?"

"No."

"You're just in the wrong mood. Look, I thought Munchin was kind of a horse's ass too, but he could be valuable to us all the same. Let's—you know—keep an open mind."

"Okay," she said. "I guess there's not much else we *can* do."

Within two weeks they were back on Carl Munchin's patio, and this time four other men were there. One was a lawyer Pamela's father had recommended, one was Munchin's lawyer, and the other two—both short, dark men who seemed to look exactly alike—were introduced as Munchin's business associates. And by the end of that afternoon, after the flourishing of several dense documents and the scribbling of several signatures, they had incorporated and formed a production company.

"Is that really how these things are done?" Pamela said. "It all seemed so easy."

"It seemed easy because we have good lawyers," Munchin said, tilting a martini pitcher toward her glass. "Now all we have to do is find the backing and make the picture."

". . . So we're in business," Wilder said as they drove home that night. "We're producers."

"I know; I suppose we ought to celebrate or something, but I still don't feel right about it. I still don't trust Munchin's idea."

Soon—almost too soon, it seemed—there was a conference with the writer Munchin had secured from one of the two or three top agencies, a tall, fat, nervous man named Jack Haines.

". . . I see him as a married man," he said, soundlessly treading Munchin's patio in a pair of desert boots that must have looked just like Munchin's when they were new. "He's unhappily married and he's got kids he can't relate to and he feels trapped. He's solidly middle class.

I don't know what he does for a living, but let's say it's something well paid and essentially meaningless, like advertising. When he gets out of Bellevue he's scared and lost but he doesn't know where to turn. Maybe he gets involved with a quack psychoanalyst, that'd give us an opportunity for some humor—black humor—and then he meets a girl. The girl—"

"Hold it right there, Jack," Carl Munchin said. "I can see you've given this a lot of thought, but I can't help feeling there's a quality of cliché about everything you've said so far. Unhappy advertising man, gray flannel suit and all that. We can't have a character who meets his downfall out of some cockamamie, two-for-a-nickel *Weltschmerz*. This is a *dark* story. We need a man who's *doomed*." And Helen Munchin said "Oh, yes."

Jack Haines blinked and looked wounded, but not for long. "Well, Carl, I think the quality you're looking for will be there in the writing. All I'm giving you now is the briefest kind of summary; I don't see how you can make a judgment like that on the basis of—look, can I go on? Okay. The girl tries to help him. She offers him hope, and for a little while it's a happy affair—that gives us the upbeat flavor we need for the ending of part two; then, zap! In part three everything falls to pieces. He can't handle the hope the girl's given him; he's emotionally tied to the past. He *is* a 'dark' character, as you'll see, and he brings on his own—"

"Does he commit suicide?"

"No; worse, in a way. He systematically destroys everything that's still bright and promising in his life, including the girl's love, and he sinks into a depression so deep as to be irrevocable. He winds up in an asylum that makes Bellevue look like nothing. And I think you'll see, Carl, when the whole thing's on paper, that there's an inevitability to it. The seeds of self-destruction are there in the man from the start." His performance was over, and only his trembling hands—quickly corrected by the lighting of a cigarette—betrayed his anxiety.

"I don't know," Munchin said. "Something's missing. Something's lacking. What do you people think?"

Wilder had been made so uneasy by the first part of the writer's recital (Who the hell *was* this Jack Haines? How did he know so much?) that he almost welcomed the chance to reject him—then they might get another writer with a whole new set of ideas—but he didn't want to say anything precipitate. "I see what you mean about clichés, Carl; still, it's hard to judge something that hasn't been written yet."

"I think it sounds interesting," Pamela said, and Wilder looked at her in surprise. He'd been sure she would think it sounded terrible.

"And where's all this going to take place?" Munchin inquired. "In New York?"

"Mostly; I haven't really worked that out. If you want a change of scene he could take off somewhere with the girl. Could be anywhere."

When Jack Haines had been cordially dismissed ("Talk to you later, Jack," Munchin said) he drove away in a dusty white Volkswagen that looked too small to accommodate his legs.

"What did you really think, Pamela?" Wilder said.

"I told you; I thought it sounded interesting. It's the first time I've really been able to picture Carl's idea for a three-part story."

"Well, all right," Munchin said, "but remember, Haines is expendable. All I know about Haines is that he published two obscure novels some years ago and he's got a list of television credits as long as your arm. We can do better. I saw in the trades this morning that Chester Pratt's in town. He may be tied up with other things, but I intend to find out. Get a writer of that calibre, you might really see some imaginative work."

"No, that's out, Carl," Wilder said, afraid the rush of heat in his face must be visible to them all. "We don't want Chester Pratt."

"Why not, for God's sake?"

"I met him once. I've heard he's not reliable. He's a drunk."

Pamela was inspecting her fingernails.

"He stayed sober long enough to write a pretty terrific book," Munchin said.

"Oh, I don't know," Wilder said. "I thought it was a little overwrought."

"Have you read it?" Pamela inquired. "I didn't know you'd read it."

When they were driving home she said "Why were you so funny about Pratt? It *would* be a break if Munchin could get him."

"I don't want him around, that's all. I must say I'm surprised *you* want him around."

"Oh, John, he wouldn't be 'around.' He'd be holed up writing the script, and once it got into production we'd probably never see him again. Besides, whatever we think of the man personally, he happens to be an excellent—"

"Okay," he said, gripping the wheel very tight in both hands to prove he wasn't angry. *"Okay."*

"And in any case it's silly even to think about it. I don't think Munchin'll ever get him."

Later that night, walking home from dinner, she stopped and bought copies of the two trade papers.

"What's all this?" he said.

"I just want to check that item about Pratt. I want to see what they say about him."

"No you don't." He stopped on the sidewalk. "You're not bringing those fucking papers into the house."

"Are you out of your mind?"

It wasn't their first quarrel in Hollywood but it was the most abrupt, and it was the first to happen on the street.

"All right, *read* 'em!" he shouted. *"Read* 'em—they won't have what *you're* looking for; they won't print his *phone* number."

"John, this is the most utterly pointless, ridiculous—if you don't stop this, I swear I'll—"

"You'll *what?* Take your daddy's money and move out? Fine! Go shack up with Chester Pratt again! Get him together with Munchin and the three of you can make a movie about *me!* Oh, I'm a Dark Character, all right, baby; I'm Doomed; I've got the fucking Seeds of Self-Destruction coming out my *ears* . . ."

She was walking quickly away from him, and several gaping adolescents in bright-colored T-shirts—two boys and a girl—had stopped to watch. There was nothing to do but turn and walk in the opposite direction, fast, in search of a bar to hide in.

He found a cheap, loud, crowded place that was evidently a hangout for young actors—it had a much-used call-board instead of a mirror behind the ranked bottles —and after fighting his way to the bar for two shots and a beer, he left quickly. The second place was better, and the third was the best—so agreeably dark and somber that he felt he could stay here forever, signaling the courteous waiter for refills and hearing of how Tony Bennett had left his heart in San Francisco.

Soon he would go home and apologize—he would wake her up, if necessary, to do so—but not right away. It was very important to think things out.

"Sir?"

"Yes, please. Another double."

He was faltering, staggering drunk by the time he got home. He thought at first that instead of waking her to apologize he would crawl in beside her and pass out, but he couldn't even do that. He wasn't sleepy.

He sat on the living-room sofa, tapering off on beer, waiting for sleep. And he was still there, awake and whispering to himself, when daylight crept through the Venetian blinds.

". . . Good news," Munchin said on the phone a few days later. "It isn't final yet, but I think we're going to get Pratt."

"Oh," Wilder said.

"His agent asked for the script yesterday, and Pratt's reading it today. So listen: assuming he likes the property, what day do you think you two could come out here? To meet him and talk it over?"

"Well, don't count on me, Carl," he said, and the phone trembled slightly in his grip. "I don't want to see him at all. Hold on, I'll ask Pamela."

She was sitting in an armchair across the room. She had been reading *Sight and Sound* but she'd dropped it when the phone rang, and now as he relayed the message she drew a section of her lower lip between her teeth and bit it. Her eyes were wide. "God," she said. "*I* don't know."

"She doesn't know, Carl," he said. "She'll call you back in a few minutes when she's made up her mind, okay?" And when he hung up the phone he said "Okay, baby. It's up to you."

"I won't go at all if you don't want me to," she said. "You know that."

He hadn't known it, and it pleased him, but he didn't want to show it. "No, you'd better go," he said. "You're one of the producers."

"Well, so are you. If you go alone he might never even know I'm connected with it."

"He already knows. Your name's on the script."

"Oh. I didn't think of that."

In the end she called Munchin and agreed to go on whatever day was most convenient.

On the appointed afternoon she took longer getting dressed than usual, trying different dresses, until he said "Anybody'd think you're worried about how you look."

"Oh, you're right," she said. "This is silly. I'll just wear a shirt and some old slacks. You sure you don't want to come?"

"I'm sure."

But after she was gone he walked the floor with his fist in his mouth. Why *hadn't* he gone along? Wouldn't it have been better to let Pratt see she had another man? He had a drink—just one, he promised himself, because he wanted to be alert and keen—and settled down to wait for her.

When she came back he studied her closely, weighing her every answer and every glance for signs of duplicity, and he had to admit there were none.

"How was it?"

"Oh, it was—pleasant. At least he was sober."

"How'd he act when he saw you?"

"He was very discreet. He just said 'We've met' when Munchin started to introduce us, and after that it was all —you know—strictly business. I thought he had some interesting ideas. I wish you'd come along."

Chester Pratt was retained to write the screenplay, and since it would take him a few months to finish it they were left with nothing much to do. They spent time at Munchin's, meeting several directors, and they spent time with real-estate agents in futile search of "a nice little house in the hills," but for the most part their days were empty.

"We might as well do *something* with all this time," she said. "Do you want to go up to San Francisco for a few days? Or down to Mexico?"

But they did neither.

9

"And what seems to be the trouble, Mr. Wilder?" said Dr. Burton L. Rose of UCLA.

"There's no real trouble, doctor, but I suppose you could say there might be. I really only came to get my prescriptions refilled—here, look, I've brought the bottles—and then on the way over here I thought of a few things I'd like to talk about."

As soon as he'd said that he regretted it. Dr. Rose was a very small, slight, pale man who couldn't have been over thirty, with humorless eyes that stared unblinking at his visitor. His office, deep in the labyrinthine complex of the Medical Center, was barely big enough to contain a desk, two chairs, and a psychiatric couch that looked obscenely out of place. How could anyone "talk" to this solemn, staring boy in this claustrophobic room?

The doctor frowned over the labels of the pill vials and reached for his prescription pad. "How long have you been on these medications?"

"These four, you mean, or medications in general?"

"These four, to begin with."

"Oh, let's see. About three months. Before that I was taking something else, another combination of drugs. Dr. Brink used to change the prescriptions quite often, you see. I've been on drugs of one kind or another for two and a half years."

"And what did you want to talk about?"

Wilder's hand went involuntarily to his brow and a small patch of skin near his eye began to twitch. "I don't know; it's very complicated. If I started telling you everything it would take all day."

"You've been feeling a good deal of anxiety?"

"I'm not sure if 'anxiety' is the right word; but yes, I guess that's about it. It's just that there's so much I'd have to tell you to explain it—even begin to explain it. For one thing I haven't been sleeping well and I think I've been drinking too much."

"Didn't Dr. Brink tell you not to drink when you're on these medications?"

"He said one drink would have about the same effect as two. Look, maybe I don't want to talk to anybody. Maybe all I need is to have my prescriptions changed again. Could you help me there? Could you put me on a stronger antidepressant or a stronger psychic energizer or something?"

"I'm not a magician, Mr. Wilder. And in any case I can't change your medication without knowing more about you. If you'll sign a records-release form I can write to Dr. Brink and have him send me an abstract of your history."

"Okay."

The doctor opened a desk drawer in search of records-release forms, and now, freed from his scrutiny, Wilder let his eyes roam around the tiny office. On the desk blotter were scattered half a dozen bright, foil-wrapped chocolate mints, the kind sold at check-out counters for two cents apiece, and by leaning forward and peering over he could see many crumpled foil wrappers in the bottom of the tin wastebasket. Maybe Dr. Rose was trying to quit smoking. Or maybe he was a candy freak; maybe when he had no patients to stare at he sat here alone, staring at the wall and masticating the chocolate and the cheap cream filling, compulsively easing some dark and secret neurosis of his own.

"If you'd like to arrange a series of appointments for psychotherapy," he was saying, "let me know. In the meantime I would suggest very strongly that you stop the alcohol."

On the way home Wilder thumped the steering wheel several times with his fist and said "Shit! . . . Shit! . . ."

"What's he like?" Pamela inquired.

"He's a jerk. He's not much older than you and he has an office about as big as a phone booth and he stuffs his face with chocolate mints all the time. The hell with him. At least I got my prescriptions refilled."

"Did you ask him to put you on something stronger?"

"He says he can't until he writes to Brink."

"Oh." She was reading a copy of *Newsweek*, probably the "Movies" section.

He fixed himself a drink without asking if she wanted one; he was reasonably sure she'd say it was too early.

"I've got an idea," he said after a while. "Let's go to one of those big, opulent restaurants on La Cienega where they have fountains and strolling violinists and the whole works. Just for the hell of it."

"No," she said. "We've been eating out too much. I'm going to fix dinner here tonight. Do you want to come along to the market with me, and help?"

He had always hated supermarkets, and the one she took him to was a giant—more aisles and more check-out stations than he could count, with acres of brilliant overhead lights trained on the eggs and carrots and toilet paper. She wheeled her double-decked shopping cart briskly down one aisle in search of meat, and he followed her, staring at the passing merchandise and into the petulant, bewildered faces of other shoppers. He guessed he ought to push the cart for her—was that what she'd meant by "helping"?—but when he offered to take it she said "No, it's easier this way; I know just where I'm going and where I'm going to stop." But she hadn't allowed for all the stops she would have to make for traffic jams, where the carts and the people blocked the aisle.

"Excuse me," she said helplessly. "Excuse me."

"Jesus," he said. "At this rate we'll never get out of here."

"I only have a few things to get. Just be patient."

He wanted a drink, and chain-smoking cigarettes didn't appease his thirst as he followed her through the enormous store. The Muzak system was playing "I'll Never Smile Again," and when that was over it played "All the Things You Are."

"Aren't you about finished?" he said.

"No. I need bread and paper napkins and something to make a salad with; also we need some Comet cleanser and some toothpaste and a few other things. Why don't you wait for me at the front?"

"No, that's okay."

"Please," she said. "I don't *want* you tagging along and suffering this way; you're like a little child."

On his way to the front of the store ("Excuse me . . . Excuse me . . ."), he passed Duz and Oxydol and Brillo; then he passed Grape Nuts and Post Toasties and Cheerios and a great many other bright things until he found what he suddenly knew he'd been dreading all along: a tall revolving display of Marjorie Wilder's Chocolates. It was a six-sided rack, mechanized by some mysterious electric motor in its depths; it held hundreds of candy boxes, and it seemed to be turning to the slow, seeping rhythms of the Muzak system. "To have . . . to give," read the cardboard sign; "The aristocrat of fine candies."

What would happen if he pushed the damned thing over? Would women scream? Would men come running? Would somebody call the police? He kept both fists tight in his pockets to restrain the impulse. Several of the boxes in each row were open to reveal their plump and succulent contents—nougat, coconut cream, English toffee, nut fudge—and he remembered sitting in wholesale offices long ago with the salesman who said "Taste one—just taste one. Be our guest." How fine it would be to see the whole elaborate structure toppled to the floor, boxes dented and smashed, chocolates spilled and rolling in the dust under people's feet.

"I'll be through in a minute," Pamela said, pushing her cart up close to him. "What're you looking at? Oh."

"Hey listen," he said, plucking a box of chocolates

from the rack and dropping it in the cart. "Let's give Rose some *decent* candy to eat."

"Let's do what? Give who?"

"Rose. My little buddy out at UCLA. Here; let's get him two."

That was when it happened. He was leaning with one hand on the edge of the cart; with the other he reached for the second box, and when the cart rolled forward under his weight he lunged heavily into the display rack and down it went, scattering boxes, spilling loose chocolates in a spectacular crash on the linoleum floor. A woman did scream—one of the check-out girls—and two or three young men in white did come scurrying from different directions.

"Come on, quick," he said, grabbing her arm. "We gotta get outa here." And he forced her through the crowd, around the last of the check-out counters and through a big automatic door marked OUT.

"John, this is *crazy*," she said breathlessly on the sidewalk.

"Quick. Hurry. Get in the car. Those slobs are gonna call the police."

"Why would they do that? It was an *ac*cident."

"It was an accident-on-purpose. I've been wanting to knock over one of those fucking racks for years. Never quite had the guts." He wrenched the car into "Drive" and winnowed swiftly out of the parking lot, nicking the bumper of another car.

"Will you watch your *driving?* John, I left all my *shopping* in there."

"Tough. I don't happen to feel like spending three hours explaining the story of my life to some supermarket manager while the cops take notes, that's all. If you gave a shit about me you'd see what I mean."

Swerving through traffic, driving foolishly and fast, he took her to La Cienega and to the very kind of restaurant he'd suggested before: opulent, with a trickling fountain in its vestibule and a group of violinists strolling among its rich tables.

"Something from the bar, sir?"

"Yes."

"Oh, please. Couldn't we just order some food?"

"No. I'll have a double bourbon on the rocks."

"I've never done anything quite so silly in my life," she said. "Running away from that store like a pair of thieves. How can I ever go *back* there?"

"Nobody'll recognize you. It's a big town."

"I'm worried about you, John," she said. "It's not just the drinking, though God knows you've been drinking too much. It's something else. Something worse. I think you're—I don't think you're well."

"Thanks for the information," he said. "I believe I'll have another drink."

Then at her insistence they ordered "New York Strip Sirloins," which turned out to be the heaviest slabs of meat he had ever seen. He looked fixedly at his portion and knew that if only he could cut into it and eat it some balance might be restored to the evening, some act of self-rescue might be performed, but the sight of it was nauseating. So was the sight of his huge baked potato, its own bulk overwhelmed by a gout of sour cream and chives, and so was the glistening amplitude of his salad. Close beside him, Pamela was tucking into her food with apparent relish, and he didn't want to watch her. The only thing on the table that held any appeal for him was his half-finished whiskey. He picked it up, swirled the ice and drank; then he sliced out a small wedge of meat and chewed it mightily, but it was almost impossible to swallow.

"You enjoying that?" he asked her.

"Yes; it's delicious."

"Good. I'm not hungry, is all. You go ahead and eat. I just don't happen to feel like watching you, is all. Makes me a little sick to watch you, as a matter of fact."

She laid down her knife and fork, still chewing, and then she swallowed. "All right, tell me," she said. "What's the matter now?"

"They're doing it again."

"Who's doing what?"

"Everybody in this whole place. Staring at me. Look at the fat guy over there in the silk suit. Don't look now. And those two painted-up old whores in the corner. And that bunch of flaming faggots near the door."

"John, nobody's 'staring' at you. You're hallucinating."

" 'Hallucinating,' huh? You like that word? You planning to have Chester Pratt work that into the screenplay? Look now. Look at the guy in the silk suit. Look at every single person in this—"

"John, this is absurd. You're acting—"

" 'Paranoid,' right? Is that another of your favorite words?"

"I wasn't going to say that at all."

"All right, look *now* if you don't believe me. Everybody in this whole fucking restaurant is—"

"They're *not.*"

"Yes they *are*, God damn it. What the fuck do you

think I am, *crazy?*" And from the corner of his eye he saw the waiter advancing on their booth with quick little steps.

"Sir, I'll have to ask you to keep your voice down." The waiter was old and soft and Italian.

"All *right,*" he said. Far across the room the strolling violinists seemed to increase their tempo.

"Do you want to leave, John?"

"*No,* I don't want to leave. I want to sit here and finish my drink. Fuck 'em. Go on, eat. *Eat,* God damn it."

But instead of eating she covered her face with both hands.

"Oh, *Jesus,*" he said. "That really rips it. Look, I'm warning you: if you start crying here there's going to be trouble. Stop it, now. I said *stop* it, God damn it. Look. You want to get me thrown *outa* here? They can do that, you know. If you go on crying and I go on yelling at you they'll throw me *outa* this fucking faggot joint. *Stop* it, I said. . . ."

The old Italian waiter was back, holding up both hands in supplication, and now poised behind him were three younger, stronger waiters. "Sir," he said, "I spoke to you before. I *must* ask you to keep your voice down."

Wilder laid a ten-dollar bill on the table, then a second and a third. That should cover it. "There," he said. "Now why don't you go fuck yourself?"

"Oh, *John,*" Pamela said.

The old waiter stood dumbfounded, opening and closing his mouth, and the three younger men suddenly converged around him, one of them pulling the table away from the booth. "That's all she wrote, mister," he said.

Wilder was on his feet, hauling off for a swing at the man who'd said that, but his wild, looping right was neatly blocked by the man's forearm, and then suddenly all three waiters were on him, one of them clamping his neck in a painful half-nelson. They had him off his feet and struggling in their arms; they dragged and carried him among other startled diners as the violins played on. "That's all she wrote," one waiter kept saying through gritted teeth, until one of Wilder's flailing hands found his throat and he pressed his thumb as hard as he could into the man's Adam's apple. From somewhere behind him he heard Pamela crying "Oh, don't! Wait! Stop! . . ."

They were carrying him down the dark corridor and past the dribbling fountain; he felt that some semblance of pride could be maintained as long as he held his grip on the windpipe of the man who'd said "That's all she wrote." Then the heavy front door opened and they threw him sprawling onto the sidewalk; he rose and stumbled and fell again before he righted himself.

When Pamela came out he said "The car—where the hell's the car?"

"The attendant took it," she said. "Wait, I'll—"

But the attendant was already sprinting away to get it, and in less than a minute they were away from the place, driving too fast down La Cienega Boulevard.

"I want you to stop this car," she said in a surprisingly strong voice for someone who'd recently been crying, "and let me drive, before you kill us both."

But he insisted on driving himself, while she huddled in fright against the passenger's door. He took several wrong turns, caused other drivers to blare their horns at him for changing lanes too abruptly, and once scraped the fender of another car.

When they were home at last he fixed himself a drink. She had one too, and then she broke it to him.

"I'm moving out, John," she said, pacing the carpet with her glass in her hand. "I can't take this any more. I found another apartment today, while you were at the doctor's, and I left a deposit on it. I'm planning to move in the morning."

He was stricken—"Oh, baby, don't do that; please don't do that"—but at the same time he was mildly relieved: with her out of the place it would be possible to drink at any time of day, even in the morning. Besides, she would have to keep in close touch with him so as not to miss any meetings with Munchin. He'd get her back.

"There's no phone there," she said, "but as soon as I get one installed I'll let you know; that way we won't miss anything with Munchin. I'm sorry, John, but I can't *live* this way."

"Listen," he said. "I'll take my emergency kit."

"Your what?"

"Brink gave me a special set of pills to take in emergencies—times when I feel I'm about to—I'll take them now."

"Oh, John, you're too much. Do you honestly think pills are the answer to everything? You can't change your whole personality with *pills.*"

"I don't want to change my personality. I just want to get so you can go on living with me."

"Well, you'd better forget it. No pills are going to fix that. Do you want to sleep on the sofa, or shall I?"

"I will," he said. At least the sofa would give him easier

access to the liquor supply. "Listen, Pamela, please reconsider this."

"I've been reconsidering it for weeks. Now I've made up my mind."

For the fourth night in a row—or was it the fifth?—he hardly slept at all. No amount of whiskey could make him drowsy as he sat or sprawled on the sofa and tried to think things out, and he watched the morning break through the closed blinds.

"I'll just make some coffee," Pamela said, coming sleepily out of the bedroom. "I don't want to go through a whole *breakfast* scene before I leave." And they went through no scene at all. They decided she would keep the car—he could rent another one—then he helped her with her suitcases and she was gone. There wasn't even a chance to wonder whether he should kiss her goodbye.

The first thing he did when he was alone was go to his own suitcase and find Dr. Brink's emergency kit: three vials of pills with names he forgot as soon as he'd swallowed them at the bathroom sink. Then he found a hard-boiled egg in the refrigerator and wolfed it down, and then he sat on the sofa with a light whiskey and water and tried to make plans.

It was on the third day that things began to close in. His watch had stopped, but the Venetian blinds showed that it must be past noon, and he decided he'd better get out. Once he was out, walking along Santa Monica Boulevard, he decided he'd better have some food. He had eaten only scraps from the refrigerator and cheap hamburgers from a corner stand since Pamela left. There was an all-day restaurant within walking distance, one that he and Pamela had often gone to, and he went there now determined to stuff his guts: he would have a big Western breakfast of steak and eggs.

"Something from the bar, sir?"

"No, thank you. Or wait—yes. I'll have a Bloody Mary."

And over his second Bloody Mary, while trying to work up the courage to attack his cooling food, he discovered that everyone in the place was staring at him. It *was* true this time; but these people, unlike the ones in the other restaurant, didn't seem unfriendly. They seemed to be pitying him. They turned quickly away when he caught their eyes, but it was clear from their expressions that they'd been staring as if to say Look at *that* poor guy.

He sat up straighter in his chair, put his hands on the table to steady them and tried to imagine how he looked to others. He was dressed well enough—a clean shirt, clean corduroy jacket and clean slacks—and except for the fact that he hadn't shaved this morning he thought there could be nothing the matter with his face. But there it was, every time he glanced up to test it: somebody looking away with a barely perceptible shake of the head or a little exhalation of breath— That poor bastard's *really* suffering.

One man especially, plump and bald, sitting alone and pretending to read a trembling newspaper, had him under constant sympathetic surveillance. And there were others: two long-haired youths in T-shirts and jeans seemed to be discussing him in whispers, as if debating whether to come over to the table and speak to him, and a motherly woman with blue hair and a pink pants suit seemed ready to cry for his sake.

When the waitress brought his check she seemed reluctant to approach him, and her heavily made-up eyes said Are you all right, sir? He wanted to assure her that he was, or at least that he would be if everybody quit looking at him, but instead he kept his gaze fixed on his plate.

"Something the matter, sir?"

"No, no; I'm fine. Just not very hungry, is all."

When she was gone he laid a big, crumpled paper napkin on the plate to conceal how little he had eaten, left too much silver on the table for a tip and glanced up again. There they were, all the quickly averted faces. He got up and made his escape, feeling many eyes on his back.

Outside, the afternoon sun was blinding. He moved through it as slowly as if it were a sandstorm, shielding his squinted eyes with one hand.

A grey, curly-haired man was waiting on his doorstep, and after blinking several times he recognized him as the man from whom he'd rented the apartment, the building manager.

"Are you all right, Mr. Wilder?" he asked.

"How do you mean?"

The building manager looked embarrassed. "I just mean, are you feeling well? The ladies next door thought you might not be feeling well."

"Why'd they think that?"

"They said you were groaning and whatnot last night; said it sounded like you were in bad pain."

"Oh."

"And I mean I know you're new here in town. We have this doctor looks after the tenants in all the apartments, Dr. Chadwick; I could call him for you if you'd—"

"No, that's okay. I'm fine. Thanks anyway."

And at last he was alone, safe in his own place with the door locked. A phone call had to be made, and after he'd fixed a drink to steady his hands he sat at the telephone table and dialed.

"Neuropsychiatric."

"Dr. Rose, please."

"Is this Mr. Wilder?"

"How'd you guess?"

"Just a moment, please."

"Dr. Rose speaking."

"Doctor, this is John Wilder. Listen: I think you'd better help me, if you can. The point is I just went out to eat and everybody was giving me these very funny looks, and then when I got back the building manager said— look. Could you come over here and give me a shot or something?"

"Mr. Wilder, these phone calls are becoming a little bizarre."

"Whaddya mean? This is the first time I've—"

"You called me four times yesterday, three times at the office and once at home, and you called twice the day before. I've heard a great deal about 'emergency kits' and 'shots' and all sorts of disconnected talk, and I've given you the same advice each time: stop the alcohol. If you want to come and sign into the unit for a few days, that's something we can discuss during your appointment tomorrow."

"The 'unit'? What the hell's the 'unit'?"

"The ward. I can arrange to have a bed for you, if that's what you—"

"Oh *Jesus*, no, that's not what I want."

"Well, stop the alcohol, Mr. Wilder. I'll see you tomor-row."

He sat breathing hard into the phone for a few sec-onds; then he said "All right, Rose—thanks for nothing," and slammēd the receiver into its cradle.

He must have slept a little after that, because when he looked up again the Venetian blinds glowed with the colors of sunset.

". . . Operator, I want to make a person-to-person call to Dr. Myron T. Brink in New York City. I don't have the number but it's in Manhattan, on the East Side."

"Dr. Brink's office."

"Long distance calling Dr. Myron T. Brink."

"Who's calling, operator?"

"It's okay, operator, I'll talk to that lady. Hello?"

"Is this Mr. Wilder?"

"Did I talk to you yesterday?"

"Yes, sir. Several times. I told you Dr. Brink will be out of the country until the second week in June."

"You did? Well, look: did I ask to speak to one of the other doctors?"

"Sir, I told you Dr. Grady was handling Dr. Brink's patients but you said you'd rather not talk to him."

"I did? Well, scratch that, okay? Now we're getting somewhere. Put him on."

"Dr. Grady here," said a voice with an Irish accent, and Wilder did his best to tell him what the trouble was. When he got to the part about the emergency kit the doctor made him stop, go and get the bottles and read their labels aloud. Then he said "You mean you're drink-ing with *those* in your system? It's a very bad idea, Mr.

Wilder; all I can tell you is to cut out the alcohol at once. Beyond that there's nothing I can do for you at this distance. . . ."

The sky beyond the Venetian blinds was black when he made his next call—or at least the one that seemed like his next. "Person-to-person to Mr. Paul R. Borg in New York City, operator. I don't have the number. I used to know it like the back of my hand, but I've forgotten a lot of things."

". . . John! Where are you?"

"Out in Los Angeles. Listen. Things aren't so good out here, Paul. Not so good at all."

"You finding it hard to crack the movie business?"

"I'm finding it all too easy. Trouble is the movie business is about to crack me. I'm a co-producer of a movie that's going to crack me wide open."

"I don't follow you, John."

"You don't? That's funny; everybody else is following me like a dog. Another thing: my girl's gone. I can probably get her back if I want her, but she's gone for now. Moved out on me. Listen: did I just say 'if I want her'?"

"That's what it sounded like."

"I'll be damned; I guess I did say that. Thought I was crazy about that girl—when she left me before I damn near died—but now I guess I really don't know if I want her back or not. Funny. The trouble is she's too damn ambitious for my blood. She's on the make. I don't mean sexually on the make, though I guess she's probably that too; I mean nothing's going to stop her until she—until she's the first female Samuel Goldwyn or something. Listen. I'll tell you why I called, Paul. I wanted to ask you a question. How do you think it'd be if I called Janice?"

"Well, John, I think that would depend entirely on what you have to say. Also on the way you say it. If you've been drinking I don't think it'd be a good idea. Why don't you wait until you've had a good night's rest, and then—"

"Are you kidding? Who the hell can 'rest' when their nerves are screaming? Listen. Remember the time you took me to Bellevue? Do I sound like that now?"

"You sound very agitated, John, and very—well, disturbed. Are you in touch with a doctor out there?"

"Oh, shit, yes. I'm in touch with more doctors than you can count. So you don't think I ought to call Janice, right?"

"Not tonight, I'd say. If you're asking my opinion."

"Okay. You know something, Paul? You're probably the best friend I have, but I've never liked you very much. Say hello to Natalie."

And he hung up. There would be no more phone calls. "Pamela," he said to his glass of whiskey, "I don't like you very much either." He got to his feet and threw the glass high against the far wall of the apartment with all his strength; there was a satisfying crash and the whiskey slid down the wall in a long wet stain. "Sorry, baby," he said, picking up his last bottle of bourbon, which was nearly two-thirds full. "Sorry, baby, but it's time. Down the drain." Slowly at first, and then more quickly, he emptied the bottle into the bathroom sink. "Down the drain," he said as the last of it gurgled away; "it's all down the drain, Pamela sweetheart. I may have loved the hell out of you but I've never really *liked* you very much." There was nothing to do with the empty bottle but break it, which made another fine crash; then he started back toward the telephone table and the living-room floor hit him in the face. The crystal of his wristwatch was shattered; that was the last thing he saw.

When his eyes came open everything was white and green. He was naked and struggling in a hospital bed with three or four white-clad people bending over him, holding him down, trying to stick something into his arm. One of them was a young nurse whose left breast hovered close to his mouth. He bit it, and she said "Ow" in a restrained way, as though her nurse's training came before everything; that struck him as so funny that he was still laughing when he passed out again.

Then all the struggling was over and he was alone except for an orderly who was adjusting the intravenous bottle over his head.

"Excuse me," Wilder said. "Can you tell me where I am?"

"You're in Hollywood Presbyterian, sir."

"And is this a psychiatric ward or a medical ward?"

"Oh, it's a medical ward, sir."

"Good. Thank you."

A medical ward. Maybe he had injured himself in the fall that broke his watch; or maybe he was being treated for simple exhaustion, with no need for psychiatric care. In any case it was a medical ward. Nobody was fooling with his brains here, and there was no lock on the door.

". . . Mr. Wilder?"

The orderly was gone and Dr. Burton L. Rose was standing beside the bed, looking very small.

"How'd you know I was here?"

"Dr. Chadwick called me. Apparently he found my number beside your phone."

"Dr. who?"

"The physician who brought you here. His name is Chadwick. I understand he looks after the tenants in your apartment house."

"Oh. Well, what do you want from me?"

"I think we ought to arrange a new appointment as soon as you're—able to."

"Okay; I'll call you." And he closed his eyes to get rid of the man.

When he came awake again he felt fine—fully restored to health and strength, as if he'd undergone some miraculous cure—and he wanted to be up and into his clothes and out of here.

"Excuse me," he said to the orderly—a different one. "Am I still in Hollywood Presbyterian?"

"Yes, sir."

"How long've I been here?"

"Since night before last, I believe."

"And this is still a medical ward, right? Doesn't that mean I can sign out whenever I want to?"

"I believe so, sir; but you've been very—"

"I know I've been sick, but the point is I'm well now. How about cranking up the bed."

"Certainly."

"And you might as well take that tube out of my arm; I don't need that."

"I'll have to ask the nurse, sir; I can't—"

"Okay, let's get the nurse, then."

Soon he was fully dressed and downstairs at the cashier's office writing out a check, checking out of Hollywood Presbyterian as easily as if it were a hotel.

"Where can I get a cab?"

"We'll call one for you, sir."

"Thanks." And in the taxicab he felt as if he owned Los Angeles; he felt as if he owned the world. For some reason he had a lot of money in his wallet—well over two hundred dollars—and he felt like spending some.

"Stop at a florist's," he told the driver. "Any florist's."

He bought an expensive bouquet of mixed spring flowers, and on second thought he bought two. Then he had the driver take him home, where he pressed the bell on the building manager's door.

"Well, Mr. *Wilder*; you're looking much better. How're you feeling?"

"Feeling fine, thanks, except that I'm sorry for all the trouble the other night."

"Wasn't any trouble. I figured you needed medical attention, that's all, so I called Dr. Chadwick."

"You did the right thing. Here, I brought these for your wife."

"Oh, nice. Well, that's very—thoughtful, Mr. Wilder. Would you like to step inside for a few minutes?"

"No thanks; some other time. Do you know if the ladies are home? The ladies next door to me? I want to apologize to them too."

"Oh; very nice. I think they're home, yes; why don't you just ring their bell?"

He had expected old ladies; instead the older was only about fifty, a pleasant, crafty-looking woman with a henna rinse, and the other, apparently her daughter, was a pretty blonde in her twenties. Maybe they had come to Hollywood to try and get the daughter into the movies.

"Excuse me," he said. "I'm John Wilder; I live next

door here. I just wanted to say I'm sorry about all the noise and the trouble—here, I've brought you these."

The older woman's eyes looked him carefully up and down before she broke into a pleased smile. "Well, that's very nice. Joy? Come and look. Aren't they lovely?"

At last he was alone in his own place, rich with a sense of having paid his debts. There was some broken glass to be cleaned up and a few tumbled chairs to be righted, and something would have to be done later about the tan whiskey stain on the wall, but generally things were in order. He couldn't remember having felt so well in years. Pouring that bottle down the drain was the smartest thing he had ever done.

But it was much too fine a morning, or afternoon, to stay indoors; very soon he was outside in his shirtsleeves, strolling up Santa Monica Boulevard, wanting to smile and wave at every passerby. He came to an especially sunny patch of sidewalk and stood slowly turning in place for a long time, holding his face up to the health-giving sun. Then he came to an Orange Julius stand and bought a paper cupful of the stuff. It tasted sweet and cheap, but the orange flavor reminded him of all the good, nourishing things he'd missed in all these years of alcohol. He stopped at a small neighborhood supermarket—really just a grocery store; not at all the kind of place Pamela had taken him to—and decided to buy whatever looked appealing. When he came out he was carrying a bag of twelve fragrant peaches in one arm and twelve small bottles of club soda in the other: just exactly the right combination of food and drink to get him through the day.

Back in the apartment he took a ravenous bite out of

a peach; he broke out the ice and made himself a plain club-soda highball. "Down the drain," he said, sitting back in an easy chair with his shoes off. "I'm sorry, Pamela, but everything between you and me is down the drain."

When the phone rang he thought it might be Pamela, or Munchin, and he took his time getting up to answer it; he wanted to be ready for anything.

"Mr. Wilder? This is Dr. Chadwick."

"Oh, hi there. I guess we haven't formally met, but I want to thank you. I feel like a million dollars."

"Very good. I was surprised to find you'd left the hospital."

"Didn't see any point in staying, that's all. Felt too good to stay."

"I see. And what are you up to now?"

"What am I up to? I'm eating peaches."

"Very good."

"And I'm drinking enormous amounts of club soda."

"You're drinking what?"

"Sparkling water."

"Ah, very good." And the doctor chuckled. "I'll drop by to see you in the morning, all right?"

"If you want to, okay. And thanks again, doctor."

This was the only kind of doctor he needed—the only kind he had ever needed: a thoughtful general practitioner who would pack him off to a medical ward when he was unconscious and chuckle approvingly on the phone when he was well again. The hell with psychiatry! Fundamentally, John Wilder knew how to take care of himself.

The telephone became faintly oppressive, sitting potent and ready on its little table. It might ring at any second—or, worse still, it might tempt him to make a call, as it had tempted him to call Paul Borg. He might call Carl Munchin; he might call Dr. Rose; and unless he was very careful he might call Janice and Tommy.

When evening came he found he was tired but not sleepy, and the fine glow of his well-being had begun to fade. The only way he could sleep was to have a drink —just one or two, taken as medication—so he walked down to the liquor store and bought a fifth.

"Hey, you forgot your change," a voice called after him from the cash register. "Hey, mister; your *change.*" But John Wilder couldn't be bothered with trivialities; he had important things on his mind. He had to figure out not only how to extricate himself from Munchin's and Pamela's movie, but how to prevent the movie from being made—and beyond that there were still graver matters, issues that hadn't yet defined themselves, that would have to be dealt with in the morning.

He took off all his clothes and brought the whiskey bottle to the bedside; then after a while he got in between the sheets and lay like a corpse until sleep over- came him.

It seemed only a few minutes later that he woke with a sense that the world was coming apart. Things couldn't wait until morning. He leaped from bed before he quite knew what it was he had to do; then when the knowl- edge was clear he found there wasn't time to get dressed. Still naked, he ran to the kitchen and got a carving knife; then he ran to the telephone and cut the wire. He was just in time: if he'd hesitated a heartbeat longer the phone would have rung, and a voice sounding like Mr. Epstein's at Marlowe would have told him he was the new Messiah.

From outside in the night streets he heard a child's scream and then a police siren, and all at once he realized the enormity of what he had done. Communications had broken down all over the country—all over the world—and he had to act quickly. He pulled on his pants and zipped them up but there wasn't time for any more clothes; he was out in the dead, deserted street and running barefoot for Santa Monica Boulevard, hearing nothing but the wind in his ears and his own gasping breath. There was a sidewalk phone booth two blocks away; he sprinted for it, clambered inside and grabbed the receiver off the hook.

"Listen, operator, *I'm* the one; *I* cut the phone wire; it's *me; me; me*. My name is John C. Wilder and I'm only a man, do you understand? I'm only a man . . ."

And he hardly dared to look, but it did seem that the streets had come to life again; people were moving, and some were even talking and smiling as if nothing had happened.

"Hey, buddy . . ." A long-haired young man in a Levi jacket, smiling and frowning at the same time, was hurrying after him as he left the phone booth. "Buddy, *I* can't let you be alone after what I just heard."

And Wilder backed away from him, gesturing for him to keep his distance. "Yes you can, buddy," he said. "Yes you *can*."

Because it was very important to remain alone as long as possible. If it wasn't true, let them leave him alone. If it was, let them find him. Let them all hear whatever the young man had heard; then let them find him. He walked steadily away from home, going west along Santa Monica with his head down, watching his naked feet tread the pavement. Once he stumbled and went down on one hand, and his thumb picked up a trace of dogshit. He wiped it on his pants but the smell remained, and the smell soon became his sole proof that he was mortal and earthbound—only a man. No second coming of Christ would have dogshit on his thumb.

". . . The man is said to be in Los Angeles," Walter Cronkite was saying on television screens all over America, "and is said to be walking the streets alone. Los Angeles police have been cautioned not to be misled by impostors . . ."

The only way to silence that voice was to smell his thumb. An adolescent boy sat in a doorway playing a guitar, and Wilder sat down beside him. The boy was barefoot too, and he was playing mortal, earthbound music.

"Don't let me interrupt you," Wilder said; "that sounds nice. You just go on doing what you're doing, and I'll do what I'm doing."

"What're you doing?"

"Smelling my thumb."

And the boy got up and walked away.

If it wasn't true, he was making a fool of himself. But what if it was? He was heading toward the Strip now, walking up a long shallow hill. A cop in a crash helmet stood tensely astride a motorcycle at the curb, his radio crackling, and Wilder approached him—first smiling and waving both hands to show he meant no harm, then pointing to his own naked chest. "It's me, officer," he said.

"Don't touch me, mister; don't come any closer." The cop's hand rested on his loaded belt.

"No, no; you don't understand. It's me. I'm the one."

"Move along, mister. . . . I said move *along.*"

So he walked on, climbing toward the lights of the Strip. If the police were all afraid of being misled by impostors, how could he ever establish his identity? He dropped his ring of keys on the sidewalk; then he pulled out his wallet and began dropping means of identification as he walked: his driver's license, his credit cards, his Social Security card. When they were all gone he resorted to dollar bills, which he dropped at measured intervals—singles, then fives, tens, twenties. He was up on Sunset, walking east toward home. People were clustered at the sidewalk tables of late cafés or strolling both ways under the bright street-lights, and nobody seemed to notice what he was doing.

"There is still no word from Los Angeles," Walter Cronkite's voice said. "The man is still at large . . ."

All his money was gone by the time he turned down his own street, which he found more by instinct than design. The door of the apartment was standing open and he padded inside, shutting and locking it behind him. He had given them every chance; let them come and find him here.

". . . either one of the greatest events of all time," Walter Cronkite was saying, "or one of the cruelest deceptions. Only time will tell. . . ."

He paced the apartment with both hands over his ears,

but when he closed his eyes he saw a tabloid newspaper headline:

SAVIOUR
OR
FRAUD?

There was nothing to do but walk around the apartment and wait. "Come *on,"* he said as he walked. "Come *on;* come *on."*

Toward dawn he heard a police helicopter hovering over the building and he had to smell his thumb for a long time before the sound went away, but it wasn't until the first light of morning that he separated two slats of the Venetian blind and peeked outside to see if a crowd had formed. It hadn't—at least not yet—and he went back to pacing the floor while the windows slowly changed from blue to yellow.

". . . The search has narrowed to a single residential block in Los Angeles," Walter Cronkite said, "but police have not yet revealed the location for fear of drawing a crowd that might well be unmanageable. CBS camera crews are standing by for what may be the greatest moment in . . ."

WILL HE
SHOW
HIMSELF?

"No, wait," Wilder said. "Listen: I'm only a man." And he would have gone out and walked the streets again to prove it if he hadn't been afraid of opening his door.

Soon he could hear the crowd—a dense, heavy sound

like the sea—and he parted the slats just enough to see that the police had erected barricades across the street.

He went to the door, opened it and looked out blinking for a split second before he slammed it shut and went back to walking the floor.

A GLIMPSE!

Walking, he insisted to himself that it wasn't true. If it was true the tumbled apartment wouldn't look this way: these ashtrays wouldn't be overflowing with butts and there wouldn't be this tan stain of whiskey on the wall. The clothes in this closet were John C. Wilder's clothes —anyone could see that—and the dirty feet that padded this carpet were John C. Wilder's feet. John C. Wilder was short. He was thirty-nine years old and he came from New York, where he sold space for *The American Scientist,* and he had a faint scent of dogshit on his thumb.

But what had driven him out of here last night? What had made him walk all that distance and drop all that money? What *was* the phone call he had stopped by cutting the wire?

The attraction of the front door was powerful. He let himself go to it again and open it, and this time he let his shy, blinking face be seen for a whole second or more.

The crowd gasped—a sound like a great wave—and he could hear the whirring and clicking of many cameras before he shut the door.

IS HE

OR

ISN'T HE?

And he was walking the carpet again with his head in
his hands.

". . . We have now had two very brief glimpses of the
man, enough to convince many skeptics that the whole
incredible story is a hoax. . . ."

"No!" Wilder said. "I mean *yes!* I mean wait; just
wait." He stood with his hand on the doorknob, breathing hard; then he opened it and looked out and ducked
quickly back out of sight for the third time.

                    THIS IS
                    GETTING
                    SILLY

He was hopping and bounding around the room now,
whimpering, and he had left the door slightly ajar. For
what seemed a very long time he stood pressed against
the far wall where the whiskey stain was, trying to gather
courage, until at least a serene inner voice said Go ahead,
John.

                    WAIT . . .

And there was more than dignity in the way he walked
across the carpet; there was a kind of grandeur. He
opened the door all the way and stepped out in the
sunshine, letting the crowd and the cameras feast on
him. He stood with his hands at his sides for a while; then
he raised two fingers in benediction, and then to leave
no shadow of a doubt he raised both naked arms as if he
were hung from a cross and let his head fall to one side.

                    THE
                MILLENNIUM!

He held the pose of crucifixion for a while; then he dropped his arms again and turned his head slowly to the left and to the right. There was no cheering; there was only a vast, solemn hush and the sound of many cameras.

A middle-aged Negro carrying a small black satchel emerged from the foreground and approached him, followed by a heavy Negro woman in a maid's uniform who held one hand pressed to her mouth. "Mr. Wilder?" the man said. "I'm Dr. Chadwick. Can we go back inside now?"

It was only natural that they would want to authenticate the miracle: the doctor would probably check his heartbeat and other vital signs, and the maid was there as a witness. When they came in they flooded the place with sunlight.

"You've been through a great deal, Mr. Wilder," Dr. Chadwick was saying, "and you're very tired. Now you need a good rest." He set his black bag on the coffee table, opened it and took out a hypodermic syringe.

"You gonna shoot me out?"

"I'm just going to make you more comfortable." He squinted at the needle and sank it into Wilder's upper arm. "He'll be all right," he told the maid, who was still clasping her mouth. Then he picked up the phone and said "Oh" when he saw the wire was cut. "I'll have to call from the office." The maid said something Wilder couldn't hear, and the doctor said "Oh; all right, we'll take care of that now. Mr. Wilder? Will you step over here, please?" They were escorting him to the telephone table, and he collided with it so heavily that the dead phone clattered to the sunlit floor. "If you'll just sign this," the doctor said, "we'll fill out the rest." At first

Wilder thought he was handing him the hypodermic needle to write with; then he saw it was a ballpoint pen.

"I get it," he said. "This is to establish that I'm alive, right?"

"It's to establish that you're alive and well and fully aware of your responsibilities."

The first time he tried to sign his name it came out in shaky capital letters like the writing of a child. "That's no good," he said. "Let me try again." The second effort looked more like a real signature, and the third was better. While writing, it struck him that maybe he wasn't certifying the identity of the new Messiah; maybe he was certifying himself as the first man in history to make a full recovery from madness without psychiatry. And maybe the two were the same.

Only after four or five signatures did he notice that the slips of paper he'd been writing on were pages of his checkbook, each one patiently turned and held for him by the maid.

"He'll be all right," Dr. Chadwick said, snapping his bag shut. "Just stay with him for a few minutes; I'll be right back." And he was gone.

"You want to sit down and take it easy, Mr. Wilder?" the maid said.

"No." He was still intently pacing the floor, and she took him by the arm to slow him down.

"You want to get dressed? Put on a nice clean shirt?"

"No." They were standing by the open door. "Where did all the people go?" he said. "What happened to the crowd?"

"What crowd is that, Mr. Wilder? Ain't no crowds around this time of the morning."

"There was a big—there were a lot of—there were cameras and—oh my God!"

"Now, you just relax, Mr. Wilder. I know about people like you."

"Oh my God!"

"*I* know what's good for you," she said. "I *know* people like you." She led him stumbling to the bathroom door, ducked inside and turned on both taps of the bathtub full blast. And he couldn't account for it—did he take off his pants or did she?—but the next thing he knew he was sprawled in the tub, thrashing his limbs, sloshing warm water over the side.

"Oh my God!" he said again and again, because it was clear now that he was guilty of some monstrous crime. Where had he been and what had he done last night? The night before? The night before that?

". . . The man who trifled with the faith of millions throughout the entire Judeo-Christian world earlier today," Walter Cronkite was saying, "may turn out to be not only an impostor but a criminal, possibly a murderer. . . ."

The maid would be of no help in finding out what he'd done: she might not even know, and if she did she would only jolly him along, waiting until Dr. Chadwick got back from calling the police. He struggled for purchase and climbed out of the tub.

"Don't get out; nice warm bath'll make you feel better."

"Oh my God!"

He pulled on his pants without drying himself and tried to make a run for the front door but she stood blocking his way, and when they collided she put her big arms around him. She was very soft and strong.

"I'm not trying to escape," he told her. "I want to turn myself *in.*"

He wrestled free of her and got to the door, but she was right after him. She caught him and grabbed him just as he was stepping over the sill and they clung struggling together all the way down the short path to the sidewalk. Several people on the street had stopped to watch.

"I killed—I killed Kennedy," he said.

"No you didn't, Mr. Wilder; Oswald killed Kennedy."

"I killed Negroes. I killed Negroes all over Los Angeles . . ."

"No you didn't . . ."

Still grappling with her, he thought of the worst thing he could possibly have done, and said it: "Oh my God; I killed my wife and baby."

Her face changed. "Yes you did, Mr. Wilder," she said, "and that's why we're tryna help you."

He broke free of her at last and started to run down the sidewalk, and he ran straight into their waiting arms —not the police, but four young Negroes dressed in white.

". . . That's right, Mr. Wilder," one of them said, "you come along now." Two of them had him by the arms and two by the legs, and the last thing he saw as they loaded him into the back of their ambulance was Dr. Chadwick, standing outside the building manager's door and watching with a look of stern approval.

". . . In you go, Mr. Wilder." They slammed the doors and the ambulance moved quickly away. He couldn't see out; all he could see was the four attendants—two of them smiling at the success of their capture, two looking grim. Had he really murdered Janice and Tommy? How?

It wasn't a very long ride. Soon they had him out and stumbling down a swaying, tilting corridor; then a door opened into what looked like a hospital room and another Negro, tall and slim, was standing beside the half-raised bed. "Is this Mr. Wilder?" he said. "Bring him in. Welcome to El Dorado." And in no time at all they had him in the bed, sitting up, wearing a white hospital gown and strapped down at the wrists and ankles by white restraining bands. He thought of the blind man at Bellevue, the man who had cried "Ah got lucidations!" but it was clear that this was no hospital: the men's smiles were too sinister for that. He was a captive.

". . . wanted for questioning in the brutal slaying of his estranged wife Janice and their infant son Thomas," Walter Cronkite was saying, "and has eluded police only to be kidnapped by members of an underground cell of the Black Nationalists, who are holding him for ransom. . . ."

"My name's Randolph, Mr. Wilder," the Negro said. "I'm in charge here."

"I've got to go home," Wilder said. "I've got to see if I—"

"You won't be going anywhere, Mr. Wilder. You'll be staying here with us. Have you noticed I speak Perfect English?"

"Did I kill my wife and baby?"

"Don't ask me. That's between you and your conscience. And it's no use struggling against those bands; you're tied down."

"How long—how long are you gonna keep me here?"

"Until we get tired of you. Probably longer than that."

"What are you gonna do with me?"

"Keep you tied down for the time being, until you start acting right. Then we'll see. We could do any number of things. Care to watch a little television?"

"No. Don't turn it on. Please don't turn it on."

But the big tube was right there, craftily suspended from the wall so that it faced the bed, and Randolph was busy with the dials. When the picture came in it showed the sole of an infant's foot, marked with thin black lines in four or five places to show where it had been broken.

"Turn it off! Turn it *off!*"

"Mr. Wilder, if you don't shut up I'll have to *shut* you up."

"Oh, Jesus, let me die. Just let me die."

"I'm considering that, Mr. Wilder. I'm taking it under consideration."

The dead foot was still there, being slowly turned for the camera, but Walter Cronkite's voice was mercifully silent.

"I can't get the sound," Randolph said. "Damn. Does that mean I'll have to listen to *you* all afternoon?" He turned off the set, and Tommy's foot evaporated.

Soon a stocky, frowning Negro came into the room and said "Okay."

"This is Henry, Mr. Wilder," Randolph said. "He's going to look after you for a little while. Henry, this is Mr. Wilder. He says he wants to die."

"That should be easy to arrange," Henry said, and when Randolph was gone he sat down beside the bed. "You've heard of the electric chair, Mr. Wilder," he said. "Well, this here is an electric bed. All I have to do is press this button." He held up a small control panel that was connected to the bed by a thickly insulated wire. "But I don't believe I'll press it just yet. I've got a few questions first. You don't have much use for black people, do you, Mr. Wilder?"

"That's not true; I've always—"

"Oh, you've always voted Democratic, I know, and you believe in Civil Rights and good stuff like that, and you admire Dr. King and you thought it was Just Awful about Emmett Till, but that's not what I mean. I mean deep down, where it counts. Deep down you wish we'd all go away. You think our lips are too thick and our noses are too flat and you shudder at the thought of our kinky hair. Isn't that about right, Mr. Wilder?"

"No . . . No . . ."

"Oh, you don't mind us too much when we speak Perfect English, like your old friend Charlie at Bellevue, isn't that right? Well, I have a message for you from Charlie, and he said to tell you he's sorry he can't be here to deliver it in person. The message is this." He held up the control panel and pressed a button. There was a hum, and the raised part of the bed began to sink back. When it was halfway to the flat position he released the button and it stopped. "And now I have another message for you, Mr. Wilder," he said. "This one is from Clay Braddock—remember him? The man you suckered into acting in your little art-house movie? Up at Marlowe College? Clay Braddock said to give you this—and he said it in Perfect English." The hum came on and the bed reclined still farther; then it stopped again. Henry leaned over and brought his big face up close to Wilder's. "Do you know what you are?" he said. "You're the worst enemy a revolutionary can have. You're a liberal. And now for your final message. This one's going to take you all the way. Are you ready, Mr. Wilder? This is the big one. This is from all of us."

The hum began again and the bed slowly sank flat. He couldn't feel the voltage coursing through him, any more than a man with the muzzle of a shotgun in his mouth can hear the blast when he squeezes the trigger. He felt nothing at all, and heard nothing, and saw nothing. It came as a bewildering surprise to find he was still breathing.

"How's our man?" Randolph inquired, coming back into the room.

"Didn't shut up the whole time you were gone until just now," Henry said. "Talking about liberals and revolutionaries and Emmett Till and I don't know what-all. He's quiet now; maybe he'll sleep."

"No," Randolph said, "I don't want him sleeping now or he won't sleep tonight. Mr. Wilder?"

"Please. Just let me die."

"Not a chance. You don't deserve a break like that. We've got something worse in mind for you, Mr. Wilder." The hum came on and the bed was slowly raised to a sitting position. "Something much, much worse. You're going to *live*."

". . . And Hollywood Presbyterian refused to take him back," Dr. Chadwick was saying, "because they don't treat alcoholics there—and that's how they'd diagnosed him, you see—so I had to send him to El Dorado. I had no choice."

"What's El Dorado?" Pamela asked.

"Oh, it's very nice, it's just that they don't have any

facilities for dealing with something like this. It's a private geriatric home—a nursing home. He's been there nearly two weeks now. He's getting twenty-four-hour nursing care there, but that's all. And they tell me he's become a discipline problem: he makes so much—well, noise, and so forth, that he's disturbing the regular patients. So you see it's imperative to get him out of there, from everyone's point of view."

"I see," Pamela said, and chewed her lip. They were sitting in the building manager's office, and the building manager and his wife were hovering somewhere in the next room. Their television set was on but she suspected they weren't watching it; they were listening to every word of this talk.

"Now, Dr. Rose has given me this." He laid a printed form on the table. "All he has to do is sign it, and he'll be committed to UCLA on a voluntary basis. That's certainly the best place for him. But I've brought him this paper three—no, wait—four times, and he's refused to sign it. He seems to think it's a check. I had him sign a couple of checks that morning, you see, for my own fee and for whatever the maid wanted to charge for looking after him, and now whenever he sees me he thinks I'm trying to get money from him. Anyway, that's where I thought you could help. If *you* take it to him, it might make all the difference."

"All right," she said, "but what if I can't get him to sign it either?"

"It's worth a try. Shall we go, then?"

"I have to make a phone call first," she said, and after dialing a number she said "Chet? Listen, this has gotten sort of complicated. I have to go and—well, I'll explain it when I see you; but the point is I may not see you for a while. I'll be late. . . ."

She followed Chadwick's car with her own, in which she carried a suitcase containing all of John Wilder's belongings, and in a very few minutes they pulled up to the big three-story structure of El Dorado.

Dr. Chadwick took the suitcase from her and led her down a richly carpeted corridor. They passed several young Negroes in white, all of whom looked busy, and through the open doors of rooms on either side she could see vases of flowers, the gleaming spokes of wheelchairs and occasionally the white head of a very old man or woman.

"God," she whispered. "Isn't this very expensive?"

"That's still another disadvantage," the doctor said. "It's very expensive indeed. Here, he's right around this next corner."

They could hear him from several doors away. He was singing, and his voice sounded terrible—not at all the light, funny Eddie Fisher or the heavier Fred Astaire she remembered, but hoarse and cracked and out of tune, like the singing of a street derelict.

". . . Buy me some peanuts and Crackerjack; I don't care if I never get back . . ."

He was sitting up with both wrists fastened to the bed; his song was addressed to the blank television set, and he sang so intently that he didn't notice them come in.

"Hello, Randolph. How is he today?"

"Hard to tell when he's like this, doctor."

". . . For it's one, two, three strikes you're out at the old—ball—game." With the song ended, he strained forward against the wrist bands and spoke as if into a microphone. "All right, Tommy boy; that's enough songs for tonight. You go to sleep now, fella. Cut!" And he closed his eyes.

"He thinks the TV is a camera, you see," Randolph said, "and he's singing to his son. But it's worse when we turn the set on; every time that shoe commercial comes on he thinks his son's dead. You know that children's shoe commercial? Where they hold up the little kid's foot? Hey, Mr. Wilder? Mr. Wilder. You've got visitors."

"Hello, John," Pamela said.

"So you're working for Chadwick and his friends now, right? As well as for Munchin and Chester Pratt?"

"Of course I'm not. You know better than that. I just came to see you." And she turned to Randolph. "Is it really necessary to strap him down this way?"

"Wouldn't be if he behaved himself, miss. Last time we took the bands off he picked up a chair and broke the TV screen. Had to get a whole new set put in."

"Oh. Well, you can take them off now. He won't break anything." When Wilder's hands were free she sat down beside him and gently massaged his pink-blotched wrists. She hoped it would make him feel better, but at the same time she couldn't deny a faint revulsion in touching his flesh. She looked up into his face, but that was no help. He was clean and freshly shaved, but his shining, protruding eyes looked—well, crazy—and the effort of singing had left a trickle of saliva from one corner of his expressionless mouth. Was it possible that she had ever loved this man?

"John," she said, "would you like to get out of here?"

"And go where?"

"To a much better place where they'll give you medicine—the kind of medicine you need, so you won't have these terrible dreams any more. Doesn't that sound like a good idea? And I've brought your clothes; we can leave right away if you want to."

He was silent for a long time. Then "Okay," he said, and she could feel the happy smiles of Dr. Chadwick and Randolph on her back.

"All you have to do," she said, "is sign this. Here, I've even got a pen."

"No. Forget it. I'm not signing any more contracts with you and Carl Munchin and Chester Pratt. Make your own half-assed movies; I don't want any part of 'em. Is that clear?"

"Oh, John, you're just fooling. I *know* you know better than that. This doesn't have anything to do with movies. It's just a piece of paper to make you well."

And it took twenty minutes or more, but at last there was a scrawl that looked something like "John C. Wilder" on the proper line of the printed form.

"Wonderful," she said. "Now we'll get you dressed."

"I'll go make a phone call," Dr. Chadwick said. "Tell them we're on our way."

"He ought to have a bath," Randolph said, "but the last time we tried that it took three men to hold him in the tub. He thought we were trying to drown him. I never heard such yelling and screaming; had complaints from all over the building."

When he was dressed and standing up he looked better; he looked almost normal, except that it was clear from the fit and hang of his clothes that someone else had put them on for him. Pamela took one arm and Randolph the other, and they guided him carefully out of the room. Chadwick was waiting in the hall.

Randolph went along on the drive to UCLA: he rode in the back seat with Wilder, holding his arm. Chadwick sat in front with Pamela, who drove.

"We going to the airport?" Wilder inquired.

"No, John; I told you. We're going to a place where you'll get medicine to make you well."

"Why we taking Randolph?"

"Because he cares about you. We all care about you, John."

"In a pig's ass."

"That's no way to talk to a lady," Randolph said.

She thought she would never find her way through Westwood to the university campus, and then she thought she would never find the building, but Dr. Chadwick was a steadying influence: he guided her into the right parking lot and put the right amount of change in the meter. Then they were all four in the elevator, and then they were in Neuropsychiatric.

"Rose," Wilder said. "What the hell's *Rose* doing here?"

"If you'll just come this way," Dr. Rose said, "I'll show him to his room." But he looked nervous as he ushered them through the open part of the ward, where a woman wearing her hair in curlers played Chinese checkers with a young boy who must have weighed four hundred pounds. When they were all in the room that had been prepared for Wilder a nurse appeared with a hypodermic syringe.

"All right, Mr. Wilder," Rose said, "if you'll just take off your coat and roll up your—"

"Fuck you, Rose. Go eat your chocolate mints. You're not *big* enough to shoot me out, and you're not smart enough either. And fuck *you*, Chadwick, you simpering nigger bastard. Wipe that shit-eating grin off your face and tell your friend to get his black hands off my arm. Motherfuckers! Motherfuckers! And you know what *you* are?" He turned his wild eyes and wet mouth on Pamela. "You're a *cunt*. You're a *cunt*. You're a *cunt* . . ."

In the end Randolph had to wrestle him to the floor. The nurse brought a straitjacket; Randolph and Chadwick stuffed his arms into the sleeves of the thing, rolled him over and tied them behind him. When the straitjacket was secure they all retreated into the hall and Rose shut the door, which locked with an efficient click.

"He'll quiet down now," Chadwick said.

"Not necessarily, doctor," Randolph said. "Not if *I* know him. He's liable to go on like this for days."

"In any case," Rose said, straightening his coat with trembling hands, "I doubt if we can keep him here."

It was hard to tell, from the thumping and shuddering of the locked door, whether Wilder was hitting it with his shoulder or his head.

Through friends—and it often surprised him how many friends he had left—Chester Pratt had found a nice little house in the hills. It overlooked a foggy canyon, with the tops of palm trees rustling just below its porch, and it suited him perfectly: a good place to work, a good place to sleep, a good place to sit with a lemon Coke in his hand and watch the sun go down.

All the poison was out of his system now. He was working well, if you could call writing a movie script "working," and as soon as this job was over he would get back to his second novel. He would have to throw away a lot of what he'd done in New York and almost everything he'd done in Washington—bad work; bad work—but if he was lucky and careful he might finish the book in a year. And it would be good; maybe even better than *Burn All Your Cities*.

Sometimes, bored with Munchin's screenplay, he would get an idea for the book and drop everything until he'd written it out in the form of a note and stowed it away, face down, on the little pile of other notes that lay under a paperweight on one corner of his desk. And he took a miser's pleasure in the accumulation of those papers: he liked to pick them up and test their thickness with his thumb. He was doing that when the phone rang.

"Hi, baby," he said. ". . . Hell, that's okay; take your time. I won't expect you till I see you. . . . Okay."

And he'd scarcely gotten settled at his desk when it rang again.

". . . Oh, hi, Bill," he said. ". . . Tonight? Well, of *course* we'd like to; it's just that I don't know what time Pam'll get back here. She just called and said she'll be late. Well, look, let's leave it this way: if you haven't heard from me by six, that means we can make it. The Beverly Brown Derby at seven thirty. . . . Okay, Bill, thanks for calling. We'll look forward to it. . . . Right. Okay, Bill. . . ."

Finally he was free of the phone and back at the manual labor of Munchin's screenplay. How did a nice middle-class advertising man go crazy? Simple: he did it in a hundred and twenty-five pages of script, the first third of which were an easy rewrite of Jerry Porter's turgid little Bellevue piece.

At first he had planned to live in Hollywood only until he'd made enough money to go back East, but recently he'd changed his mind. He would stay here. This was, after all, the place where his luck had changed: the gentle climate, the good house, the lucrative job with Munchin, and best of all the marvelous coincidence of finding his little New Frontier girl again and getting her back. He didn't quite trust her—she had left him before and might leave him again; and even though it had worked to his advantage he didn't much like the way she'd treated this poor bastard Wilder—but it was fine to have her for the time being. She was like the glass of cold milk he drank at eleven o'clock each morning: she made him feel young and strong and full of good health. The future would take care of itself. He had learned in AA to take things a day at a time.

He worked without interruption for two or three hours; then he heard her car pulling up to a stop outside and got up from the desk.

"*God*, what an afternoon," she said. "I don't know if I can tell you about it or not."

"Sure you can tell me," he said, "after you've had a drink."

He fixed the drinks—bourbon on the rocks for her and a lemon Coke for himself—while she arranged herself in one of the canvas chairs on the porch.

"Oh, lovely," she said after her first sip. "God, I needed that." And then she told him everything: Chadwick, El Dorado, UCLA, and Rose's saying "I doubt if we can keep him here."

"So where will they take him?"

"I don't know." She closed her eyes and held the bridge of her nose between thumb and forefinger. "Oh, Chet, I don't know, and I know it's awful of me but I don't much care. They're doctors; they'll work something out. At least he's in good hands."

"Yeah," Chester Pratt said. And he guessed she was right—there probably wasn't anything she could have done—but he had to study her face for a second before deciding he still liked her.

". . . And I can't help feeling this enormous sense of relief," she was saying. "His problems are just—beyond me, that's all; too much for me. He needs professional help, and that's what he'll get."

The sun was low. The light on the porch was the color of dry vermouth, and it flattered her face. How could anyone dislike a girl with cheekbones and eyelashes like that?

"Are we eating in or out tonight?" she asked.

"Out. We're meeting Bill Costello at seven thirty."

"The awful little television man, you mean? The 'Let's Ask Daddy' man?"

"Come on, Pam, that's not fair. He's a good friend. God only knows where I'd be if he hadn't been my sponsor, first in New York and then here. He's done more for me than I can ever—"

"Oh, that's nonsense. You did it yourself."

"I never could have done it without his help. Besides, he's getting older and he's lonely. The least we can do is—"

"All right. If you're in one of your sentimental moods

there's nothing I can do about it. Do I have time for a shower?"

"Sure."

"What'll I wear?"

"Doesn't matter. You always look good."

But nothing prepared him for the way she looked when she came out of the bedroom wearing a short, backless dinner dress: she looked stunning. He wanted to tear the dress off, pick her up and carry her back to the bed; instead he settled for a courtly little kiss on the neck.

"Oh, Chet," she said, stretching up on tiptoe to receive the kiss. "You're so nice and tall."

10

Janice Borg agreed with her husband that Southern California was much less interesting, much less stimulating than the northern part of the state. In San Francisco they had stayed in the Fairmont Tower; they had ridden the cable cars and visited North Beach, where they'd browsed in the City Lights Bookstore and sipped espresso in an Italian café that featured old Caruso recordings. Then, in keeping with the leisurely pace of this long and happy summer vacation, they had taken their time driving down the coast. Janice pronounced Big Sur the most utterly beautiful place she had ever seen, and Paul made her laugh by saying she had better look hard and remember it well, because there would be nothing but plastic and palm-lined squalor when they got to L.A.

What neither of them mentioned, because they had discussed it thoroughly before leaving New York, was that she would want time alone in Los Angeles to go and visit her former husband.

It was 1970, a troubled year in many ways but one in

which Janice Borg could count her blessings. The unspeakable war in Vietnam was still going on, but she thanked God for Tommy's student deferment. Richard Nixon had become President—a thing that could almost certainly never have happened if Robert Kennedy had lived—but Paul said he might grow in the job.

Paul had been silent for many miles when they turned off the coast highway onto Sunset Boulevard, and his profile looked a trifle grim, but Janice knew better than to interrupt his silences. They often meant he was thinking about Natalie, and that was understandable: there were times, less often, when she was quiet because she was thinking of John. They never lasted long, though, these little breakdowns in communication; that was one of the many wonderful things about their marriage.

"Which sounds better?" he said at last. "The Beverly Wilshire or the Beverly Hilton?"

"You decide. You always know best about hotels."

He always knew best about everything. She didn't say that aloud for fear of sounding silly, but it was true. She had never known anyone whose judgment was so totally reliable.

"Oh, I think this is charming," she said as the palm trees swept past their car, and when they pulled up to the Hilton she said it was "lovely."

Their room was lovely too, and so was their dinner; everything was lovely until the following afternoon, when the time came for her to leave Paul and make the drive alone out to Camarillo.

"I won't go if you don't want me to," she said. "He'll never know we were here."

"No," Paul told her. "You'd better go. It's the right thing to do."

It wasn't that she dreaded seeing him as she negotiated the Freeways and then the dreary local roads, it was simply that she didn't know what to expect. That was what made sweat break out in her scalp and under her arms.

The state hospital looked pleasant enough from a distance, but up close you could tell what it was. Patients dressed in grey or green twill work clothes idled in the sunshine around the main door of John's building, and on the lawn near the parking lot a couple of heavy, slow-moving parents were bathing their grown son. They had removed his twill shirt to wash the upper portions of him, using a soaped washcloth and a plastic bucket of steaming water; then, after his father had turned him to face the building, his mother dropped his pants and carefully swabbed between his legs.

"Hey lady, gimme a dime for a cuppa coffee?" a toothless old man asked her in the doorway, and before she got to the elevator another old man plucked at her sleeve.

"Hey lady, gimme a dime for a piece a cake?"

The linoleum of the waiting room outside John's ward was being mopped, and the angry-looking black man who mopped it talked steadily to himself as he worked. There were only three or four other visitors sitting at chrome-and-plastic tables around the room. A short, grey-haired man in green came out, and she didn't recognize him until he drew a chair out from her table.

"Hello, Janice," he said.

It wasn't only that he'd turned grey; his face had gone

slack and his eyes bland. He looked like a middle-aged man to whom nothing had ever happened.

"It's good to see you, John," she said. "You're looking very well."

"You too. What're you doing in California?"

"Just a vacation." There was a pause. "Tom said to give you his love. And wait—look." It was a relief to busy herself with her handbag. "Here, I've brought you some pictures of him." She laid three snapshots on the table. "I took these at Harvard. Isn't he a fine-looking young man? I know his hair looks a little strange, but that's the way they're all wearing it now."

"Yeah. Yeah, he looks good. He looks tall."

"Five foot eleven. Almost six feet."

"Wow. That's really something."

"And in another year he'll be ready for law school. Isn't that wonderful?"

"Yeah. You want these back?"

"No, they're for you. I want you to keep them."

"Thanks." And he put the pictures away in his shirt pocket. "How's Paul?"

"Oh, Paul's fine. He said to give you his—very best."

"You two getting along well?"

"Very well."

"Good."

For a little while they sat like strangers sharing a table in a cheap cafeteria. Then she said "John? Is there anything you need? Anything I could get for you while I'm here?"

"No, thanks."

"You have plenty of cigarettes?"

"Oh, sure. Anyway, I've cut 'way down. I smoke less than a pack a day now."

"Well, that's wonderful. Are there any—you know—activities for you here?"

"Oh, they keep us pretty busy. In the mornings we generally have OT."

"What's that?"

"Occupational therapy. I'm in woodwork refinishing. Tables, chairs, things like that."

"I see."

"Then in the afternoons we have sports. I'm on the softball team."

"Oh? Does that mean you get out and play teams from —other hospitals, or whatever?"

"No. It's intramural."

"Oh."

"And when it rains we do different things. Sometimes we have dance therapy."

"Well, I imagine you enjoy that; you always were a good dancer."

"Oh, this isn't social dancing. It's interpretive."

"I see."

She knew her next question would be a difficult one, but she decided to ask it anyway. She might never be in California again; she might never see him again. She had to wait for a swelling in her throat to go down before she could trust her voice. "John," she said, "have you made any plans or—you know—given any thought to what you might do when you leave here?"

He looked puzzled, as if she had asked him a riddle. "Leave here?" he said.

That was when an orderly came out and announced that visiting hour was over.